Jubi Stone:

Saved by the Vine

Jubi Stone:

Saved by the Vine

Yvonne J. Medley

URBAN
CHRISTIAN

www.urbanchristianonline.com

Urban Books, LLC
78 East Industry Court
Deer Park, NY 11729

ISBN 13: 978-1-60162-762-9
ISBN 10: 1-60162-762-9

First Printing July 2013
Printed in the United States of America

10 9 8 7 6 5 4 3 2 1

Distributed by Kensington Corp.
Submit Wholesale Orders to:
Kensington Publishing Corp.
C/O Penguin Group (USA) Inc.
Attention: Order Processing
405 Murray Hill Parkway
East Rutherford, NJ 07073-2316
Phone: 1-800-526-0275
Fax: 1-800-227-9604

Jubi Stone:

Saved by the Vine

by

Yvonne J. Medley

This book is dedicated to my armor bearers, Robert G. Medley, Sr., Robert, II, Renesha, Rashad, and Rachel; and the second tier, Zachary, III, and Zavier.

Also in loving memory to the mighty matriarchs, my grandmothers, Mattie L. Tomlin and Audrey L. Johnson; Minnie L. Lewis, my grandmother-in law; and my great-aunt, the Reverend Margaret Deans Floyd.

Acknowledgments

As a Christian journalist and a member of the universal body of believers, I arrived at an obvious conclusion: that the church is God directed, administered by mortals, many times flawed, but immeasurably worth it. That revelation, and others, provided the inspiration for *Jubi Stone: Saved by the Vine,* as well as my first novel, *God in Wingtip Shoes,* and its upcoming sequel. So above all, to my gracious Lord and Savior, Jesus Christ, I thank you. At the onset, I promised to give you all the honor, praise, and glory throughout this journey, with its triumphs and challenges, and during every opportunity for honest discussion and fellowship. Know that I will continue to do so.

To my earthly lord and savior, my husband, Robert G. Medley, Sr., thank you for not only cheering me on, but also for showing me your constant love, understanding, and care for me and our children. I believe that's called unconditional love, and it's a rich blessing. I will forever appreciate my family and friends who have shown me that "faith is the substance of things hoped for, and the evidence of things not seen" (Hebrews 11:1). Even when I encountered frustration, doubt, and disillusionment, you carried me until I felt strong enough to keep it moving.

Thank you to my sister, Yvette Cetasaan; my brother-in-law, Kwaku; my sister-in-law, Cheryl Medley McKinney; Tom Saunders; Billy Medley; Leon and Patricia

Dorsey; Nathaniel Williams; Love and Angela Smith; Cynthia Mazyck; Renée Dames; Pastor and Mrs. John Lewis; Bishop and Mrs. Forrest Stith; Peggy Evans; and Cornell and Gloria Evans.

Thanks to my parents, Juanita Freeman and the late Will S. Freeman, and Anita Medley-Anderson, my mother-in-law, for making certain I focus on joy, not pain.

Thank you, Dr. Maxine Thompson, my literary agent, for showing me that an author must be the first champion of the dream. Thank you to acquisitions editor Joylynn Jossel-Ross and Mr. Carl Weber for taking my faith and making it tangible. (Even if the meticulous process caused me to rub some of the skin off my forehead, it was worth it.) Thank you to the editor who got everything off the ground, Karen Sorenson-Bartelt, who continues to encourage me.

To my international encouragers—Katerina Llioglou in Australia; Michelle Higdon in London; Tokombu Oladeinde, simply a Nigerian Yoruban queen; and Maysa Elshafei, an Egyptian beauty inside and out—a heartfelt thank-you.

Thank you to my literary angels of the Life Journeys Writers Club; Emily Ferren, director of the Charles County Library System (and her diligent crew); the Lifelong Learning Center; the Enoch Pratt Free Library in Baltimore; Carolyn Anderson; and author Ann Crispin and her husband, Michael. Not only did you encourage, mentor, and critique, but you also imparted life wisdom.

And thank you to the shepherds who ushered me in His presence: the late Reverend Mannie L. Wilson of Convent Avenue Baptist Church in Harlem, New York, and the Reverend and Mrs. William C. Calhoun, Sr., of Trinity Baptist Church in Baltimore. And my gratitude goes to the shepherds who keep me in His presence, Pastor and Mrs. Darin V. Poullard of Fort Washington Baptist Church (FWBC) in Fort Washington, Maryland. Thank you for sturdy lessons in integrity, love, and patience, as well as grace and mercy. Also thank you for your willingness to address the tough questions. To the FWBC deacons and especially the FWBC Women's Ministry, I'm grateful for your covering, objectivity, and support.

What Others Are Saying about *Jubi Stone: Saved by the Vine*

"*Jubi Stone: Saved by the Vine* is a colorful and intriguing testament to the importance of communication in family relationships. In this prequel to *God in Wingtip Shoes,* Medley shines a heartfelt spotlight on the personal lives of those who work to maintain the church—before the church drama starts. It draws out the importance of faith and family legacy."
—Angela Dion, counselor, professional writing coach, and author of *Let's Talk about Race* and *Dear Son: Letters from a Birth Mother*

"Readers will want to know how this one turns out, and about who's telling the story. *Jubi Stone: Saved by the Vine* crosses the generational divide. The story skillfully unfolds to bridge the gap. It's definitely a must-read."
—Derrick N. Terry, president and founder of Edvocare Consulting, LLC, specializing in the arena of secondary and higher education; and author of *I'm Not*

Complaining . . . I'm Just Sayin': Memoirs of the Good and Bad in the Education System

"Yvonne Medley has provided the reader with a powerful narrative with interesting characters who are struggling with real-life issues. This story captivates and weaves a rich tapestry of a family's love, heartaches, complex relationships and heartfelt faith during times of adversity. The story is compelling in that it tells the tale of many families who have faced the dilemma of addiction. I was captivated, left wanting to immerse myself further into the lives of the Stone family and to be a witness to their journey toward salvation and healing. A transformational reading experience!"

—Dr. Lorri Glass, associate professor and undergraduate social work coordinator in the Department of Social Work at Governors State University in University Park, Illinois.

Table of Contents

Jubi Stone:
Saved by the Vine

"I am the vine, and you are the branches. If you stay joined to me, and I stay joined to you, then you will produce lots of fruit. But you cannot do anything without me. If you don't stay joined to me, you will be thrown away. You will be like dry branches that are gathered up and burned in a fire." John 15:5–6 CEV

Chapter One

Sapphire's Escape

1993 · · ·

"What's that you just slipped in your pocket?" Esther said to her daughter, Jubi. Esther kept her eyes on Jubi's hands when she said it, too. Jubi was a medium height, leanly built nineteen-year-old who was going to turn twenty in a month. She looked frail and actually too lean these days. And the corners of her eyes and lips were crusty. She stood there trying to look dumbstruck at her mother. But her dumbstruck look failed. Instead, she managed only to re-create the look of the beat-up, old whisk broom propped up in her mother's living room. Jubi's straw-like hair had little curlicues here and there. Every strand practically stood on its own.

Esther stood there thinking, *Has this child been in a fight or something? I mean, electric shocks couldn't have pointed those rusty antennae with any more precision.* But she pondered this for only a second due to the pressing matters at hand. "So what's that you think you're walking out of here with this time?" she asked sarcastically. Then she answered her own question. "But you're not."

Jubi was silent, thinking up something to say or something to do. Jubi feared that perhaps if Esther

moved in a little closer, there might be some spicy BO—
bad odor—to behold. But Esther stood firmly where
her feet had planted her. It was a position from where
she could accurately assess the total picture. She also
stood blocking the path to Jubi's front-door freedom.
She wasn't about to budge.

Surrounding them both was the projected glee of
family portraits. There were grouped images of Esther;
Jubi's daddy, James; and Jubi. They depicted happier
times and tracked Jubi's years from birth to tween.
Each portrait doubled as history and decor to fill out a
beautifully decorated front room. Had those pictorial
scenes been rewrapped in flesh, they would have felt
shame over this present scene.

"Uh-huh," was Esther's audible response to Jubi's silence and lame dumbstruck expression. "I'm gonna ask
you again," Esther said smoothly. She worked to keep
her demeanor smooth, as smooth as her beautiful olive
skin. She spoke calmly, remaining as calm and col-
lected as she was always expected to be around those
who knew her. Jubi tried to make a dash for the door.
Esther blocked her. She still kept her cool.

Esther's general demeanor and appearance took on
a classy, regal air. It was second nature. And Esther
liked to look stylish, too. Dressing for church earlier
that day, she felt that the bracelet now stowed away in
her daughter's jacket pocket, and about to be smuggled
out the door, was the perfect addition to the new outfit
she planned to wear. That was why the bracelet had
been exhumed from its hiding place. It had been inadvertently left out, and ultimately snatched by Jubi,
Esther's gift from God.

When Jubi was around fourteen or so, all the rebel-
lion and trouble started to invade the Stones' world.
"That's when the devil moved into our house," Esther

shared one Tuesday night during a weekly ministry group meeting at her church. Forest Unity Memorial Church of Baltimore was a pillar in the Forest Park community, where the Stones lived. And it was a saving grace to Esther. She had not long been voted in as chairperson of the group, aptly christened the FISHH Ministry. FISHH! It stood for "Fellowship, Intercession, Study, and Healing Hurts."

Responding to her mother's disbelief at the present moment, Jubi said, "What?" She draped it in a fake laugh, one that verged on a cackle of disbelief. Jubi's stale, cracked voice was once the voice of heavenly angels and sweetness to the ear. For the final touch, Jubi worked to paint an incredulous look on her face. She used it to season her laugh as she let her mother's bracelet plummet into the pocket of her worn-out, armpit-stinky jacket.

Jubi's maternal grandmother, Adele, had sent the bracelet to Jubi's mother when she married. And so that gold bracelet, encrusted with glistening sapphires, had been in the family since forever, it seemed. According to family folklore, the bracelet had slavery blood on it.

"Whaddaya talkin' about?" Jubi said, letting go of the bracelet and thrusting her empty hand into the realm of plain sight like a magician. She made a motion with her hand that seemed to say, "This conversation is over, and I'll be leaving now." "Mom, you seein' things again. You know you gettin' old," Jubi said. She gave a phlegmy laugh that caused her to clear her throat and wipe her runny nose with a dusty hand.

And it was true. Her mother was getting old. In truth, Esther was well into her fifties and looking around the corner at her sixties. She somehow managed to look better than she felt, which was run-down, because her beloved was a thief and a crackhead.

Esther hard-eyed her daughter. "If you think you're gettin' outta here with that bracelet you got there in your pocket . . . ," Esther said. Her death-ray stare targeted Jubi's pocket for just an instant. Esther kept her voice smooth, even toned, but she executed a mean black-woman neck roll for visual emphasis. Her hair, with its abundant, healthy brown waves fashioned in a flip, bobbed on her shoulders when she rolled her neck at her daughter. She aimed her eye again on the very pocket that harbored their family's heirloom. She declared, "If you think you're gettin' outta here with it, you're sadly mistaken."

Esther wore a purple-print housedress. It was neatly pressed, even though she wore it only in the house. She had on house slippers to match. Her hairdo still looked fresh from church because she hadn't yet had the chance to take that power nap she'd promised herself. She'd planned to fry up some pork chops for James's dinner once she was reenergized. But Jubi had come knocking on the door, messing up the groove of things. Esther had barely gotten out of her church clothes when she heard the knock. James had to work, so she had gone to church solo that day. Jubi had their routine committed to memory. She had timed her visit perfectly. She didn't want her daddy around when she came to ask for money or to lift what she could from the premises.

It was nearing the middle of the month, and Jubi was short, real short, on the rent and some other ne-cessities. If she couldn't make up the shortfall from her parents' place, then she'd have to make it up in other ways—ways that lately had begun to turn her stomach and were almost unbearable. The parent savings and loan was fast becoming her first and only option, her desperate option.

"Mom," Jubi said as if settling a contract dispute. "Hey. Look . . ." She shook her head while moving toward the door. "Look here, I just came over to say hi. Ya know? I thought that maybe we could talk or something. But I see you trippin'. So I'ma just go. All right? Get out of your hair. Okay?"

She gibbered some more and sidled forward until she had just about met up with her mother and was nose to nose. Perhaps it was the last bit of home training that stopped her. Who knows? Esther would wonder about that later. But right then, Esther neither abandoned her silence nor backed up. There was a slight, brief dance between the two of them. When Jubi attempted to glide around her, Esther blocked her. They danced to the left, then veered to the right.

"Hey, Mom, I said I'm leavin'. What you doin'? Huh?" They were now eye to eye, nose to nose for sure.

"I told you you're not leavin' here with my bracelet," Esther said. "Oh, *you* can go," she heard herself clarify, "but that bracelet—and whatever else you're hiding that belongs to me—is staying." Esther let a meditative moment lapse, for Jubi's benefit. Then she sprinkled a little paprika on her prior statement, you know, for dead-on clarity. "You got that, right?" Esther questioned Jubi. "I mean, you understand what I'm sayin', right?"

Mother and daughter stood their ground, equally stunned and steamed at the other's growing gall. Neither could believe it. Television murmurs and familiar commercial jingles played innocently in the background, but that didn't lighten the mood. Suddenly, Esther stepped forward and gave Jubi a good push. Jubi was caught off guard and almost tripped backward over the maple coffee table. The coffee table tipped over, and one of its wooden legs fractured. Jubi's arms pinwheeled, and she searched frantically for leverage in the air. She found none.

In what felt like an out-of-body experience, Esther made another quick decision to take advantage of the situation. Her primary goal was to end it all right there. While Jubi struggled to reclaim her steadiness, Esther lunged forward like her body was not tired at all and yanked at Jubi's jacket pocket. It ripped. The bold move caused the sapphire-encrusted bracelet to break free. It dropped to the hardwood floor, rolled, and swiveled under the couch like a runaway slave.

Jubi was incensed. She became crazed. She cursed. Cursing was an offense she had never before perpetrated in front of her mother. Jubi dove to the floor, her hands and knees hitting first, then her belly. She dove to where she thought she'd seen her future bankroll disappear under the couch.

"Oh, no, you're not," Esther yelled. Her cool was gone. It was another out-of-body experience. Her physical strength had come from . . . Well, later, she'd recall that she didn't know from where it had come. Because in the old days, Esther would not have ever raised her voice or her hand in such raw anger toward her child, let alone started a brawl. But on this day, the bracelet represented the last straw. Esther felt like shaking her baby about the head and shoulders until some godly, good common sense filtered in. And, if she'd wanted, she could have done it, too. Esther was a longtime registered nurse. She was used to tussling to restrain patients when she had to. But such strength was reserved for the job, not the home. The overwhelming sensation of wanting to violently shake some sense into her daughter was real, but not readily recognizable to Esther.

God forgive me, she thought in the rush of things. *James, where the heck are you?* She pounced on the back of her baby girl like a Roller Derby skater in the midst of settling an argument. She aimed to draw Jubi back away from the couch, and away from the bracelet. But the bracelet, having been through much worse for sure, kept still and sufficiently hidden. Thoughts of shaken baby syndrome consumed Esther while she had Jubi in her clutches. At the moment, it actually seemed like a possibility.

"Jubi, stop all this mess," Esther shouted as she pulled Jubi away from the couch with little effort. "Stop living like this! God don't want this mess outta you. You've lost your mind," Esther yelled as they tussled. Jubi huffed and puffed and tried to scramble away. Esther mercifully allowed Jubi to get to her feet, hoping this would lead to a cease-fire. But all mercy did was allow Jubi to attempt to get the upper hand in the situation. The two became interlocked. They fell and rolled on and off the couch. They grunted and screamed, and a lamp on the end table crashed to the floor.

"God!" Jubi shouted, breathing hard, surprised. She saw herself pulling her mother's hair. In the back of her mind, this was an out-of-body experience for her, too. She was assaulting her mother. It was something she couldn't believe she was doing. "God!" Jubi shouted again as she took a stinging slap across her face from Esther. It came shortly after they both had climbed to their feet. The slap drew tears from them both.

But the tussle wasn't over. Jubi threw a wild punch that caught the side of her mother's head. Jubi's jagged fingernails scratched her mother's cheek as she drew back her hand. Jubi, stunned, wanted to shout, "I'm sorry, Mama!" But instead she bellowed, "You always shouting about some God. Like that's supposed to do something." Her voice screeched and quivered. "And look how you treatin' me! God tell you to do this?" Jubi challenged.

"God ain't tellin' you to mess yourself up like this," Esther said as the two of them managed to stand their ground. Their fists remained on guard and clenched tight. A quick survey would show that the living room had taken quite a hit. It had become a battlefield.

Just then, James appeared in the doorway, astonished. "What the heck happened here?" he asked, surveying the damage, his eyes popping. "I could hear y'all shouting from the curb. Y'all gonna cause the police to come here again." He stepped between them like a Roller Derby referee.

"Mama hit me," Jubi rushed to say, trying to effect a little girl's tattletale tone. "She hit me for nothin', Daddy." She tried the doe eyes, too. That used to work on her father when she was a cute little girl, a honey-hued gingersnap. But the daddy's girl innocence had long vanished. They both knew it. Sad, but true.

Panting and staring, Esther shouted at Jubi, "You need to fall down on your knees and beg God for forgiveness for the life you leadin'." She checked the long, deep, wet scratch on her face for the blood that she knew was there. She drew in a heavy breath, searching for the calm of salvation, but there was still anger in her heart. She glared at her flesh and blood like she was a stranger when she said, "I don't know you, chile. What's gotten into you? Ever since you left the church, you've—"

Incensed at hearing the word *church,* Jubi shouted, "Church! God! Church! That's all you ever talk about. That's all you care about. You don't care nothin' about me. You only care what those fools think about you down at that stupid church." Jubi stared at her mother through intense slit eyes and said, "You didn't care nothin' about me when you left me bleeding!" Her words were clipped as she huffed. Snot dribbled to her crusty lips.

Esther just looked at her daughter as James reached for his hankie and handed it to his baby girl. Esther stood there, feeling both steamed and sorry, but she kept silent. In her head she bellowed, *You don't understand!* Esther found herself standing there in a flood of secrets and nightmares about her past. She could have explained things, perhaps. But, sadly, any brief rebuttal she was willing to give would have been useless. That awful night years ago, Esther had come home from a late-night work shift to find a bloodstained bathroom and her daughter hiding in the shadows of her bedroom. There was even a strange stench in the air, one that was very recognizable to her. What in the world made her dismiss it all, again, and go to bed, she'd never know. Or did she know the root of her behavior? For there had been times when pride and appearances won out over Jubi's drama.

James kept his daughter at bay as she wailed and accused. "You don't know, Mama," Jubi yelled in wounded tones. "You don't know nothin' about me—what I'm goin' through! All you care about is that stupid church!" Her tears gushed down her cheeks, leaving dusty trails. "Mama, that church and your God can't do nothin' for me." Jubi's voice squeaked, and she felt helpless.

Esther wanted to run to her, hold her, and wipe her tears away, but she kept herself away and still. She stood there and wiped her own tears and dabbed at the traveling trickle of blood with a tissue she'd fished out of her housedress pocket. She struggled to reclaim her composure. She looked at Jubi with fresh pain in her eyes. It was an alphabet soup of compassion, remorse, and hurt. But what Jubi saw was disdain.

Her voice was low now, but direct. Esther's total focus was Jubi's soul when she said, "Neither of us can
reclaim the past, chile. But just the same, you've hit a
new low. For some reason, you've walked away from
everything we taught you. You've thrown away everything you really are. You won't listen to reason. You
won't grow up. You won't forgive and move on." Esther
shook her head, then eyeballed Jubi real good when
she added, "And you're right. I don't understand it."

Jubi's breath caught in her chest and choked her. She
gulped a dry, bitter heave that rendered her speechless,
because, deep down, she knew her mother's words were
true. At this moment, Jubi was unrecognizable even to
herself.

On days that lacked Jubi drama, days unlike the
present one, days when she could momentarily take a
break from her maternal shame, Esther liked to fondly
remember the good times. On Installment Sunday, set
to celebrate the church officers, the Reverend Charles
A. Wicker, Jr., said, "Sister Esther, we're so blessed and
grateful to have you head up the FISHH Ministry again.
As a matter of fact, we're grateful you're our cherished
and faithful longtime warrior of this branch of Zion."
Then he looked at her and smiled and squeezed her as
he gave her a big preacher hug.

Esther remembered how her skin prickled and her
cheeks flushed warm. She then turned to her left and
hugged her husband, the good Deacon James Stone,
who stood firm in support of his lovely wife. At James's
touch, Esther's flushed, warm feeling overflowed. It
showed up as a deep maroonish color in her cheeks.
Yes, she often reminisced, *that was a very good day.*

Of all the busy work she'd done and the ministries on which she had served throughout the nearly twenty-five years of her being a part of Forest Unity Memorial, she had no doubt that this one, the FISHH Ministry, was truly her purpose. Esther was the mother of encouragers. It was sewn into her flesh with thick generational thread. And it wasn't lost on her that, strangely, as her family was moving through this valley, someone had the foresight to throw her name in the hat to be chairperson for a second time in her life at the church. She was a prayer warrior, steadfast and true. She loved to pray. And up till now, as quiet as she kept it, she felt she had earned all the stripes there were for her to earn. "Forgive me, Lord," she sometimes whispered only to God, acknowledging her slight embarrassment over such a bold revelation.

At the monthly FISHH meeting, when she made her confession about the devil moving into her house, she was teary-eyed and tired—physically and mentally. The other ladies in the group, who included two of her best friends, First Lady Beola Wicker and Peggy Gentry, who served as Reverend Wicker's administrative assistant, quickly huddled around her and drenched her in prayer. In moments of thankful release, Esther swooned in their advanced praises for the victory. The victory, they all swore, was coming.

The trouble brewing in Stone paradise, whether Esther spoke of it or not, was not exactly something that had gone undetected. Peggy and Esther were longtime coworkers, nurses at Providence Hospital, and Peggy had noticed the first signs of trouble. It was just that these signs of trouble were not discussed in Esther's or James's presence. The ladies had read Esther's frail appearance and mood correctly that evening. These women had been with her throughout her awful journey. And they patiently waited for her strength to be restored. They understood.

At home, Esther often gazed at the fireplace mantel, crowded with pictures. A huge photo of Jubi's baptism loomed over Jubi's shoulder on the day she fought physically with her mother. Jubi was baptized at the tender age of eleven, and the photo had captured the proudest day in all their lives. It outranked Esther and James's wedding day. It even outranked Jubi's birth, because at age eleven, Jubi had outwardly accepted Jesus Christ as her Lord and Savior, and she had become born again.

During that great Sunday, the congregation had leaped and hollered its hallelujahs when Reverend Wicker and Jubi were positioned in the center of the baptismal pool. The pool was positioned high up and was behind an impressive, and packed, choir loft. Standing there, one had to think that one was a tad closer to heaven. Shepherd and sheep were cloaked in carnation white on white; they stood immersed up to the waist in subtle silver water waves enjoying its biblical symbolism and peace.

The standing-room-only congregation reverently rejoiced as the reverend said to Jubi, "Your sins—past, present, and future—have been forgiven. Jubi, my darling child, no matter what happens in your life, know this. The Lord is on your side, and there's a protective covering on you." Reverend Wicker's thunderous voice wobbled with emotion while he securely embraced the little girl he'd known all her life. And that was even before he had become Forest Unity's pastor, back to when his daddy was the senior pastor. Reverend Wicker, Jr., fought for control of his emotions as he said to Jubi, "You're protected by our God, and this church."

The congregation gave a collective and a qualitative "Amen!"

"Oh, the angels sang on that day," Esther often whispered to the Lord when she fought not to succumb during her low points. The Lord and the angels could find her sitting solitarily on the edge of her bed in an empty house, clutching an over-caressed pocket photo of her only child. In those moments, she had to fight not to let anger and confusion contaminate her faith.

Jubi's baptism was the triumph both James and Esther relived and retold to any and everyone who even looked like they wanted to listen. For it was the day they officially gave their baby girl back to the Lord. If Esther mentioned it once, she must have put it on blast a million times while testifying before the church. Perhaps, they thought—or hoped—in the retelling, a new healing would take place. But who knew?

"My precious child is a gift from the Lord," Esther often declared with conviction, "but she is a gift on loan that really belongs to our God Almighty. And I know He will make all our crooked ways straight because of it."

"Uh-huh," "Amen," and "I know that's right!" would always be the responses from the church, the patient hearers of her declaration.

Esther was attractive enough in the years that she wore, but during the past six years or so, she had grown hurt and frustrated. And she constantly fought anger. It hurt her that her daughter stole from her. It hurt her to know that to steal from her was the only real reason her precious child, once so innocent and beautiful, came to visit. And it lay, sadly, on Esther's heart that circumstances forced her to be thankful for those drama-filled visits. Because at least they brought physical proof that her child was alive, out there on the streets. She felt forced to overlook the truth that Jubi wallowed around in trash and trouble like a pig wallowed in the mud.

So mostly, Esther had learned to overlook Jubi's petty larceny. She and James had also learned to be proactive about it, too. They hid their valuables and such. Still, they couldn't stash away the entire contents of their house. So stuff like knickknacks, silverware, books, and a couple of dollars from Esther's purse or James's money clip walked off on the regular whenever Jubi's visits caught them off guard. On separate occasions, the microwave and the toaster walked. It took them a minute to realize that their new camera had clicked off into the sunset. After a Jubi visit, if they weren't just weary from the drama of it all, they made a quick inventory—just to know what was missing and to replace what they could.

But on this afternoon Esther just didn't feel like it. She just wasn't having it. Esther had zipped right past sadness and condemnation. On this day she soared straight to being plain old pissed!

Chapter Two

Hindsight Confession

Jubi Stone was well acquainted with the Lord, even though she was only nineteen, going on twenty. Jubi was short for Jubilee. It was the name her mother gave her, because Jubi was a long-awaited gift from God.

Esther Stone was thirty-seven years old when she gave birth to her one and only child. Jubi's daddy, James, was pushing forty at the time. And they'd been married already for seven years when Jubi was born. The successful birth was Esther's eighth go-round at trying to flower James' seed in her belly. Anyone who had weathered a storm anywhere close to that, anyone who had been in Esther's particular situation would have given up and folded up the tent long before number eight rolled around. Esther had refused to give up. If she had, she felt that then the devil would have surely won out in her life. But life experience had grown her into a strong and beautiful woman, inside and out, one who stood tall and regal, with defining Nubian features dipped in olive skin.

During the rough time of all those miscarriages, she'd survived on a promise that God gave to her. *And I will restore to you the years that the locust hath eaten.* For years, she had worked to thrive on that Joel scripture. She had also survived on God's word that he was a forgiver of sins. Esther said that in a dream, long before she met James, God told her that she would indeed birth a daughter, and that it would solidify the promise and a legacy. It was as simple as that, she said. Her faith helped James hang in there, too.

He was a good-looking dude who stood a head taller than Esther. James had fine features, like he'd been mixed with something long ago. His deep-thinking eyes looked like marbles. His face was a smooth caramel and was chock-full of deep character lines as he gracefully aged. It hurt him to see Esther heartbroken by those miscarriages time and time again, but back in those days all men would let you see them do was stand and bear it. So in front of Esther, that was what he did. Alone, he cried and wore out his knees, praying for an understanding of the circumstances, and an offspring to fill their arms.

Sometime soon after miscarriage number seven, James had fallen to his knees one night at work, in an empty hospital locker room. He made a plea to God. "Please, Lord, no more. Please, no more. I don't think she can take this kind of heartbreak anymore. And, Lord, please forgive me, but I don't think I can take much more, either. Lord God, I don't know what to do. I don't know how to console her," he said as he felt his face flush warm. "I don't know what you want from us. What do you want us to learn? I'm supposed to be the head of my family, and here I am, unable to protect? What kind of man am I being?"

He'd sequestered himself in that locker room to maybe catch a quick snooze, or at least to sit quietly and be in supplication to collect his thoughts, midway into a double shift. Instead, he found himself in consultation with God for nearly half an hour. He knew in his flesh that if anyone had gone in there and caught him almost in tears and talking to himself, he'd have been mortified. But immersed in prayer, he didn't care about it.

James's prayer morphed from a plea to an inquiry to a show of anger. "Stop it, Lord. Just stop it. No more. Esther can't take anymore. And I can't, either. I don't know what you want from me. What do you want from us? I just know that you said you'd never leave us or forsake us. You said that what my queen sows in tears, she'll reap in joy. And you said that your promise, we shall behold in faith. Please, Lord, if it's chastisement, just which one of us are you punishing? And why? Forgive us. Answer us. Bless us!"

There was outer silence. The breathing in his inner spirit made him soundly aware of his erratic inhaling and exhaling, which slowly took on a rhythmic timing. James kept his body still, taking note of the intenseness of the moment and the challenge he made to God. Then he pulled himself to his feet. He walked over to the bathroom sink to clean his face and fiddle with his tie and lab coat. He managed all this without checking his image in the mirror, because he didn't care to see himself so angry with God. He cleared his throat and made his exit, heading back to work.

James and Esther had met on the job at Providence Hospital. Nurse Esther learned about James soon after he came to work at the hospital as a research lab technician. "How could I not know about him?" she often joked whenever she recounted their first batch of encounters to friends. She told how, much to James's bashful satisfaction, one day she sent a playful, lusty smile in his direction. Back in the day, his arrival at the hospital caused quite a stir among the females on the prowl and on the hospital payroll. The year was 1965. There were a few black doctors to be had then, but their noses were stuck so far up their behinds, they seemed untouchable—especially to the black female hospital staff. And they were often spotted sniffing around white women. But James was tall, finger-lickin' handsome, friendly, and approachable to everyone. He was a professional, besides. And so James Stone was stamped USDA prime beefcake, and he was equal-opportunity game. "What a catch!" was the general consensus.

Esther had ushered in her thirties when she met James, and had quietly accepted the fact that inadvertently, she had chosen a career over family. Yes, she thought God had promised her a child, but she concluded that maybe she had been mistaken about God's meaning. Maybe God meant that she'd become an adoptive mother one day, or a mother-like figure for someone who fell into her care through her work. It would be a child or teen who needed the love and understanding she had to give. Maybe her body could no longer withstand a physical birth.

She knew that the man was meant to do the looking and the finding when it came to love hookups. "A man likes to be the hunter." That was a spiritual tidbit passed down to her from her mother like the sapphire bracelet. And that was God's Word too. It was expressed plainly in Proverbs 18:22. "Whoso findeth a wife findeth a good thing, and obtaineth favour of the Lord." During some of her lonely, trying nights, she went to her Bible to check it again. "Well, where he at, Lord?" she'd joke when those moments sent her reading, searching, and conversing with the Lord. It was a joke to keep from falling into temptation. So since no one had yet to find her, it seemed pretty clear that the career handwriting was spray painted on the wall.

But then Esther noticed James. She noticed his handsome look, his smile, and his charisma. And she noticed that for some reason, seeing him made her stomach flutter. But he was so busy, she observed, attracting, grinning at, and swatting at female flies. She thought to herself, *Huh! That funny feeling must be indigestion.* Attending to her Word, Esther kept on task with her private business and her appointed hospital rounds.

However, her regal, sultry look, her firm hips and round backside in her fitted, sparkling white uniform, and her seeming indifference to his presence caught James's eye. James hunted Esther like there wasn't another woman in the world whose heart needed to be conquered.

"Hi. Do you mind if I sit here?" James said to Esther one afternoon in the hospital's busy cafeteria. His voice was a polite whisper, but it was a manly baritone whisper that somehow slowed up the earth when it was heard. There were other seats around, at least a few. But unbeknownst to Esther, he had hunted her down, swooping in to make his move when he caught sight of her the third time he circled the cafeteria.

Esther looked up at the sound of his smooth voice and was shocked to see his caramel hands extending from the sleeves of his lab coat, and so close to her head. He had appeared out of nowhere. She had been deep in thought as she munched on her turkey sandwich. Her innards were startled, but she held it together. Forcing herself to show no emotion, she said, "Sure. I guess so." She politely made room for James's lunch tray. They started talking, first about the weather, then about their work and the politics swarming around the workplace, and then they landed on their dreams and aspirations.

"I wanna make my mark in this field," James said, being careful not to eat and talk at the same time. Esther noticed his dilemma and thought it was so cute.

"I know what you mean," she responded. "Too many of our people don't have access to good-quality health care or information even now, today, in nineteen sixty-five."

"I know," James agreed. "Hard to believe, ain't it? But if I can do anything about it, there will not be another poor person, black or white, uninformed or be sterilized by some bigot." They shared an incredulous nod, and both vowed to be the difference that the whole of society needed. Then they said no more about this.

During another one of those impromptu, "accidently on purpose" lunch meetings, God had James move in for the kill, so to speak. When, speaking about his career mission in life, he said, "I know that's why God placed me here. So I'd be doing what I'm doing." Knowing it was a fact in his heart, he barely looked up from his sandwich when he said it.

When she heard it, Esther stopped her chewing. And without even checking to see if lettuce was stuck between her teeth or if a spot of mustard had gold-ringed a tooth, she smiled at him brightly. Her eyes gleamed. When later recounting that precise moment in their budding love affair, Esther would always laugh and say, "When he mentioned God . . . oh, it was on like popcorn loaded with the butter!" It took James about three more lunchtime sidles before the two went out on their first date.

"And, ooh weeee, the hospital ladybugs were hot about it, too!" Esther would later say, chuckling. Then she would add, "And later, when they spied the engagement ring, oooh!" That particular remembrance brought on full-blown laughter. Sometimes it was the best relayed part in the chapter of their budding love affair. Because Esther had learned in her early years how to swat back ladybugs eyeing her man—that is, if it came to that.

Anyway, all that hurt about not being able to flower James' seed washed away the first time Esther held little Jubi in her arms. She was healthy. She was beautiful. That sweet little honey-drenched baby popped out looking just like her daddy. The first thing he said when he laid eyes on her was, "My little gingersnap." Esther remembered his eyes being glazed with moisture. His smile had never been so broad. Later, as Jubi grew into her looks and personality, you could see Esther's signature smile added on. When Jubi was born, it was Hallelujah shoutin' time for everybody who knew them.

On the Sunday James and Esther dedicated their baby to God, Forest Unity Memorial Church was packed. To repay God for what He'd done, in front of everyone, Esther vowed to rear their little girl straight up in the church. That was why Jubi knew the Lord so well.

Jubilee was a true lap baby of the church. Cute, with little fat cheeks and thighs, she smiled brightly whenever one of the mothers of the church grabbed hold of her or when the teenage girls of the church fought to hold her. She was their living doll. Jubi was cuddled and nursed in the church's nursery. She was spoon-fed the Holy Word in children's church and later spent summers in Vacation Bible School. Eventually, she graduated to the Voices of Praise teen choir. Then suddenly, wounded and confused, she dropped out of sight.

Oh, the devil wanted Jubi's soul, all right. Esther was sure of it, because Jubi had talent, real talent. Esther declared it in her soul every time she thought of it. And she said it to her spiritual confidants after the drama got to be too much to handle and too big to hide. It forced her to finally deal with her false pride issue. Much to her surprise, she found that sharing the burden aided her search for solace and eased the constant sting of heartbreak.

Jubi's vocal cords must have belonged to a songbird before she got them. It was apparent early on. Even as a baby, her soft cries were melodic, Esther noted.

"Remember little Jubi in the children's choir?" Sister Gentry asked during a FISHH meeting one Tuesday. She reared back and forward in her folding chair, as if the recollection had been generated with the aid of movement. The other ladies, gathered there to discuss church business and other things, had a lot to say on the subject.

"Yes, indeed," one of the ladies added. "'Cause whenever she'd gaze with her little crystal brown eyes in your direction, then open her mouth to sing—"

There was a serenade of "aahs" and "oohs." It swelled Esther's chest.

The lady who'd been interrupted continued. "Well, there was always a spontaneous combustion that took place."

First Lady Beola Wicker jumped in with a look of kindness on her face. "I mean, your soul flamed up," she said. "And all you could do was surrender to it!"

One Easter Sunday morning, the children's choir led the program of the day. A thirteen-year-old Jubi stepped out from the ranks of blue robes. Jubi had a good, tight hold on the microphone and sang slowly but purposefully, just like the choir director, Sister Cherry, had taught her. Jubi sang the intro sweetly, "A change, a change has come over me," and the choir belted the chorus. Then Jubi took over again, in full control of her extensive voice range. She crooned again, like she'd been coached. She looked out into the congregation with her innocent-child eyes and continued the first verse. "He changed my life and now I'm free."

By the end of the song, everyone within earshot—those still in the pews, and the saints slain in the spirit and stretched out on the carpet—were certain that Jubi had commandeered the well-known Tramaine Hawkins gospel classic hit "Changed." And as far as Forest Unity Memorial Church of Baltimore was concerned, the classic would forever be referred to as Jubi's song.

While Jubi sang, Esther, almost slain herself, was especially proud of and grateful for the young choir members surrounding Jubi. They were kids her baby girl had grown up with and gone to school with and played with, and they rallied around her with praises. Her peers shouted the godly praises they had heard their parents lift up during years of good teaching, preaching, praise and worship. They encouraged Jubi unselfishly while she sang. It had been her first real stand-alone solo, and Esther knew how worried Jubi had been about it.

During those moments of doubt, Esther would talk Jubi down off the ledge of fear and had filled her with confidence. Mother and daughter would be sitting on the couch, their favorite place to be, cuddling and laughing at something on TV. "Baby, just use the confidence of Jesus," Esther would often whisper in her daughter's ear during a hug. "Jesus put that voice inside of you," she'd say. "Using it up there in that choir loft is just you tellin' Him thank you—that's all." Jubi's tears and her apprehension would cease every time she heard her mother put it that way.

During the choir rehearsals, Esther watched Jubi's friends pump courage into her daughter's lungs. *That is a special group of kids,* she'd think. Especially that little drummer boy. Esther was pretty sure that he had puppy-dog eyes for her Jubi. Will Promise was about two years older than Jubi, maybe. A tall, wiry kid, he was always smiling effortlessly, as if he couldn't help it, showing off a set of gleaming white teeth inside of a smooth chocolate face. Will was a good kid, with a good family grounding. The family lived just two doors down from the Stones' front door. And Will was as talented on the church's drums as Jubi was standing behind the microphone. In fact, Will was so good, the church took up extra offerings prior to that Easter Sunday to purchase a brand-new set of drums. Later, the church would help Will get into Morgan State, where he would study music.

"The boy can't be playin' on no set of beat-up drums," Reverend Wicker had joked one Sunday, before he preached. The congregation had nodded its agreement and howled in laughter. "That's why when these kids show talent and real interest in something uplifting, it's our job to support 'em." During his church appeal, the reverend went on to say with conviction, "Oh yeah, we prayin' for them. That's without a doubt, but we gonna do a little more than that. Amen, Church?"

And the church said, "Amen." It took about three Sundays to bring in the yield that produced a sparkling set of drums to match the gleam in Will's smile. When Jubi stole a peek at Will, seeking his approval, while she sang "Changed," Esther watched Will's eyes light up. She was glad about it.

However, *changed* turned out to be the operative word, as there were many twists and turns ahead in Jubi's life and in her family's life. And no one, less than God Himself, could have foreseen how wearying and troubling the road would become.

"Her voice was that powerful," folks who remembered would always say.

"That girl used to light up the Forest Unity Children's Choir," Sister So-and-So would say.

"Uh-huh!" would be the hearty response from another old-time member, who would add, "Then she lit up the youth choir."

"Yep. And then . . ." There'd be a regret-filled pause. "Then she dropped out of sight."

"It was a shame, too," the pastor would admit. "When Jubi sang love songs to God, you wanted to curl up like a newborn and let Jesus cradle you in his arms. Her gift was just that pure!" One time Reverend Wicker even made reference to that from the pulpit.

And that was how the story would go.

"The devil wants to swallow all that up," Esther argued tearfully during the FISHH meeting when Sister Gentry brought up Jubi's singing in the children's choir.

Her Forest Unity sisters wrapped her in prayer.

"He don't want nobody to get the glory," she said, fighting to get the words out, because this was war and she was losing. "He don't want no souls saved. Jubi can save souls with that sweet voice of hers, and the devil knows it!" She cried, hard.

Chapter Three

Alternatives and Johns

Jubi gathered a couple of breaths to pull herself together. They stood in the war zone of her parents' living room. In the recent years of her estrangement, she'd won many a battle. She'd vacate the premises with handsome hauls of stashes to liquidate. However, on this blessed Sunday afternoon she'd have to concede a pitiful loss. *Shoot*, was the defeated whisper in her head as she worked to straighten the mess that was her worn-out attire. The battle over, she was now free to head for the front door and make her pitiful exit. And it was none too soon for both James and Esther.

Jubi could feel her parents standing there, consoling one another and staring in her direction. Esther stood there dumbfounded, with her cheek puffy and blood-stained. James hurried off and fetched a dampened paper towel for her to place on her wound. He wrapped his wife up in his arms.

Before her exit, though, Jubi did a slo-mo to the front door, thinking and summoning one last bit of courage. She turned, doe-eyed, to her daddy, and said, "Well, could you at least give me a couple of dollars to hold me?" She kind of rocked unsteadily on one leg while she said it, but she fully expected to get the money. "I'll pay you back, Daddy, when I get paid, Tuesday," she said, darting her eyes on and off her father's face. She ignored her mother's glare.

James broke the embrace of his wife and moved in closer to his daughter, who was God's gift to him and Esther. "Paid!" he said incredulously. "You got a job?" He put his discerning eye directly in her gaze, which bobbed and weaved. It was his attempt to have an honest father-and-daughter conversation. But that wasn't happening. Jubi was lying and was using her tart breath to do it. And it wasn't a secret in this house. "You got a job?" James repeated.

"Yeah, Daddy," Jubi said, making it up as she spoke. "This lady around the corner from where I stay is paying me to watch her kids."

A woman entrusting plants, let alone live babies, to Jubi sounded ludicrous, even to Jubi. For one thing, she, and that no-good slug of a boyfriend, Ambro, didn't even nudge themselves toward the bed's edge until about one o'clock in the afternoon. But Jubi was proud of her quick thinking. It was a story that couldn't be checked out. The last time she lied and said that she had a job, her mother went poking around in her business, checking up on her at the 7-Eleven. The store manager was clueless about who or what a *Jubi* was. And he was perturbed about having to stop his work to answer stupid questions.

But this time was different. Jubi could serve up her great babysitter story as collateral every time she needed some ready cash from her dad. *Yeah. Yeah, that's a good one,* Jubi thought as the revelation hit her. Her satisfaction forced the slip of a smile to cross her crusty lips.

James stared at his baby girl. He couldn't believe that she was standing there, smiling at him. Not after all this. And the loan request was unthinkable. There were plenty of times when his heart buckled and over-ruled his common sense, and he would reach down in his pocket. Unfortunately, such weakness supplied the fuel for disagreements with Esther immediately after. Lately, she seemed to be taking a harder line toward her daughter. James and Esther found themselves fighting not to go to bed angry or disappointed with one another. The effort was getting harder and harder. After all, they were human, and the two were growing weary in their wait for a breakthrough. "And the devil knows we're tired of it all," James had thrown out during one of those testy debates.

Standing there in real time, he said to his daughter, "Really? Do you really think I'm gonna give you some money?"

Jubi bobbed and weaved once more. She gave him a shocked look that said, "How could you?" Her mouth dropped open, then snapped shut. "What?" is all that came out when she could speak.

"Look at this place," James said, his arms in the air as he surveyed the room. "Look at your mother!" he shouted. James rarely shouted. "I don't even know all that went on here, Jubi. But I know you must be out of your mind."

Jubi huffed her anger. "That's right, Daddy. You don't know all about what went on here. But you keep takin' her side in everything." And that was how Jubi truly felt, period. Except that this time, she was going to have to admit to herself that dividing and conquering wasn't going to get it. Things weren't going in her favor, and it looked pretty clear that she was heading out the door, empty-handed. Tears dropped as she begged, "Please, Daddy, just give me fifty dollars. Twenty dollars. Just give me a couple of dollars. C'mon. I know you got it." She walked up to him as she bargained down and grabbed his hand. Sadly, her movements mimicked what she did with her johns when they wanted to be begged. The realization hit her. She almost vomited.

He snatched his hand out of her grasp, and it hurt him to do it, but he kept up his resolve. His voice grew lower. "Get out, Jubi. Just go wherever you've got to go," he said. The room felt cold and still to all three of them. Even Esther's silence was strangely apparent. James drew a long breath before he added, "We'll be here when you need us. *Really* need us."

Jubi's eyes dropped to the floor. "This is wrong, Daddy," she said as she turned and walked to the door. James was close behind, silent. In the corner of her eye she saw her mother turn and scurry up the steps, still dabbing at her cheek. That was when Jubi slammed the front door. And when the door sealed her out and her parents in, she heard the hard clicks of the double locks being bolted behind her. She could have sworn it was a hollow sound. Hollow was what her life had come to be.

After some moments of peering through the front window, James walked past the living room mess, carefully dodging the ceramic lamp fragments on the floor, and headed upstairs, expecting to find his wife right where he knew she would be—in their bedroom, probably on her knees in prayer and crying. But she wasn't on her knees, and she wasn't crying. She was sitting on their bed, nursing her cheek with a pink-stained white washcloth, staring at nothing.

Yes, Esther had been on her knees praying many times. It had been her ritual after every Jubi visit. Esther would pray for the safety and restoration of the child they once knew. She would pray for forgiveness for the secrets she knew. She would pray for the restoration of their family. *Lord, keep her safe until she can find her way back home,* was one of the intimate thoughts she would relay directly to Jesus.

So on that particular Sunday Jubi left her parent's home empty handed. Well, that hadn't happened in a while, she noted with anger. "How could they do that to me?" she muttered through clenched teeth.

Jubi stood outside her former abode, and she waited for the next thing to happen. She didn't know what, exactly, but she waited. Perhaps her mother would run to the door, swing it open, and apologize, hug her, and pull her back inside. Maybe her father would open the door, hug her and kiss her cheek, reach into his pocket, and pull out a wad of twenties to stick in her hand. Maybe he'd add an "I love you, baby," too. Jubi stood there, in fantasyland, for the few seconds it took to run all that through her dusty head. None of it happened, so it was time to make her feet start walking.

Jubi reached the sidewalk, which was landscaped with perfect, lush green squares of baby grass through-out the entire neighborhood. She peered upward. It was sunny, and not a cloud was to be found. But her mind was full of clouds. It was misty with regret and confusion. *What to do now?* she thought, but her mind failed to offer up a solution—a plausible one, anyway. Her parent's house was situated on the dead-end curve of Hilton Road. Heading north would point her toward the main street, which was Liberty Heights Avenue. She looked north and started walking to the bus stop on the corner of Hilton Road and Liberty Heights.

Since it was nice out, a couple of her used-to-be-neighbors were sitting outside on their porches. Among them were some kids and young folks she once knew. They were enjoying the outdoors, talking, playing, lis-tening to music, and stuff. As she approached, each per-son froze and stared. Jubi invoked her pretend blinders so she wouldn't have to look into any of their faces or, God forbid, speak to anyone. Some of the neighbors had overheard the tussle in the Stones' house, and they knew the backstory. Most were members of Esther and James's church. Nearly all the young adults in the neighborhood had been lap babies, just like Jubi, in Forest Unity Memorial Church. Anyone who was still living at home or had gone off to college was still a part of that church family.

Jubi kept her head down and powered up her pace. She felt their inquisitive eyes and knew they were wondering how in the world it could have come to this. She knew it. And she knew they knew the deal about what had just happened in her mama's house. The bright sun warmed her back. But her thinking was still cloudy and clammy. *Darn, what am I gonna do now?* she wondered. Panic seeped into her bones. Jubi still had to come up with some cash, really, quite a bit of cash, to take care of her needs and Ambro's needs. And whatever were they gonna do about the rent? They hadn't paid that in a while.

She flashed back to her last glimpse of that sapphire-encrusted bracelet escaping under the couch. A curse word crossed her lips. Disbelief caused her to shake her head. The mess of her brittle sandy brown curlicues and hay-like split ends played with the wind that flew past. Jubi cursed under her breath again and thought, *If I coulda just got my hands on the doggone bracelet, everything woulda been all right. She had to mess up everything.* Her thoughts flew out of her head when she looked up and spied three or four representatives of the families that were the Stones' neighbors and fellow church members just standing in the vicinity, eyeing her like they were taking in the movie of the week.

Jubi didn't have to be a brain surgeon to surmise that they must have heard everything, or nearly everything, that went on. Her parents were always causing drama whenever she stopped by to visit, she thought. She silently accused both her parents and these inquisitive spectators gathered in her sight of being hypocrites. *Why don't they mind their own business?* She knew just what they were thinking. *Look at poor old crackhead Jubi, coming around once again to wreak havoc on her poor old parents.* She worked to avoid eye contact with any of those "churchy snoop heads," as she called them, so she didn't have to speak or wave to any of them as she made her way down the sidewalk.

Jubi's mission was to get to the corner bus stop to catch the number fifty-two bus back across town. *Freakin' stupid-behind busybodies,* was the last poison dart she leveled in her thoughts before she walked right into Will Promise, another one of those used-to-be lap babies of Forest Unity. Now twenty-one, he'd graduated from Morgan State and continued on there, doing some type of fellowship in music theory. But on that day, he was home, hanging in the neighborhood. Will was a good kid, and things were going well for him. He still played drums for the church on appointed Sundays, when he didn't have to study or be at some school event.

He was well aware of Jubi's downfall. He was well versed in her street reputation. Will knew she had some old old-man boyfriend somewhere in the mix, too. And it was no secret that the guy was a bum. Before Jubi's total disappearance from Forest Unity, they went on a couple of innocent double dates to the movies, the skating rink, and such. But a handhold here or a quick peck there was all it ever amounted to in the early days. Will had liked Jubi back then, and they used to talk a lot. These days, he wasn't waiting for her or anything like that. He had his fun, Jubi suspected. Sometimes, when she thought about him spending time with other girls, when she allowed herself to go there, her skin crawled. She missed their talks, his concern for her. Often his concern had come with innocent kisses. That must have been why she had a soft spot for him. And the feelings he had had for her had somehow remained in his heart.

Will, with his lanky chocolate self, had been outside shooting the breeze with the fellas and absentmindedly dribbling a basketball when he saw Jubi heading up the street. He put himself in her path—almost like magic.

"Hey," Will said, burying the ball in the crook of his wiry arm.

It startled Jubi so much that she came to a halt. She saw his sneakers first and slowly let her eyes travel upward to meet his smiling face. *Oh crap. This is all I need,* she thought sarcastically, and she was suddenly self-conscious about how badly she looked. "Hey," she said back, attempting to move beyond him and be on her way. But he wasn't havin' it.

"Where you headed?" Will asked.

"I don't know," she said. Searching for an answer to his question, she finally said, "Home." Jubi's voice rose when she added, "Excuse me." And then she attempted to move past him. But he blocked her. *Didn't I just go through this dance with Esther?* she thought. *Darn.*

But Will failed to read her exhaustion; he read opportunity. "Home!" he said playfully, letting the basketball drop from his underarm and bounce away. It was his signal that she had his full attention now. She caught it. She understood. She even let herself like it. "Home?" he repeated, continuing to play with her. "But you just left home. So where you going, huh?"

Frustration and anger were starting to rise up in her. She fought them, because he was about to get cursed out, and he didn't deserve it. She liked him, yes, but all that was old stuff. Now the way her life was, she could never get caught up with a church boy. That scene was long over, and she was too contaminated, besides.

"Look," Will said. He seemed not to be playing anymore.

"What?" she said sharply, backing up from him, hoping he hadn't smelled her breath or caught any foul odors from her person.

"Wherever you going, let me take you there. I can drive you."

A few seconds of deliberation flew by as Jubi pondered the opportunity that had presented itself. She smiled and said, "You got any money? Any cash on you?" Jubi had quickly moved into john mode. She recognized it and felt slightly ashamed for crossing this particular line with him. But she was desperate. If she couldn't get at least some of the cash she needed from Will, then she'd have to get it from a john, on her knees in a piss-laden alley. *This is business*, she thought, clarifying matters.

"Money!" Somehow Will hadn't expected the question. Way later, he'd wonder why he had let it shock him. "Girl, I'm a poor college kid. I ain't got no money. What I said was . . . I could go get my mama's car and give you a ride somewhere. That's what I meant." He was laughing, and still smiling, hoping to spend some time with her.

Ignoring his jabber, she asked, "But you can get it, right?" She wasn't smiling, she was negotiating. She looked about them, checking for any witnesses within hearing range. She scratched her nose and attempted to smooth back her hair.

"Well, what you talking about?" Will asked, still thinking he was playing around and missing the desperate magnitude of what was going on.

"Fifty dollars? A hundred?" Jubi asked, but she wanted to say, "One hundred and fifty." *Shoot, something is better than nothing,* she told herself.

Now Will was surveying the scene, looking for witnesses. He was seeing an opportunity, as well. "If I get it, will you let me take you where you wanna go?" He was talking low but still smiling.

His face was pretty, Jubi noted, as pretty as it had ever been. He was a pretty church boy, not worthy of the game she was running on him. But it had to be done. That pissy alley was still in her future, but maybe with a little cash, she could delay things. In the midst of her antsy behavior and her pondering, Will turned flirty-eyed and serious.

"Jubi," he said and grabbed her arms, "so if I get you some money and take you where you wanna go, can we go somewhere else first? You know, ride around some? Talk?"

"Yeah, Will. Sure," Jubi said. She was in john mode and was disgusted. *You niggers are all the same,* was her current thought. She looked into his marble eyes but said nothing more. *Just go get my money,* was her telepathic thought. He caught it. He understood.

"Can I have a kiss right now? You know, let's seal the deal?" Will whispered.

"Sure," she said, emotionless. At this point, she didn't care that her breath was tainted. Because she knew that soon, while the deed was being done, it wouldn't matter. Only the sticky results of two bodies touching would count. *Maybe I'll up the price,* she considered. *Shoot, he's gettin' the Forest Unity homeboy rate.* Her thoughts managed to produce an ironic chuckle.

Will leaned down and kissed her lips. She closed her eyes, though she didn't want to. She liked his touch, but she didn't want to do that, either. She did succeed in not parting her lips. The gentle way that he kissed her came across as alluring. His lips were as soft as a welcoming pillow to a weary head. She remembered that from way back when, too, and was sad for the memory. She didn't think it was possible for her to feel both attraction and repulsion at the same time, but that was the strange concoction flowing throughout her body at that moment. When the kiss happened, the homeboys on the stoop howled and barked. If they knew what they knew, somebody was getting lucky soon.

"Wait here," Will said anxiously. "Wait right here!"

"Okay," Jubi said. But she thought she was lying. She wanted to escape the scene before he returned, or as soon as she could determine that he wasn't coming back out. He had left her standing there, looking like a fool. She really didn't want him to turn into one of her johns. But it was that strange concoction flowing through her innards, and a tremendous need for cash, that kept her feet planted where he'd left her.

Will did a sprint to his house, vanished inside for about fifteen eternal minutes, then reappeared, panting and heading her way. When she looked up, she spied the fellas carousing on the stoop, high-fiving and laughing again. She aimed a scowl at them, because she knew just what the joke was. It was her. But when Will reappeared in front of her, he seemed either oblivious to or unconcerned about what his buddies thought.

"C'mon," he said and motioned with the car keys in his hand on purpose. He stuffed some folded-up bills in his pocket and angled himself toward his mother's car. Jubi saw those, too, and followed his lead. The two folded themselves into the driver's side and passenger side of the car, Will revved the engine, and they were off. She assumed they were headed to some secluded place in or around Druid Hill Park. She was right.

Chapter Four

Carnal Knowledge

1987 . . .

"Jubi," Esther called down the stairs, in a hectic rush. She called out from the sculptured mahogany ball atop the bannister, then scooted back into her bedroom, where she had just awakened from a power nap. Now she was frantically trying to zip herself into a lavender linen pantsuit, primp up, and get ready to head out. The debt retirement committee meeting was to start down at the church in less than an hour. Breaking stride just to get her daughter's attention was a source of major irritation.

At Forest Unity Memorial Baptist Church, committee planning was hot and heavy over a big celebration slated for the first Sunday in November. Forest Unity planned to torch the eggshell parchment paper that said "mortgage due" during a special blazing-fire celebratory church service, an evening service. The committee had already extended an invitation to Forest Unity's sister community church, the Bible Deliverance Church of God, to come and join in the glee. Next on the to-do list at this meeting was to seal the deal on the guest speaker headliner. It seemed a no-brainer.

Later, at the meeting, here was how it went down. Rushing in, aiming for the well-worked folding chairs arranged around an oblong table—a "double zone," as Sunday school teaching took place there—Esther commandeered her seat. First Lady Beola and Sister Peggy, sat amid a couple of seasoned deacons and the two new church members they had welcomed into the committee flock about three weeks prior.

"Now, you know Bible Deliverance is coming to join us, right?" Esther said, catching her breath after sitting down. A mixture of greetings and agreement coughed up in the space. She let her tiny black notebook drop on the table. "Well, it seems only right to let that young preacher over there be our guest speaker," she said, with a look that said, "Well, duh!" painted on her face.

There was a brief silence. Then those present began to deliberate.

"You mean, Li'l Rev? That young boy?" Beola asked.

"Well, look, B," Esther said, kind of laughing. "He ain't exactly a young boy. He is young . . . in his thirties or early forties, I think," Esther added, looking around for confirming nods, "but he ain't no boy—"

Beola cut her off before she was finished. Laughing and conceding, she said, "Okay, yeah. You're right on that count, but I was thinking that Pastor would preach on such a momentous occasion as burning our mortgage and all."

One of the deacons jumped in, taking a liking to Esther's idea. "No, no, no, Mother Wicker," he said. "You don't want Pastor working on that day. You want him celebrating . . . enjoying the service."

Peggy added, "Yeah. You want him standing ready to put the actual fire to that mortgage at the end of the service, not working hard throughout, having to fire everybody up."

Everyone laughed at the unintended pun.

Esther cosigned. "Yeah, that's where our pastor will come in. He'll come in on the burning and the thankful praising of it all. For the sermon and the singing, let him enjoy himself. Let the guest preacher do all the work. Li'l Rev . . . uh, excuse me, Reverend Daniel Harris," she said, clarifying matters, as if they needed clarification. They didn't.

Everyone had known who Li'l Rev was practically since his birth. He was the play son and protégé of Big Rev. And Big Rev was the Bible Deliverance Church's senior pastor, officially known as the Reverend Tommy B. Graystone. Reverend Graystone had taught his play son, i.e., his unofficially adopted son, well, had brought him straight up in the ways that he should go, which meant that Li'l Rev not only knew the Word but could also fire up a church.

"You know that boy sho' can preach," said deacon number two. He shook his head up and down like he was watching a fast yo-yo in motion. He added, "He can pack in a crowd, too." He gave a quick look to his right, at deacon number one, and asked, "We takin' up an offering, ain't we?"

Deacon number one gave a confirming nod and a grin, then said, "You got that right."

They laughed. But everyone in the circle knew that sustaining a church and getting it to the place of ongoing operations was serious business—if it wanted souls to be saved.

"Then you'd better get Li'l Rev over here," Esther joked.

Beola cringed a bit at the remark but kept silent.

Li'l Rev and his spiritual gifts packed a church and caused congregations to be grateful and generous. And you had to be deaf, blind, or dumb not to know it.

"He can pack in the women, can't he?" Peggy threw in. "What else do they call 'em? Behind his back, I mean. Oh yeah, Buttercream Beautiful!" She cracked herself up, because she was being naughty, and she knew it.

The women laughed.

The two deacons chuckled and threw up their hands in playful defense. They said in unison, "Look, I don't know anything about that." It was a lie, in jest, of course. They knew all about it.

Deacon one said, "All I know is that the boy can preach and pack 'em in. So what are we gonna do?"

Esther play smirked at her friend Peggy and said, "I should have known you'd take it there, lady. Okay, so we've established that Reverend Harris can pack in the women. And the women will bring in their children and their men. So in my book, that's a crowd. And Li'l Rev is definitely a crowd pleaser. Plus, we can also ask them to bring one of their choirs along. So is this settled?"

"Amens" and "Uh-huhs" filled the room. Esther surveyed the expressions of those present, threw an extra eyeball at Peggy, and said, "Well, Buttercream Beautiful aside, can we bring this discussion back around to our Holy Ghost Party as a whole, please?"

"Sure," Peggy said. "I was just sayin' that's all."

"Well, the guest preacher is set," Esther declared.

"Great," Beola said. "Peggy, will you draft a letter of formal invitation to Bible Deliverance, its choir, and to the Reverend Harris, please?"

Peggy nodded yes and scratched it down on her to-do list notepad. The meeting moved on.

But first, before all that good stuff could happen, Esther had to get her body over to the church meeting. It wasn't out of the norm for Esther to be down at the church, busy in one committee meeting or another, especially throughout the summer months. Church members didn't have to worry about their children's school days or homework, and older siblings were around to be rankled babysitters for their younger siblings. This was a good thing, because the church liked to solidify lineups for its fall and winter schedules. For this special planning, the meetings had kicked into high gear. It was already September 1987, and this committee's meetings marched on in full gear right up to November.

"Jubi." Esther had returned to the top of the staircase one more time to holler down when she detected no rustling and no response.

"What!" Jubi responded.

Esther's eyeballs journey-rolled to the back of her head as she tried to let the brazen insolence slide off her next-to-the-last nerve. Jubi knew full well that the correct response was, "Yes, ma'am?" And the argument could have started right there.

For some reason, Jubi's obstinate behavior was fast becoming the norm in the Stone household. Both James and Esther had noticed it, but they figured that at fourteen, Jubi was probably just beginning to smell herself—assuming erroneously that the world owed her something because she lived in it, and that, naturally, the world revolved around her. Of course, the fact that Jubi possessed an enormous singing gift didn't simplify matters much. Even so, they both chalked up Jubi's stanky behavior—and that was what Esther called it, "stanky," not stinky—to being a growing-pains thing. For they knew their Jubi was a good girl at heart, a talented girl. They knew for sure she'd outgrow it, or so they both thought.

Let it go, Esther. Let it go. Giving herself a pep talk, Esther slowly massaged her head, which made her testier, because she didn't have the time to be slowly massaging anything. She was in a hurry to get to the church.

Jubi was sitting on the couch, munching on crumbling barbecue potato chips. She was making a mess all over the place and was watching a repeat episode of *The Facts of Life,* a television sitcom. Whether or not it was intentional that she hadn't budged at her mother's first calling, no one knew.

"Jubi!"

"What!"

Let it go. Let it go. I'm not going there. I'm running late. Esther was screaming in her head at this point. Esther asked, "Did you wash those dishes and get the dinner warmed up in the oven yet?"

"Ahhh, yeah," Jubi answered, knowing she hadn't. And yet the lie had not prompted an urgent move on her part to make it true.

"Well, how come I don't smell anything?" Esther challenged.

"Dang, Mama," Jubi threw back, disgusted. She slammed the chips down. The flimsy bag burst open. She got up, brushed the crumbs off her lap and onto the shiny hardwood floor, and stomped toward the kitchen. "Why I gotta do everything around here, huh?"

"Girrrl, we're not tramplin' around that barn again," Esther stressed, upset that she had to stop what she was doing, again, to have this conversation in the first place. "Get on it, girl. Now!" On that note, she heard Jubi clanging dishes, pots, and pans in the distance.

Now, lately that last obstinate move on Jubi's part was a guaranteed invitation to a mother-daughter confrontation. Because girlfriend was begging for it, and both of them knew it. But Esther had to be at the church in twenty minutes. It was at least a thirty-five-minute drive to the church, so she fought temptation and declined the invitation to ring the starting bell for a crisp round one. Instead, she retreated into her bedroom, thinking, *Lordy, I don't know what's gotten into that girl. I don't understand her. More and more, she won't listen to anything we tell her to do. Why, Lord? Why?*

Reruns of their prior battles had started to invade Esther's dreams, as if she was now searching her subconscious for solutions. None came. But this much she knew: the situation was getting worse, something she had once shared with her friend Peggy. "It ain't gettin' any better. And it's gettin' embarrassing," she'd confessed. That was hard for a proud woman like Esther to admit.

Peggy had looked puzzled on purpose. "What do you mean?" she'd said, prodding Esther to drop that load off her chest. Peggy had served with Esther on many of the same Forest Unity ministries down through the years. The debt retirement committee was just another on the list. And Peggy was a fellow nurse at Providence Hospital, where Esther worked. She'd been around Esther and Jubi practically all Jubi's life.

"Well, it's getting so that we'll be in public, I'll say something to her, and she'll snap back some fresh comment, especially if she's got an audience," Esther explained. Her new truth came out with a great deal of difficulty.

"Oh, my gosh," Peggy said, artfully pretending not to have noticed such incidents on her own.

Peggy had conceded the fact long ago that Esther was one of those funny parents who acted like her child could do no wrong. Esther didn't want anybody chastising Jubi since, at least prior to this latest development, she was perfect. And you know how it went;

usually it was those parents who birthed the monsters in training. Still, to be fair, though Jubi was no saint, she wasn't no hell-raiser, either, at least prior to. But as she moved through those early teens, everybody but James and Esther, it looked like, could see that something bad was up.

Peggy had been drooling for an opportunity to tell Esther what was what for a while. So, suddenly, because Esther actually opened the door, Peggy saw it as her duty to walk a little honesty right on in. "You know what you'd better do, don'tcha?" Peggy said quickly, bringing Esther's explanation to a halt. "Knock a couple of those pretty pearly white teeth out. And I bet it'll put some good second thoughts in her." *Ooh, Lord.* Peggy sighed as her eyebrows went up in the middle of her afterthought. *Oops. I guess I went too far.* Peggy didn't want to hurt her friend's feelings, but getting the truth out did feel rather good. *Well, she asked,* Peggy silently assured herself, *and I told her.* Unfortunately, both she and Esther knew that Esther would never raise a hand to her baby girl.

"Huh?" was Esther's only comeback to the suggestion of violence.

It was a hat-pin prick in Peggy's truth-telling balloon. *Frustrating,* was Peggy's next inner thought. They both let out an ambiguous chuckle, then smothered the uneasiness in a gravy of weak smiles. And the conversation was over. The two were at work when the conversation took place, and since nothing really was being resolved in that matter, it was time to move the meds to the patients on the third floor.

For some reason, the communication gap in the Stones' household had become the great divide, and it grew with each passing month, week, even day. Both Esther and James remained clueless. The change in

Jubi seemed to have started sometime that summer. Mother and daughter could hardly have a word of agreement for any length of time. And James's role as referee grew bigger. Esther wondered if it wasn't perhaps because she'd grown busier between her church work and her new supervisory position at Providence. Their impromptu hug fests on the couch were nonexistent now. These days when Esther came home, she either plopped herself down on the couch, exhausted, or crawled upstairs to her bedroom, with the intention of pulling off her bleached white uniform, kicking off her polished white shoes, and plopping her body on the bed for a power nap before something else had to get scratched off her agenda.

Besides, Esther just figured Jubi was getting too old for hug fests, anyway. "You know teenagers," she'd said, laughing it off one day, when Jubi turned her back to a public hug Esther had reached out to give her. They'd been standing in the church's vestibule, and everyone had seen it. Esther had played it off, but she was mortified. She felt her cheeks marooning. Peggy witnessed the whole thing too.

"C'mon, lady," Peggy had said, coming in like the cavalry. "You know we'd better get downstairs and start servin' up those chicken wings before the line gets too big to handle. You know church folk get ravenous after good preachin'," Peggy had joked. They both chuckled a bit. Peggy saw how Esther's smile was forced, and how her eyes wanted to relieve themselves of moisture. Peggy's hug and her effort to keep the moment light kept Esther's tears at bay.

Or maybe it was because Jubi's body was changing and budding. It was true that nearly every day Jubi looked slightly different to Esther, but she couldn't put her finger on it. When Jubi caught Esther's eye from certain angles, Jubi's breasts appeared fuller. Her face seemed a little rounder or something. *Maybe puberty is at the root of this changed appearance,* she thought. It was a curious thing, but finally Esther decided not to dwell on it. *Don't make a mountain out of a molehill,* was her ever-passing thought. Their relationship was already teetering on shaky ground. There was no sense in asking Jubi pointless questions about nothing. What would happen if Jubi thought her mother was stalking her, and for no good reason? Invading her private time for no good cause?

Esther settled the curious matter in another private thought. *Maybe Jubi doesn't know how to handle the growing attention swirling about her due to her physical appearance—attention from boys, and men.* Esther knew she had needed to sit down and have a special talk with Jubi ever since the emergence of breast bumps on her chest. A second special talk, that is, about how to handle the attention of the opposite sex and such. They had had a first special talk to get Jubi ready for her menstrual period. And that was hairy enough. Esther knew she'd never forget it. She suffered the flashbacks often.

Esther recalled that first talk. "So why do I even have to have this period?" Jubi had asked her mother. "Sounds messy." Jubi was ten, going on eleven.

"So you can have a baby," Esther had answered. "It's your body . . . you know . . . gettin' things ready."

"But suppose I don't wanna have a baby? Can I skip it?" Jubi had asked, earnestly deliberating whether or not she felt like having a baby—as if the decision needed to be made right then.

The two were in Esther's bedroom, sitting on Esther's bed. Jubi loved to play grown-up using her mother's jewelry. And Esther loved watching her daughter do so. Back then, one of Jubi's favorite things to do was to watch her mother get dressed. During the talk, Jubi had moved the jewelry box to the bed so she could play, imagine, and quiz her mother, again, on how and when she'd acquired each significant bauble. Some expensive pieces were mixed in. The one piece of jewelry that never failed to elicit the juiciest story was the beautiful, shimmering bracelet encrusted all around with sapphires.

"How did you get this bracelet, Mama?" Jubi asked. The inquiry came out of her mouth like it was a new one. All her mother's jewelry and trinkets were spread out on the bedspread before her. It made Jubi feel rich, like a fairy-tale princess.

Esther enjoyed her daughter's company and pretended to busy herself folding and putting away clothes while they talked. She always answered these inquiries like it was her first time. A small TV provided some colorful white noise. Before the bracelet story got started, Esther decided, impromptu, that this was as good a time as any to have "the talk." Esther sat down on the bed with a half-folded blouse buried in the well of her lap.

"You know, Jubi, you're getting older now, growing up before my eyes. And one day soon your body's gonna make some big, big changes because of it too."

"I know, Ma," Jubi said, neither impressed by her mother's words nor distracted from playing with her mother's jewelry. "I'm getting boobs. I know. You're late. They're already comin' in." She snickered. "They're gonna be big ones too." She laughed.

"What!" was all Esther could say, trying not to laugh.

"Yeah. Like yours!"

"Oh, Lordy," Esther said. "Well, good for you, smartypants, but that's not what I'm talking about, fresh missy." Esther laughed. "When you become a woman, you're gonna wanna have a baby," Esther explained, "and soon your body's gonna start preparing for it."

It was at that remark that Jubi threw out the notion that maybe she didn't want to have a baby. Esther had prayed, literally, for years, for the coming of motherhood, so the notion of non-motherhood seemed ludicrous.

"Of course you're gonna wanna have a baby, like I wanted to have you. Like me and your father wanted to have you," Esther said, reasoning with Jubi.

Adding James to the stew proved to be a boo-boo, because it took them away from the menstrual period prep and caused them both to tread a trench of pain and anguish. The subject turned sharply to sex. Suddenly, the discussion detoured to the naked procreative mechanics of doing it. "The talk," and how it evolved, would go down in the annals of Esther's most horrified moments—at least until future horrors topped the list.

"Has Daddy ever seen you naked?" Jubi asked.

"What? Well . . ." Esther fell into a ditch, something for which she was totally unprepared. She started fidgeting with the half-folded blouse, turning it into a ball of confusion. She could have ripped it to shreds. For she knew she would have this talk, this kind of talk, with her daughter sooner or later, but she hadn't expected it not to be so direct or personal. She expected to use the birds and the bees, maybe even some pollen and some trees, for examples—not the naked, defenseless silhouettes of her and James. *Where are those doggone birds and bees when you need 'em?* she pondered out of desperation.

"Did you and Daddy get naked to do it?" Jubi asked, shifting her attention away from the baubles and bracelets and totally focusing on this incredible idea of her parents being naked in front of each other, and maybe worse. Her expression begged the question, How could you do it?

With a feeling of revulsion, Esther, deciphering her daughter's expression correctly, went into defensive mode. "Well, we had to . . . to . . . to undress. Um, as you say . . . we had to, to get you, darling. We had to."

Disgusted and inquisitive at the same time, Jubi asked rapidly, "Did he get on top of you? While you were naked? And . . . ?"

The room grew hot and stuffy for Esther. Breathing became a chore, and she could feel sweat beads materialize across her forehead. She used her freshly cleaned blouse to wipe her forehead. Now, the poor defenseless blouse bore streaks of make-up. She wanted to forget about the whole thing and deflect her daughter's attention to something funny happening on the television screen, but she couldn't think quickly enough. So she deflected her attention to the unseen and the impersonal. "You see, Jubi, a man has a thing . . . kind of like a pole. . . ."

"A pole," Jubi cried out, her face contorted in incredulous fright. She tried to visualize her daddy coming in from work, now knowing that he had a pole hiding in his pants. "A pole?" she cried out again.

"Well, no, maybe not a pole. Maybe . . ." Esther struggled for words, wishing she had a hammer so she could hit herself in the head with it. "Maybe it's a thing like a pencil." She was dying here. "Something like a pencil pole. I don't know. Something straight, you see." Her hands awkwardly gesturing, she drew in the air some kind of surgical tube device or something like it.

"And what happens then? I mean, what does he do with it exactly?" Jubi asked, like she was waiting for the suspenseful end to a murder mystery, because this had to be murder. And it surely was a mystery. *Her mother and father, naked in a room, on a bed, with her father on top of her mother and her father using his pencil pole. Did she like it? Was it fun? It couldn't be.* Those thoughts roamed in her mind, but she'd save those questions for later, after her mother first got straight what her father did with his pencil pole. She had bits and pieces of the sex story from what she'd seen on TV. But people were always under the covers, or the show would cut to a commercial. She just couldn't snag all the prickly particulars. Jubi kept her eyeballs zeroed in on her mother's face and lips.

"Look, my Jubi." Esther tried to start anew, hoping to steer the conversation away from herself and James. "A man has a thing, like a pencil-pole thing." She started over, this time using the visuals again. She held up her index finger to symbolize the pencil pole, or the pencil pole–surgical tube, and then she shot it out into the air. "And he puts that into the woman, the woman's vagina, to make a baby."

"Ohhh, nooo!" Jubi exclaimed. "Daddy didn't do that to you, did he? Did he?"

"Well, dear." Now Esther wanted to rip the blouse she was wringing in her hands for strength. Or maybe she'd twist it around her own neck until she fainted. For years, she had envisioned "the talk" to be a soft bonding moment between mother and daughter, and here it was a slow walk inside a house of horrors. What in the world had happened to the rhyme she had practiced in her head? First, she would talk about the love; second, she'd talk about the marriage, and throw in the blessings of God; and third, she'd talk about the baby in the baby carriage.

But instead she was trapped, talking about buck-naked sex. She was talking about it in terms of herself and James. And she was traumatizing her daughter. *Where the heck is the manual for this stuff?* her head screamed. Stalling for time, Esther started singsonging in her head, *First comes love. Then comes marriage. Then comes a baby in a baby carriage.*

"Mama!" Jubi yelled, being rude and interrupting Esther's inner thoughts. "Oh no. Daddy didn't do anything like that to you, did he?"

The last thing Esther remembered about the entire debacle was emphatically saying, "Well, he had to, darling, if we were going to get you! We had to, sweetheart!"

Thinking back, she couldn't remember if they had ever totally clarified the menstrual period protocol or not. She'd like to think that later on, she had. Esther did remember vividly how James had cracked up when he heard about it later that day. But he'd declined to go into the trenches to straighten any of it out.

"Oh, no, no, no," he'd said, laughing. "That's women's talk." Before he ran out of the bedroom to escape an airborne pillow, he'd joked, "Ain't nobody tell you to go and have a girl. That's your fault!"

Fast-forwarding to Jubi's moody condition, Esther knew a much-needed second special talk—or was it a third?—was going to have to take place. Esther started that talk on several occasions, but there just didn't seem to be adequate time. *My baby's barely fourteen.* The denial streamed in her head. She made excuses. *I'll get around to talking with her soon*, was the thought that often ransacked her mind. That reasoning popped up when she witnessed curious phenomena, like boys and men in the act of fingering her daughter's anatomy with their eyes in unwholesome ways.

On the day of the church debt retirement committee meeting, Jubi cleaned the dishes poorly, and she
shoved the dinner into the oven, half prepared. She
scooted back to *The Facts of Life* and what was left in
her ripped barbecue potato chip bag barely before the
commercials were over. As a result, she overcooked the
dinner, which was dried out and rubbery. And those
were the events that proved ripe fodder for the fresh
war of words, rounds one, two, and three, that Jubi and
Esther would have when Esther returned home, tired
and church-folk irritated. And so went the new norm in
the Stone household. Most of the time, if James wasn't
refereeing, he simply ran for cover.

"I mean, I don't know what's gotten into that girl,"
Esther said to her dear friend Beola. After another debt
retirement committee meeting devoted to celebratory
planning, the two had slowed up to have a private talk
in the pews. Everyone else but the custodian had left
the church, and he was busy running around, checking
doors and hitting the lights. The sanctuary would be
his last stop.

"I know what you mean. We went through it with our
girl, Cecil. It's something, naw. No joke about that,"
Beola said. "But it ain't nothing new." Beola threw her
head back in relief. She chuckled. "Thank God that
child is married now, with her own kids. Ha, she might
even get some of it back!" They both shared a playful
laugh at the thought. Then Beola felt a slight sense of
guilt over the relief she felt, because her Cecil wasn't
nearly as bad as Jubi seemed to be shaping up to be.
Beola was hopeful Esther couldn't read the relief on
her face.

"Yeah, B," Esther said without looking at Beola, "but
your baby grew out of it and went on to do well in school
and everything. Y'all got a great relationship, right?"

"Well, yeah, Esther. And have no fear about your baby. Have a little faith," Beola replied, trying to console her. "Jubi will—"

Esther interrupted Beola because faith was a little hard to grasp at the moment. "But Jubi is starting to fail her classes. She ain't even showing up at school some days. Teachers are calling," she said. "We argue every Sunday morning, when we're getting ready for church. She acts like it's a surprise about where we're going. And she's awful sassy, too. That's on the regular. So far James and me have been trying to ignore it. So we don't argue with each other about it." There was a curious lump in Esther's throat, because that last part wasn't altogether true anymore. There was loads of arguing all around, going on everywhere. Esther continued, "You know, we're praying on it, and we're hopeful it will go away. Calm itself down. But . . ." Esther's words trailed off as she became consumed by private thoughts.

Beola stood there quietly, listening to Esther, because she understood that at that moment her role was to be a sympathetic ear rather than a conveyor of empty solutions or promises. Besides, Beola didn't really have any answers. She'd heard it through the grapevine that Jubi was running amok in school, acting frisky with boys, and possibly even skipping school. How could she break that news to Esther, the news that their business was all out in the street like that? Beola didn't quite know yet. Esther was a good woman, but she was so proud, and her baby, Jubi, was her world.

"Hey, baby," James called out to Jubi. He had just come home from work. He was working the day shift that week. Esther was still at the hospital, working the evening shift, but the two had managed to cross paths long enough to finalized birthday celebrations for their child. Esther had cleverly assigned James the task of giving Jubi the news that the celebration was going to be a slightly belated one.

"Yeah, Daddy?" Jubi dropped her social studies textbook on the floor to come a-running. Like a rabbit yanked out of a hat, she was standing before him, grinning from ear to ear, within seconds. "Yeah, Daddy?" She was in full doe-eyed mode.

"Come here and sit down on the couch a moment. I've gotta talk to you," he said.

He wasn't exactly smiling, but good news was on its way, Jubi knew. So there were no worries on her part. *Yea!* she thought, but she held that sentiment close to the vest.

"Look, baby," James said, looking into her beautiful, soft gingersnap face, "you know we're gonna celebrate your birthday. You know that. But we're not going to be able to celebrate it right now."

"But it's this weekend," Jubi said.

"I know. However, it's Memorial Day weekend, and the hospital's short, and there's some other stuff."

"So? My birthday is May twenty-ninth!"

James let out a quick laugh. "Jubi, I know when your birthday is. I was there. And I'm the one who told you!" He laughed again. At this point, he was hoping to lighten up the mood with silly banter. He knew his daughter wasn't used to being disappointed about anything, least of all the biggest celebration of the year, her birthday. Mainly because they just wouldn't stand for it. He and Esther and Jubi loved to put on like it was a national holiday.

"But didn't you guys take those days off, like always?" Jubi was reasoning with her father like she was his coworker or his supervisor. And James, feeling guilty, was obliging.

"You see, baby, I've gotta work, and your mother and I have been so busy down at the church that—"

"Ugh!" Jubi screeched, coming close to a toddler's temper tantrum. She was losing all manner of respect. "That church!" she shouted.

James snapped back into parent mode. "Watch it, Jubi. This conversation is about to be over right here and now." His voice was stern.

"No, Daddy, no. I mean that church. You guys are always there, and when you're not there, you're at work!"

"As far as work is concerned," James reminded her, because they had gone around this barn before, "where do you think all the nice things you have come from? The gimme fairy? And what's with this new attitude about church, young lady? We didn't raise you up to be jealous of the church."

Jubi had no answers, just facial contortions to convey her combative thoughts. James didn't like being caught in the butt crack of a confrontation like this. It made him angry, frustrated, and slow on comebacks. If she had responded in the right way, his plan was to tell her about a special amusement park outing that he and Esther had planned. It was a trip to the Kings Dominion just a few weeks later, in June. But Jubi was sitting there with her arms folded and her lips sticking out in a pout, and he didn't feel like discussing the matter anymore.

"Look, go on back upstairs to your room," he said "Your mother and I will talk to you later.

"Fine," Jubi declared. She got up and stomped up the stairs to her room. She got on the phone and complained about her postponed birthday to every girlfriend she knew. And they all egged her on and proclaimed it a major offense.

Later Esther shared the birthday-outing news with Jubi. That was a near battle before she could get out the good news. And sometime around mid-June, the Stone family headed out for a day of fun at the Kings Dominion Amusement Park. School had just closed for summer vacation. The day was hot. The food was good. And Esther and James were busy running around, making all of Jubi's wishes come true. The park was crowded, and while Jubi stood in front of a roller coaster, sizing it up and figuring out how she would go about convincing her daddy to accompany her on the ride, James saw the handwriting on the wall and quickly made himself scarce.

"Hey, baby girl, I'm going over there to get some lemonade," James said.

Esther read the wall too and said quickly, "Yeah, that sounds like a great idea. You wait here, Jubi. We'll be right back." And the two ran off like runaway mice, chuckling.

Jubi didn't catch on to the ploy, for she was too busy mapping out a plan. The soda cart line was long. James and Esther stayed gone for a while.

"Hey," a male voice said. It was kind of smooth, and Jubi didn't recognize it at first.

"Hey?" Jubi said, like it was a question. She was uncertain about whether the greeting was meant for her. Perhaps it was for somebody standing behind her.

"What you doin' here, Songbird?" the young man said, smiling from ear to ear.

"Trouble? Is that you?" Jubi said, all shy and surprised.

Trouble was his nickname, and he had graduated from their high school two years prior. Trouble stood tall, and he was muscular and cute. He had played football in high school, and he played the piano—and all the girls—at Forest Unity. His strange mix of talents made him even cuter. Jubi knew him from afar. She wasn't in his league, so she hadn't actually talked to him much or anything.

Trouble's real name was Ty. Of course, he was the popular type, and he had popular-type parents at the church. They held some kind of high position at Forest Unity, complete with name tags, Jubi knew, and all during church service they'd be running around doing stuff, looking official and whatnot. Trouble's parents thought he could do no wrong too. So it was funny that the boy's nickname was Trouble. But that was what it was.

Jubi had had a little secret crush on him when she was about twelve. She hadn't known what to do with it, so she just held on to it right up to her fourteenth year. That year was 1987. But when, some time before that, Trouble started taking up serious with a young lady named Cheryl Kenny, who was closer to his age, another strange emotion had invaded Jubi's being. Jealousy. She had kept it to herself, but she hated seeing them together, smooching and smiling at each other. It made her sick. And from then on, she hated going to church.

At the amusement park, when Trouble called her Songbird, she felt weak in the knees. Seeing him so close up, with all his attention on her, she got light-headed. That had never happened before. "I'm here with my parents," she said, kind of rushed and unsure. "We're celebrating my birthday." She giggled. She forgot about the roller-coaster line, along with her plan to bamboozle her father into riding the Rolling Jaws of Death.

"Oooh." Trouble smiled. His eyes gleamed. "So you're having a birthday, Songbird, huh?" he said. He gave a quick survey around their space to see who was watching. It was just his way. "Well, I'ma have to give you a birthday kiss." And before Jubi could respond, gush, or faint, Trouble bent down and planted one on her cheek, then pecked her again, quickly, on the lips. Then he watched her eyes fill up with satisfaction, which in turn satisfied him. He knew he was a young girl's dream. Well, he was pretty sure of it, anyway.

Jubi stood smiling, frozen and speechless. Her sneakers felt heavy, as if they had been mounted in the ground. The rims of her crew socks squeezed her ankles. If she wanted to, and she would later, she could count this as her very first kiss. And here it was from the boy she had had eyes for all this time. Had she died and gone to heaven or what? she thought.

Trouble enjoyed every minute of it. He had always loved being the center of attention. He was used to it. "How old are you, Jubi?" he asked.

First, elation filled her, because he knew her name. Then worry settled on Jubi's face. Was she too young for him? *Oh no, that could ruin it,* she thought. Suddenly she heard herself say, "Sixteen," instead of fourteen.

Doggone, his teeth are pretty and white, Jubi said to herself. Her body got warmer than the warm day called for.

Trouble's eyes gleamed again. He shook his head in slow-motion approval and said, "All right, all right. That's a sweet age, Songbird. Do you like to enjoy yourself?"

"Yes," Jubi responded quickly, trying not to give away her confusion. *Why wouldn't I like to enjoy myself?* she thought. "Yes," she repeated as a reaffirmation. Then she changed the subject. "Why they call you Trouble?" she said. It was a question she had always wanted to ask, but she had never got close enough to him to actually say more than a generic hi or bye.

Trouble laughed. His smirk was sexy. And he looked like he was up to something. Actually, he always looked like he was up to something. That was another thing that made him look so cool, Jubi noted in her private thoughts about him.

"What's your number, Jubi?" he asked, reaching for a wrinkled-up piece of paper in his front jeans pocket.

Jubi, enamored again by the sound of her name traveling through his juicy lips, rattled the numbers off so fast, it nearly made her head spin. She was slightly embarrassed, but she was fully committed now. *He knows my name.* Her thoughts electrified the neurons in her brain. She stood there staring up at him and thinking. But what she didn't think was that it was no surprise that he knew her name. Everyone in the church knew her name. Everyone in the church who had ever heard her sing knew Jubi Stone's name. And after they heard her sing, they were destined to never forget her name.

Trouble jotted the number down and folded the paper carefully. "I can call you, right?" he asked, serious and alluring, his sultry stare bearing down solely on her face, as if his eyes were eating it.

"Yeah," Jubi said in a serious whisper. She wore a look that confirmed she was daydreaming. *Can this actually be true?* Later, she'd ask about his girlfriend and such, but those thoughts didn't come to her at that moment.

Trouble tucked the piece of paper with Jubi's phone number back into his front jeans pocket as he leaned over her to kiss her forehead. When he backed up, he saw in his peripheral vision Jubi's parents walking slowly in their direction. It was time for his good-bye.

"I'll call you, Songbird," he said with a huge smile.

Her grin almost cracked the ozone.

"I'll see you later," he said while backing up. "Hey," he called out as if it was an afterthought, but it wasn't. "They call me Trouble because they tell me, I never got over the terrible twos." He laughed and shrugged his head and raised his hands. The last thing he said before he disappeared into the crowd was, "And I like to get my way!"

Jubi laughed, delighted at a dream come true. She was still grinning and staring off in Trouble's direction when her parents sidled up beside her.

"What you grinnin' at, baby girl?" her daddy asked. "Look," he said, because a long pull on his lemonade now gave him the strength to say it, "I don't think that a roller coaster, especially a roller coaster with the word *Death* on it, is a good idea."

Jubi laughed and hugged him. Then she said, "Oh, Daddy, I ain't thinkin' about that thing."

"What? You're not?" James said, surprised and relieved.

"No, Daddy," Jubi said, grabbing his free arm and turning him around. "C'mon, Mom. Let's go do something else. How about the fun house or the house of horrors?"

Esther had been standing there sipping on her lemonade, watching Jubi's sudden change of heart like it was a movie. But the idea of changing venues brought forth only mild relief. She didn't care for the fun house or the house of horrors. Esther liked stage shows. They were entertaining, indoors, and air-conditioned. Her sarcastic comment as Jubi grabbed them both by the crook of their arm and pulled them in a new direction was, "Ummm, the house of horrors. Great. Just where I've always wanted to go—on purpose."

They all laughed, and that was just where they all went, with Jubi leading the way.

Chapter Five

Trouble Calls

Trouble made good on his promise to call Jubi. In fact, much to her relief, Trouble called her two days after they met at the Kings Dominion Amusement Park. The two gabbed for a full hour about nothing.

"So what do you like to do, Songbird?" Trouble said. "Besides sing, I mean."

"Oh, I don't know . . . watch TV, I guess," Jubi responded.

"Like what?"

"Umm, *The Cosby Show*," Jubi said. "Oh, and I really like *A Different World*," she added to impress. She wanted to sound sophisticated.

Trouble ejaculated a sultry laugh deep into her ear and said, "Yeah, I like that too. Did you see it last week?"

"Yep."

"So whaddaya wearin'?"

"Huh?"

"Never mind." He chuckled.

Jubi struck a pose across the fluffy white comforter with lace trim on her canopy bed, as if he could see her. She tightly wrapped the swirly phone cord to her new pink Princess phone around her finger. Rhythmically, she wrapped it, then let it fall, then wrapped it again. As if she were onstage, Jubi talked, giggled, and cheesed. Her Princess phone was in the mound of birthday presents she had received. It was by far her favorite gift. It kept her sequestered in her room, barely coming out for meals. James and Esther were just thankful to see a happy, slightly more agreeable Jubi bouncing around the place. And, lately, Jubi couldn't wait to get to church.

Perhaps the growing pains were coming to an end, they thought.

Trouble and Jubi talked about school stuff. "Trouble, you didn't even know I went to the school, since you were some high-and-mighty football player and all that," Jubi joked, jazzing up her voice.

"What? Naw," Trouble said, denying the allegation. "I knew you." He knew his claim was weak. Trouble knew she was an underclassman, because it just made sense, but that realization had just come to him. At school, he had spent most of his time in the gym. Jubi really had not been a concern in his world.

Later, at the church, they talked about it again, and Trouble continued denying that he hadn't noticed Jubi in school. They were playing around in the church's vestibule after choir rehearsal. Jubi was waiting for her mom to pick her up. They gabbed about school some more, but they also shared things that had made them laugh during church, like how Sister Cherry, the choir director, got happy all the time.

Jubi wondered why he was still hanging around in Baltimore, instead of being off somewhere at some big-time college. In fact, she thought she had heard that that was where he was. She wondered about it, but she kept it to herself. Maybe he got hurt or something. Who knew? "And what about your girlfriend?" she wanted to ask. She'd rehearsed the question in her mind, but she was having trouble getting up the nerve to say it.

Finally, Jubi got around to asking some stuff during their next phone conversation. "So what's up with you and Cheryl?" Jubi asked, getting comfortable on her canopy bed, and getting more comfortable talking to Trouble.

"Cheryl?" Trouble said the name like he didn't know it. "Oh, girl, she's outta here."

"Oh yeah?"

"Yeah," he said, "She's gone down south to that school. I told her not to go to. 'Cause I was stayin' here."

"What school?" Jubi asked.

"To Spelman, I think." He sounded irritated. Jubi hadn't heard that tone before. "Shoot, I don't know. But she's outta here," he said, then paused to change gears and be playful again. "What? You worried about something? You jealous, Songbird?"

"No," Jubi said quickly. "I ain't worried about nothing. I just wanna know what's goin' on, that's all."

"Why?"

"What you mean, why? 'Cause I know you ain't here talkin' to me when you've got a girlfriend. That's why," Jubi said. There was playfulness in her voice, but she was serious.

And Trouble got serious—so she could hear it. He said, "Jubi, you wanna be mine?" There was silence on the other end of the receiver. So he kept at it. "Well, I want you to be mine. So how 'bout it?" he said smoothly.

"Yeah. Sure," Jubi said slowly, stunned and happy. "Okay," she said, thinking to herself, *So I guess I'm going steady, huh?* When the fact settled in, she became ecstatic, but she tried hard to play it cool.

"Good. Then let's make this thing official."

"What you mean?" Jubi asked in earnest.

"Girrrl," Trouble joked, "you sixteen naw. I know you ain't gonna turn into no baby on me, naw. When can I come over there?"

"Over where?"

"Over your house, Songbird. When can I see you, girl?" he said. He paused, then said, "I wanna see you sing for me. Just for me."

Panic set in on Jubi. She didn't know how to react to that last thing he said. And she hadn't shared with her parents that she was talking to a boy, much less that she had a boyfriend. *Oh, Lordy, how am I gonna break the news to them*? she wondered. How was she even going to bring up the subject of boys and the fact that she wanted to have boy company? The good news was at least it was someone they knew. That would soften things. And it was someone from the church. But the bad news was that he was older, maybe even twenty. And here she was, barely a minute past fourteen. *Will they go for it?* she asked herself.

"Jubi? Jubi? Where you at, girl? You done hung up on me or something just 'cause I asked to come over?" Trouble said playfully.

Jolted out of her inner turmoil and deliberation, Jubi said, "Huh? No, no, Trouble. Sure, you can come over."

"Okay, cool. When?"

"Look, soon. Lemme call you back, okay? My mama's callin' me."

"Okay, girl. But call me," Trouble said. "We gotta make this thing official. Ya hear me, Songbird?"

"Uh, yeah, yeah, I hear you," Jubi answered, not really listening or understanding. She had to think about how she was gonna work this whole thing out, including the part about her lying about her age. That could upstage everything and end it all. Finding solutions was gonna be tough. "I'll talk to you later. Okay, see ya," she said, and she hung up without hearing his good-bye.

Since the thought of telling her parents that she wanted to have boy company was overwhelming at the time, the strangest thought rolled through her mind. She lay there, resting her head on her pillow and gazing out her front window at the neighborhood's tree-lined street, thinking, *Uh, it's funny how calling him Trouble seems so normal.*

Two afternoons went by before she felt the time was right to engage her mother in an impromptu conversation. Esther stood at the sink, rinsing off dirty dinner dishes, placing them with care in the dishwasher. James had moved from the dining room into the living room, where he had planted himself on the couch to watch the ball game. The Orioles were trying to have its way with the Yankees. It was a good evening to have that conversation because both James and Esther happened to be off at the same time, and there were no church meetings that they needed to rush off to. Jubi had followed her mother into the kitchen when she left the dining room. She plopped into a kitchen chair, plotting. Then she popped up.

"Here, let me do that, Mom. You rest." Jubi said it like it was normal.

Esther's eyes widened, and she chuckled. "Say what? Little girl?" she said, standing stock-still, holding a soapy plate, which dripped on the floor. "You gonna do *what?*"

"Oh, Mom, you're so funny. I help you all the time," Jubi said without giving her mother any face-to-face. She just grabbed the dishes out of the sink, ran them under the water, and placed them carefully where they needed to be.

"Well, I see you do know how it's done," Esther said with a chuckle. "Yeah, you help, all right. But that's after I pulled a tooth, either yours or mine," Esther joked, then laughed. She stood there, and it took her only seconds to realize that something was up. "So cough it up, baby girl," she said, now standing with her hands mounted on her hips.

"What?" Jubi said, still working on the dishes and looking dumbfounded. "What? Cough up a tooth?"

"No. Cough up what it is that you want," Esther said. "You know what I'm talkin' about, little missy."

Jubi stopped what she was doing. She had finished the dishes and was down to the soapy silverware. Slowly, she put everything down and cut off the water. Her mother sat down at the kitchen table, following her daughter's lead, as that was where Jubi was headed.

"Well, Mama," Jubi said, pacing herself and being selective about each word she uttered. "Well, Mom, there is something I wanna talk to you about." She fiddled with the sugar bowl and the salt and pepper shakers, which stood between them like a tennis net on the table. As she fiddled, she intermittently looked up into her mother's smooth olive face, trying to read it.

"Okay. What's on your mind, girl?" Esther was serious now.

"Boys." Jubi let the word out before she meant to. And that wasn't the word she was planning on saying first.

Oh, Jesus, Esther thought. *I knew we should've had that darn talk.* But out loud she laughed and said, "Boys! Is that all? No. Not until you're sixteen." Her eyebrows pointed toward her forehead, but there was no malice in her voice, and just a slight smirk on her face.

"Mama, don't make fun of me," Jubi said, a little tender about being laughed at. "I don't mean boys. I mean one boy. A boy I like."

"Well, Jubi," Esther said, straightening out the baby blue tablecloth, "I'm not laughing. Jubi, really, I'm not. But truth is, you're only fourteen, barely fourteen."

Jubi whined, "Ugh, would everybody quit saying that? Fourteen is fourteen!"

"Esther quipped, "Everybody who?" Then she regrouped and went back to the statement she had planned to issue. "Now, your father and me had hoped to wait on this boy thing till you turned at least sixteen. You know, that's the—"

Jubi interrupted again. "Mama, that was in the old days," Jubi complained. "People don't wait no long time just to have a boyfriend and stuff."

"Boyfriend! And stuff! What stuff?"

"Well, I mean," Jubi said, "I mean having company, that's all." She put on her doe-eyed look, forgetting that that worked better on her father.

"Company!"

"Can I, Mom?"

"Can you what?" Esther could utter only short, stubby sentences at the moment.

"Have company? Have a boy over. Can I? Can he? "

Esther scratched her head with one hand and rubbed her arched brow with two fingers on her other hand. This was getting as bad as "the talk" they'd had, and she dreaded even more the second talk they needed to have.

"He's a church boy," Jubi interjected quickly and studied her mother's face as it slowly relaxed into a smile.

"Yeah?" Esther said with a slight hint of relief.

"Yeah."

"You should've started with that. Do we know him? How did this all come up?"

"Yeah, you know him . . . I think . . . and we've been talkin' on the phone," Jubi said.

"What?" Esther said, astonished about all this blooming puppy love going on, unbeknownst to her and James. *But at least this is a church boy. So how harmful can it be?* she thought. "Well, baby girl, who is it? Don't keep me in suspense," she said playfully.

"Well—" Jubi started in, but Esther cut in out of excitement.

"Oh, I know," Esther said most assuredly. "It's that little drummer boy." Esther smiled.

"Who?" Jubi said. Her mother caught her by surprise with that one.

"C'mon, you know," Esther said, displaying showy teeth like a cartoon hyena. "That Promise boy. Will Promise!"

"Will?" Jubi said, surprised. She chuckled. "Ahhh, Ma . . . Will . . ."

Esther was busy staring at her, her grin and her arms frozen in place. *What's wrong with Will?* she thought. Her thoughts were the only thing that moved.

"Will!" Jubi laughed. "That nerd ball?" she said. "Heck no, Mom. Whatever made you think of him?" Now little Jubi's gingersnap face had the nerve to look disgusted. Truth was, she had had a little crush on him too once. But now, with Trouble, she had moved up to the big leagues.

When Esther regained her composure, she asked, "Well, who then? I mean, I'm confused."

"Okay, Mom," Jubi said. She got serious, sensing that her mom's hesitation was an indication that she really had no clue. But she let herself think that once her mother got used to the idea, everything was gonna be all right. "Ma?"

"Yeah?" Esther eyeballed Jubi's lips, waiting on the edge of her kitchen chair."Trouble."

"Who?"

"You know, Trouble . . . Ty . . . Ty Custis."

"What?"

"Ty. Trouble! I mean Ty!" Jubi kept repeating his name in an effort to clarify matters. *How come you can't get this?* was all she thought. "Trouble," Jubi said again. "You see him playing the piano almost every Sunday, right, Ma?"

"Trouble!" Now Esther was confused. "What the heck?" she said, immediately asking God for forgiveness because *heck* wasn't the word she was thinking of. Esther shook her head no and pushed herself away from the table, because as far as she was concerned, the conversation was about to be over.

"Mom?"

"Don't 'mom' me, girl." Esther drew in a tired breath and said, "Besides his little nickname being Trouble, that boy's way too old for you. Heck, naw, that's out of the question." Esther said.

"Oh, Mom, that ain't nothin'. His name ain't nothin'. You just being old-fashioned," Jubi yelled.

"I don't know what's the matter with that Will boy. He's what? About one or two years older than you maybe? You oughta be glad we think that's all right!"

And that was the last word Esther said. Jubi's news had caught her off guard. Finally, she got up and headed toward the kitchen door. Maybe later, when she calmed down, she and Jubi could have a thoughtful conversation about it all. Maybe there'd be the second talk. But she hadn't face it just yet.

"Mom," Jubi called out again. She was still seated, and she started to cry. Later anger would set in, but she hadn't come to that yet.

Esther said, "Look, Jubi, that boy's too old for you. He's practically a man, and a disgusting one, if he's lookin' at you, a fourteen-year-old girl! I don't know how all this came to you, but it better stop right here."

"Mom," Jubi yelled, "you're not being fair!" She wasn't finished making her case, but her mother had made her final point.

"I've gotta talk to your father about this one." Esther was rolling her neck now.

"Tell Dad?" Jubi yelled. Just then they both heard James yelling his approval at somebody's home run. If this whole thing hadn't been a total disaster, James's enthusiasm for the game would have provided comic relief, but all it was, was white noise. "Why you gotta tell Dad!" Jubi squeaked out through tears that fell on the crystal sugar bowl top.

"He'll set that boy straight too," Esther yelled. And then she was gone.

As Jubi heard her mother stomp right past her father on her way up the stairs, two thoughts roller coastered in and out the tunnels of her mind. One, *Thank God Mom is bluffing about telling Dad.* And two, *Oh, I'm gonna see Trouble. I don't care what you think.*

Seething with anger, she exited the kitchen and passed by her father, who was still engrossed in his ball game. He was about to swing an imaginary bat in the air. Jubi walked up the stairs, calculated, and headed for her room. She threw herself upon the fluffy white lace comforter and grabbed her Princess phone to make a call.

"Hi," she said in a kitten voice. "May I speak to Trouble, please?"

A deep voice responded, "Girl, you know it's me." He chuckled. So you callin' *me* now?" He laughed. "What's up, girl? I didn't know you knew the number. You like to make me do all the work," he said, belting a laugh this time because he had cracked himself up.

Jubi listened but ignored the banter. She had a mission and needed to keep moving before she lost her nerve or her anger.

"You wanna come over?" Her voice was a monotone. The question was met by a brief silence.

"Yeah, girl," Trouble finally said. "I asked you, didn't I?"

"You wanna come over Thursday night?"

"Shoot, yeah. You gonna be ready?"

"Fine. Then I'll see you around seven," Jubi said, after quickly deciding that all the nosy neighbors would be indoors by then.

"Fine, baby. I can't wait," Trouble said. Then he took a breath, as if he was easing himself back, relaxing on something and ready for one of their hour-long chats. "So what you doin', girl?" He chuckled. "What you wearin'?"

Definitely not in the mood, because the mission was over, Jubi said, "Hey, listen, my mom's calling me. I gotta go now."

Stunned, Trouble said, "Okay. Dag!"

"You know where I live, right?"

"Yeah, I gotcha."

"Good. Call me Thursday, if you want, but I'll see you then. Okay?"

"Bet!" He was about to say some sweet thing before letting her go, but the click interrupted him. The conversation was over. "Doggone, baby," he said to the dial tone. He smiled a smile of anticipation. "That's how you gonna treat your lover man?" The abrupt hang-up didn't ruffle his feathers none. He went on to doing something else.

***

Thursday came. Jubi had hardly slept a wink the night before. She was nervous and excited. *My boyfriend's coming over.* The sweet thought rushed through her mind. The biggest dilemma of the day, she eventually decided, would be what to wear. Around midday she made it to her closet to scope out the right outfit.

Esther and James hadn't left the comfort of their bedroom yet. They both had getting ready for work on their mind. Both were on the three-to-eleven shift at the hospital. Getting the same shift didn't always happen, but when it did, it was kind of good, because at least they could ride to and from work together. And Jubi was fourteen now, and she had long ago proven herself old enough and mature enough to be home alone.

Esther had calmed down from the other evening, but she still hadn't revisited the subject of boy company with Jubi, though she knew she would. And she still hadn't said anything to James. She figured she wouldn't until she and Jubi had had a chance to talk again . . . calmly. There was no rush.

Of late, Jubi had taken an interest in the new next-door neighbor, who had moved in about three months prior. Her name was Victoria. The young woman was twentysomething. She was unmarried and had a young son about two years old. Initially, Esther had raised an eyebrow about that fact but had decided not to judge. The young woman was so nice, and so nice to Jubi, that she decided to help bring her to the Lord instead. And Victoria had easily obliged when the invitation was extended to come to church one Sunday. She had come a couple of times and had looked as though she liked it.

Victoria was cinnamon hued, had a sleek and shiny black bobbed hairdo, and stood about five foot six up from the ground. She was attractive and voluptuous, bordering on curvy and thick. She had a main squeeze and a couple of suitors, as well. Jubi entertained herself watching Victoria come and go, all dressed up, on dates. Often, Jubi babysat her little boy. Jubi loved when that happened, because not only did she make some good pocket change from it, but also oftentimes she'd get to come over and watch Victoria get ready for her evening out. They talked "the talk" during those times too. Victoria generously unloaded all the ins and outs about life, men, and sex. Jubi supped on the insights like they were manna.

"I'm here," Jubi called out to Victoria on one particular evening. She'd come over to babysit. Victoria often kept her front door unlocked. A lot of folks did in the neighborhood. Nothing ever happened on that street, or even anywhere close, to make anyone want to do otherwise.

"I'm in here," Victoria called. "In the bedroom. Come on back!" Her son was in the living room, in his playpen, which was parked in front of the TV. That was where he seemed to stay most of the time.

Jubi slammed the front door, made a pit stop to playfully acknowledge the little boy, then scurried into the bedroom. The door was open, and she walked right in.

"Oh my God!" Jubi yelled. She stopped short and slapped both hands over her face. In a muddled voice, she shouted, "I'm sorry. I'm sorry!" Her body was frozen.

Victoria was standing in front of her brass bed, before her bureau mirror, with nothing on but the bra she had wrapped around her upper torso. The fastener was clasped in the front, and she was in the leisurely process of moving the cups around her waist to the "get ready, get set, and go" position before putting her girls in their proper holsters. Jubi wouldn't know this fact for another, say, oh, ten years or so, but had she known, she would have understood Victoria's need for an EE-size brassiere. The girls were huge, their brown nipple eyes pointed toward the mirror, and when Victoria swung around to look at Jubi, they seemed to have minds of their own. Surprised and startled again, Jubi spied robust pubic hair, Victoria's prominent backside, her thighs, the whole works. Later she'd recall that until then she had never, ever seen anybody, a grown person, naked.

Victoria never missed a beat. She holstered herself and started laughing, while Jubi, still unable to move, continued apologizing profusely for the invasion.

"I'm sorry. I'm sorry," Jubi kept saying.

"Come on in here, girl," Victoria said, now down to a chuckle. "I told you to come on in." Now holstered, but still not wearing bottoms, she fumbled through some clothes on the bed, fishing out her panties for the next step in the process. "What are you so upset about? I'm just naked. You ain't never been naked before? Naked is natural," she informed Jubi, still getting dressed.

"Oh," was all Jubi said. She had finally regained movement in her legs, but not her sight, and she bumped her forehead on the door frame while trying to escape the entire teachable moment.

Once they both found themselves in the living room, they both acted like the little life lesson had never occurred. Jubi sat on the couch, holding Victoria's son on her lap, and Victoria was now fully dressed in a slamming cobalt-blue minidress that caressed her every curve. She was ready to hit the street. A horn beeped outside. Victoria's date was waiting.

"Okay, I'm leaving. You know what to do, right?"

"Yeah." Jubi nodded.

"Good. My mom's number is on the fridge, in case of any emergency. Don't let anybody in," Victoria said. "You can stay here, sleep on the couch, if you want to, until your mom comes home from work, or you can go home in the morning. Just let your mama know."

"Okay. I will."

Victoria gave her baby boy a hasty smooch, said her good-byes, and was out the door. The last thing she said was, "Your money's on the bureau."

"Thanks," Jubi hastened to reply, but the front door had closed shut.

Another teachable moment came when Victoria and Jubi and the little boy were at Mondawmin Mall. They had gone to the movies together and had had lunch. They had done that on several occasions. It was great. James and Esther felt it was safe. And they thought it was great that Jubi, being an only child, had taken such an interest in the little boy. She acted like a big sister. It was cute to watch.

Victoria was probably looking for something mean-ingful in her life, James and Esther assumed. That was why she never seemed to turn down an invitation to go to Forest Unity. Victoria's mother seemed very nice too, even though she appeared to be a bit highbrow. She seemed the total opposite of her daughter. But once, during a private moment when she was feeling vulnerable, something that would never occur again, Victoria's mother had revealed to Esther her initial heartbreak about her daughter becoming an unwed mother. But she did add proudly that she loved her new grandson to pieces. "I pray every day for my daughter to get it together," she'd said, which was code for "I wish Victoria would get a husband." Esther had a rare aura about her that caused people to confide in her like that. Other people's heartbreak often found her soothing ear. They found her sympathetic.

"I dreamt about your baby three nights ago," Esther told Victoria's mother when she saw her coming down the street one day. Esther had run from her front door and across the lawn to greet her. She was wearing her favorite lavender housedress again. She had about three of them that looked exactly the same.

"You did?" Victoria's mother had smiled, surprised and hopeful.

"Yep," Esther confided. "Your baby's gonna be all right. She's gonna be in the hands of Jesus soon, one day." Esther was sure of it. And perhaps Victoria's mother wanted to inquire a bit about the dream, but Victoria and Jubi came out of nowhere to greet them, and the conversation was over.

Back at the mall, Victoria and Jubi were strolling around, doing a little light shopping and heavy window-shopping, when they ran into an old college friend of Victoria's. Jubi watched the grown folks' interactions and listened with intrigue to their conversation. Victoria, Jubi noted, seemed genuinely happy to see and catch up with her friend.

When the friend walked away, Jubi said, "She was nice."

"Uh-huh," Victoria responded and smiled. "She's very nice. She's a whore too."

Jubi stopped dead in her tracks and, bug-eyed, stared at Victoria.

Victoria laughed. She loved schooling her sweet little protégé on the facts of life and catching her off guard. "Calm down, girl."

"But you said she was nice," Jubi remarked. "How could you say that about her? You said she was nice."

"C'mon, girl. Step it up." Victoria had never stopped her window-shopping. "That's right. She is nice," she said. "She just likes to have sex, that's all. She likes men—a lot of 'em." She turned to look back at Jubi, who still hadn't moved. "She's a whore, but I didn't say that was a bad thing. Did I? Now, c'mon. Step it up, girl. We got a lot of ground to cover." Victoria laughed.

And there it was—another life lesson that left the flies free to roam in and out of Jubi's mouth however they wanted.

"Oh," was all Jubi could muster up, again. She picked up her pace.

Clothes were scattered all over Jubi's bed by the time she finally settled on just the right outfit for her first boy-company affair. It was a pink and purple wrap-around skirt and a pale pink blouse that had ruffles and a button-down front. *I'll just wear sandals,* she thought. *Or just be casual. I'll just be barefoot.* That was how she walked around the house, anyway.

The phone rang. *Oh no, he's breaking the date,* Jubi thought, staring at the phone. On the third ring, she picked up.

"Hello?"

"Hey, Jubi," Victoria said on the other end.

Jubi gave a sigh relief. "Oh, hey."

"Listen, Jubi, you feel like babysitting tonight?"

Shoot, Jubi said to herself. "Well, uhhh . . ."

"Pay you double, little girrrl," Victoria said playfully. She hadn't let Jubi finish what she was trying to say. "Look, I think Buck's gonna pop the question. That's right. So I planned a quiet dinner at my place, if ya know what I mean." She giggled. "So, look, girl, let the baby stay over there tonight. Sleep over. All right?"

All Jubi could do was listen. She couldn't get a word in edgewise. "Well . . ."

"Good," Victoria said. Perhaps in her mind she had heard a yes. "Remember, I'll pay you double. And I'll tell you all about it tomorrow." She was excited.

"Okay," Jubi said feebly. *Shoot.* Her inner voice stressed. This felt like a ripple in her plans.

"I'll bring the baby over there about six," Victoria said. "And his stuff." That came just before the click.

"Shoot," Jubi said out loud, trying to come up with a plan B. She paced the floor. "Okay. Okay. Calm down, girl," she said aloud. "This doesn't have to change any-thing. My parents won't be here, and what problem could a little toddler be?" Then the cloud lifted. "Shoot, Trouble can help me babysit." And there it was, all worked out. Jubi smiled and commenced cleaning up her room. It was still gonna be a good night.

The sun was momentarily hiding behind some clouds, but the summer eve still held on to its heat. It was 6:30 P.M. Victoria had come and gone, dropping off her special delivery. Jubi thought that with Victoria coming by, the nosy neighbors would be thrown off the scent when Trouble got there. At 6:45 P.M. the phone rang. With the toddler straddling her hip, she rushed to the phone.

"Hello?" Jubi said, trying not to sound anxious.

"You ready for me, girl?"

"You still comin'?" she asked.

"You know it."

"Good," Jubi said. Hesitantly, she added, "Well, I got a little surprise for you." But she didn't say what.

If a grin could be audible, then Jubi would have heard Trouble's. "Oh yeah, girl? What?"

Now Jubi tried to keep the baby boy from making a noise. "You just get over here," she said. "That's all."

I'll be right there!" There was a click, and none too soon, because baby boy let out a rousing whoop at the sight of some cartoon character that he fancied on the television.

It was 7:00 P.M. on the dot when the doorbell rang. Baby boy was safe in his portable playpen. Jubi tried smoothing her fluffy brown hair, an impossible feat. Its natural curl was invincible. She smoothed her blouse instead, straightened her skirt, and answered the door. And there he stood. *Trouble, in the flesh,* she thought. She broke out in a big grin.

"Hey," he said.

"Hey. C'mon in," Jubi responded.

Trouble entered slowly, Eddie Haskell-style, surveying the place. He was expecting to see some parents and preparing for them to come out of the woodwork somewhere.

"You can sit down on the couch," Jubi said, polite and nervous. But he didn't.

Trouble stood in the middle of the living room, finding himself in front of a playpen and an inquisitive little baby boy. "You got a brother? I didn't know that."

"I don't," Jubi said, sitting down on the couch, expecting him to follow her lead. But he didn't. He kept surveying the room. "I'm babysitting for my neighbor. I told you about her."

"Oh yeah," he said. So this is the little rug rat."

"Yep."

"So when are your parents comin' out of their hiding place?" Trouble said, craning his neck to see around corners and such.

"They ain't," Jubi said.

"Say what?"

"They're not here."

This was indeed incredible, Trouble decided. "Well, where they at?"

"At work!" Jubi said like it was nothing. "Sit down. Relax. Help me take care of this cute little chipmunk." She laughed.

Oh, man, baby girl really is ready, was his thought. He smiled. He grinned. He had expected it sooner or later, but he didn't expect to get it this fast. This was favor. He sat down real close to her. "What we lookin' at on TV?" he asked.

"I don't know. *Columbo*'s gettin' ready to come on soon."

"Good," he said, but he wasn't paying any attention to the television set or the baby in the playpen. He leaned over and gave Jubi a slow kiss on her lips.

She felt awkward about what to do with her hands, her body, but she let him kiss her. And when he felt no resistance from her, he pressed her lips open and pushed in his wide, sappy tongue. Jubi reared backward and attempted a muffled noise of mild protest when she realized the two of them were slowly lying down on the couch. That was when she gained some control of her arms and hands and raised her arms, spread-eagle, to clutch the arm and top edge of the couch, like a cat catching itself while falling. The sudden protest caused Trouble to break free and look at her. It jolted him from his thoughts of sexual pleasure. He licked his lips, regrouped.

Catching her breath, she said, "Hey, wait a minute." Her blouse was mussed. Her skirt had bunched up. She had to regroup too. The baby remained oblivious, playing with a yellow toy dump truck and jabbering to himself.

Trouble smiled and licked his wet lips again, kind of like an iguana. "What's the matter, girl? Don'tcha like it? Don'tcha like me?"

She quickly got up off the couch and said, "I think I gotta check his diaper." Her skirt was short, and she had not pulled it back down all the way, and Trouble caught a glimpse of her panties when she jumped to her feet.

"Oooh, purple," he said, convinced she'd given him the treat on purpose. "I like it," he said. Actually, they were pink with a pale blue trim.

"What?" Jubi responded, as oblivious to his excitement as the baby was to them being there. She gave him a second involuntary treat when she bent down to lift the boy up out of the playpen. "I'll be right back," she said as she grabbed a Pamper and a travel dispenser of wipes out of his diaper bag before carrying him up the steps to her bedroom.

And for a second or two, Trouble contemplated jumping up those stairs after her and following her to wherever she had disappeared. For he assumed the final destination would be a bedroom. But for some reason, he didn't. Perhaps he was enjoying this foreplay too much. Instead, he took advantage of this solitary moment to quickly survey the downstairs again to be sure they were alone. And he perused the framed family photos on the mantel. Satisfied that they were alone, he felt no need to rush things to a climax. Still, Jubi was willing, he knew, and he couldn't wait to give her his special treat.

When she returned, her clothes properly adjusted, she placed the baby back in his playpen. Later, she wished she'd let the baby roam free in the living room. Well, after she returned the baby to his confines, she awkwardly planted herself beside the playpen, not knowing where to look or what to do or say next. Trouble had planted himself in the middle of the couch, his arms spread-eagle across its black leather rim, watching her every move, looking like he was enjoying a lap dance. If Jubi sat anywhere on that couch, she would automatically fall into his huge, gangly embrace. It was like a gigantic spiderweb, a trap. Still, without fully calculating any of that in her mind, she just stood there, looking nervous.

"So where's your parents, Songbird?"

"Umm, at work," she said softly. "I already told you that."

"At work," Trouble responded, like he couldn't believe his ears. A *Cat in the Hat* grin grew across his face. His eyes gleamed, and he made no attempt to camouflage his desire. "Your parents let you have company when they ain't around?"

"Yep," Jubi said, working to look like it was no big deal.

Trouble reined in his arms and got up slowly to walk toward her. "Cool," was what he said as he moved in close. He took her hand and moved her away from the playpen, heading for a bare living room wall.

She was silent and cooperative, even when he pressed her up against the wall. It was all a slow dance minus any music, and she performed the dance in slow motion. He had a good hold on both her hands—really, her wrists—now, ready to braid her arms around his waist. Which he did. He used his thigh as a wedge to create a space between her legs so she could feel him. And she felt his pole, solid, bulging, and aimed at her. Jubi might as well have been standing there nude from the waist down. Her thin rayon miniskirt and her pink cotton panties with the blue trim were neither gatekeepers nor barriers to anything. She felt him. She felt him good.

Not knowing where to look, she stared downward at his tennis shoe.

The pole sensation was a new one, she quickly noted. It was funny, but not ha-ha funny. It was a bit ticklish. And she could see how this new sensation could be considered quite satisfying. It called up old urges to suck her thumb while she rubbed the palm of her free hand against the folded edge of her favorite blanket. That cocktail of sensations had kept her soothed for hours when she was five. This strange mental note popped up as Trouble lifted Jubi's head by her chin. He was positioning her so he could plant another openmouthed kiss on her lips. While she let him widen the space between her thighs, and he noticed her yearning to be pumped, she thought, *I need to apologize to Mama.*

Trouble ground slowly, but hard. His kiss grew sloppy and choked her, and his hold became harsh. He was squeezing her arms, and it hurt. Jubi's chest felt like a wrinkled shirt pressed between an ironing board and a steamy iron. She couldn't move, except when he let her. She couldn't breathe or think. But soon, as the no-breathing thing began overtaking the good rubbing thing, a thought managed to sneak in. *This is going too far.* Revelation snuck in, too. It was the fact that she was trapped.

Her next thought was, *Where is this going?* She was trapped just like she'd been on the couch, and she could manage only to mumble. It took some minutes to break Trouble's concentration. Then he gave her an inch or two of breathing room, but he didn't step back—not really. She tried to squirm her way free of him. But he was clutching her forearms now. He had her pinned like a wrestler waiting for a count.

"Songbird," he whispered, "you feel good? You like it?" He freed one of her arms to put his hand under her skirt for a good, strong hand feel.

That sensation didn't feel good at all. It felt invasive and embarrassing. She heard and felt a rip of her unmentionables. "Get off of me!" She struggled to push him away, but he was tall and muscular, and so he barely noticed. He never lost his footing.

Instead, he kept her in a hug lock with one arm, her blouse inching up again as she attempted to stoop, bob and weave, and wiggle away. But she had too much to do, because she was also trying to retain possession of her underpants. Trouble continued to grab and tear until her panties were completely ripped free from her body. He pinched and scratched her down there in the process. He wretched her panties out from under her tiny skirt like a magician. He waved them into the air like a trophy. Still clutching her, he bunched them in his wide palm and put them to his nose. Trouble glory-sniffed his separated pink carnation, stolen from her. "Sweet," he said and smiled. Jubi was mortified.

Trouble's smile looked monstrous to her. She wanted to cry or scream or curse, but her eyes and voice didn't know what to do. She gave him one final push, which worked, but only because he let it. He thought it was cute. And who knew if she even computed all that correctly? She wanted to yell, "Give it back," but she couldn't do that, either. Instead, curious stuff rolled through her head. *Mama said, 'Don't.' This is a sin. I'm going to hell.* The next words that moved to her mouth were, "The baby."

Trouble stuffed her panties into his front pocket almost as an afterthought and swatted at Jubi's words with his wide, opened hand. Taking a minute to sneer in the playpen's direction, he said, "Ahh, he ain't worrying about nothin'. Come here, you sweet thing." He reached to regain his two-arm grip on her again.

Jubi dodged his outstretched hands and ran toward the couch, aiming for the phone. She didn't even know who she'd call. *I'll get in trouble if anyone knows he's in here,* she thought. But she knew she needed help. Things moved fast and failed to make sense. In the same second that she thought she couldn't tell anybody and moved her hand away from the phone, she felt a hard blow upside her head. It jiggled her right eye socket. The blow was hard enough to knock her flat on the couch. The phone careened to the floor, with the receiver off the hook. The dial tone, until it surrendered to silence, blended with the sounds from *Columbo.* The detective show was by now a half hour in. Just as the phone hit the hardwood floor, startling the baby and causing him to cry, ominous music began to play. The TV murder was about to happen. A scream from the television mixed with the baby's cry. Thankfully, it took away Trouble's focus.

"Turn that off," he said, letting her up. "And do something with that baby."

"What?" she said. This was where her voice should have trembled, but she was too angry. She puffed instead. She did as she was told, though, and turned off the set. She moved toward the baby, picked him up, and comforted him. When he became silent, she gently put him down. This time her bare bottom was in full view. And Trouble was focused again.

Jubi made a mad dash toward the front door, but he caught her like a sprinter. Perhaps he was closer to her than she calculated. He grabbed her, swung her around, and slapped her again. Jubi returned the slap, her aim dead on. It stunned him good.

"Oh, Songbird," he said, smiling and smarting.

"Stop calling me that. Get out of here!" she said in a tone that suggested that she was more concerned about being caught with boy company in the house and about the baby getting hurt than she was her about own well-being. "Get out of here. Get out before my parents catch you in here."

He moved in close and somehow backed her up to the couch again.

"So you're a little fighter, huh?"

"My folks are coming home soon," Jubi said. "You better get outta here."

Unconcerned, Trouble said, "No, they not." With that, he balled his right hand and punched her in the stomach. It folded her over, and she landed flat on the couch. He pounced. Laid himself flat on top of her and whispered in her ear, "You wanna sing to me, Songbird? C'mon, sing to me, sweetness."

Jubi's pain sent her into silence. Trouble lifted himself up and stung her face with several more slaps to make sure he chased away all her fight. She kept silent and still.

He needed to take his pants off. "Now, don't you move, baby. I got something good for you. And you got something sweet and good that you promised me. Right?"

Jubi stared, silent, at him. *Oh, God,* she thought. *I just can't let anybody find out he was in here. Why won't he just go?*

"We love each other, right?" he said as he disrobed. "Right?" His smile vanished, and his eyes beamed down a threat.

"Yeah," she said, frightened.

Trouble took the time to rip her blouse open. Its pretty pastel-colored buttons flew for cover. He tugged and ripped at her innocent spring-blue bra with the pink trim, trying to tear it off her. Without warning, he gave it a strong jerk. Her chest heaved upward, and she felt as if she had received electric shocks. He snatched her bra again and jerked it until it gave up its hold. Its thin straps, not built for such treatment, snapped wildly, like fresh rubber bands. For weeks to come, the deep scratches the clasps made across her back would haunt her.

Jubi brought her arms upward to cover herself. But when he threw up a hand-slap gesture as a warning, her arms dropped to her sides like they were dead. With her upper torso totally exposed, and her skirt scrunched up around her waist like a belt scarf, her breasts felt unprotected. They had never been exposed like that before. Never, ever exposed like this in the living room.

He pushed and forced himself inside a part of her that clearly wanted no intrusion. Trouble tried to kiss her mouth like he was starving. She summoned the last bit of fight she had to advoid his direct glare. When her eyes rested upon the baby, a fresh layer of humiliation fell upon her, for the little boy had stopped his play to stare at this curious thing happening before him.

"Please, please," Jubi begged, "just let me move the baby."

Trouble continued his mission. "Shut up," he said. The puff from his whispers added further insult to injury. "Don't worry 'bout him. He ain't hurtin' nobody."

But hurt was in the air, and in Jubi's loins. A tremendous hurt. To her utter surprise, she felt like a part of her was being knifed. First, her pubic hair was pinched and strained, and then the unsuspecting lips of her vagina were ripped, and then her innards vibrated and throbbed with pain.

Trouble proceeded with great difficulty, but he was determined to gain total entry and reentry. He pushed and pushed. His nails dug into her shoulders. At one point, he repositioned her torso like she was a rag doll. His hearty efforts led to noisy satisfaction. He uttered obscenities and promises of future encounters. Jubi remained silent; hoping it would speed him up and bring this to an end. So he could get out of there.

When he succeeded at his total entry, Jubi felt a burst of horrible pain and discomfort that she could do nothing about. The sound she let out was a strange low wailing. *Oh my God!* was her thought.

"Shut up," he warned again. And he put his hand over her mouth. Suddenly, they both felt and heard a pop. They halted. She was squealing like some frail animal dying in a trap.

Having invaded her innards like a thief, he pulled himself free, lifted his upper torso a bit, and asked, "You're a virgin?"

She only stared through him and let tears flow down the sides of her face.

He invaded her once more and continued until he was finished. When he got up for good, he wiped the sweat off his brow. Breathless, he uttered, "Thank you."

She lay motionless on the couch. She was a lifeless mass, looking at nothing, not even allowing what felt like a trickle of moisture escaping from her private parts to disturb her. Trouble quickly dressed, but he couldn't manage to erase the cheesy, wimpy look on his face while he did it. Then fully clothed, he bent over and kissed the dead mass on the forehead. He moved to the coffee table and picked up the silent phone, returned the receiver to its base, and said, "There you go. You dropped this, remember?"

There was no acknowledgment from Jubi's mind, mouth, or body. She felt fully transported to hell. And what was worse, her mind would tell her later that she deserved it. It was what she asked for.

Trouble leaned down to peck her again, this time on a salty cheek. He slurped his triumph. And he whispered to her face, though they had no eye contact, "Don't let anybody ruin what we got between us. Ya here?" With eyes he warned, *Let's just keep our love to ourselves.* "I'll call ya, baby. Okay?"

His breath smelled of spearmint, an unintended, undeserved indictment, she'd come to conclude later, against spearmint gum. After that night she could no longer stand to come across its happy green packaging, the packs neatly stacked in the checkout aisles of the grocery store. But all that would come later, to add insult to her injury.

Trouble scurried to the door. In a flash he vacated the scene of the crime.

Jubi hated the sight of church, really hated the sight of church from then on. However, her hate only assaulted people, underserved. And she couldn't clarify the source of her hate to anyone. The church had done nothing to her—maybe she knew that; maybe she didn't. Hate could often cloud one's thinking. It always did. And so it hovered, festered, and accused nearly everyone in Jubi's world—God included. But that was only a sidebar to the theft that had taken place. Trouble had planted his seed.

Chapter Six

Everything, Minus the Talk

Trickles of moisture escaped Jubi's bottom half again. The uncomfortable, slithery sensation caused her to flinch and move her head sideways, which caused the playpen to come into view. Prior to that, she had been a rotten log on the couch, heavy and hollow at the same time. This was an out-of-body kind of thing now, and her brain, because it knew it had to, struggled to think. She needed to come up with something, she knew, to force movement, to turn back the clock, to cover her tracks. She needed to do something proactive. Jubi leaned to the right and the liquid, trailed along her bottom, and probably onto the couch. But it didn't feel like her bladder was the culprit. She assessed the situation. *I don't have to go,* she thought. *What, then?* Thinking was a major effort now, because she was functioning in a fog.

The baby boy was fast asleep in his playpen, she saw. When'd that happen? was Jubi's thought. It seemed he had collapsed into slumber amid his own flurry of inquisitive stares. Whatever his summation had been about what he witnessed would forever remain a mystery. He couldn't talk yet. Her secret shame was safe with him.

When Jubi's reasoning took over, she contemplated how to save the couch and return the scene to normal. "Oh God," she whispered, noticing that her voice sounded like a stranger's. Whatever was spilling out of her just couldn't ruin the couch. "I've got to clean this up," she said to herself, referring to the entire mess. The sound of this stranger disturbed her, and hatred for this intruder started to surface. So she kept silent. *Couch, the couch,* her mind urged. *My fault, my fault. All this is my stupid fault. Oh God, why did I ever . . .*

She attempted a quick move off the couch but encountered great difficulty. With difficulty, she rolled her way off the couch, on to her knees, on to the floor. The position she ended up in put her nose to nose with a slightly milky, reddish-pinkish substance clinging to the couch's cushions and seeping down between. It nearly made her vomit, but there was no time. She had to regain control and clean up this mess. Struggling to make everything right with bundles of wet, soapy paper towels, then dry ones, fetched from the kitchen, she wiped away the physical scum, but not the heaviness of Trouble's body pounding on top of her, the nastiness of his vile words and panting sodomizing her hearing, her modesty ripped bare. And the sting of his palm was still on her cheek, and the throbbing of her head and stomach from his punches continued. Her wrists still held the feeling of his tight, unwanted grasp.

She pulled herself to her feet and inspected the living room. She put everything back in its place. As she stood there, her vision was hazy, but there was no time for that, either. *No one must ever find out,* she thought. Jubi wanted to be in the living room, minding the baby, for the remainder of the night, looking like the only drama that had unfolded that night had happened on *Columbo.* In a rush, she climbed the steps to the upstairs bathroom to wash up—to wash away the hurt. She put on her pajamas, her snow-white flannel ones with little pink angel lambs flying about. She returned to the scene of the crime just in the nick of time. The doorbell rang.

"Just a minute," Jubi called out. Before she could answer the door, she had to get to the kitchen to bury the bundle that contained the remnants of her mangled clothing, bury it deep between layers of trash in the garbage can. That took several minutes. When she answered the door, brandishing a pretend smile, a disgusted Victoria stood stiffly in the threshold.

Victoria stormed inside the Stones' household, stank-eyed and perturbed. Jubi stood frozen. *Oh my God,* she thought. *Has she been knocking and knocking? Was she knocking while I was upstairs? Did she see anything? See Trouble leaving? Oh my.*

"Girrrl!"

"What?" Jubi said, scared to death for the second time that night.

"Little girrrl, don't you ever grow up trusting these no-good fools out here." Victoria walked deeper into the living room, stopped short of the playpen, and swirled around to face Jubi. "Do you know what that Buck had the nerve to ask me?"

Major relief swept into Jubi's heart. "What?" Jubi responded, closing the front door. At this point, she was forcing herself to regroup and care about this new news.

"That fool asked if he could move in with me." Victoria was neck rolling now. Jubi watched in horror as Victoria plopped down on the couch. Restless, she popped back up again. "I mean, live with me—in my apartment. Not married!"

"He did?" Jubi said, still trying to look and sound interested, incredulous, or something, but it was a struggle. And her voice, she noticed, still belonged to a stranger. Under normal circumstances Jubi would have devoured this latest teachable moment like it was a smoked sausage loaded with spicy mustard, but her appetite for learning had vanished. She'd learned enough for the night. Jubi, in a fog, suddenly noticed Victoria was standing there, waiting for her to react. She jumped to it. "So, so what did you say? Whaddaya gonna do?" she asked obediently.

"He said some crap about two living as cheaply as one. It was crap. Some bull," Victoria said, finishing up her monologue.

"So whaddaya gonna do?" Jubi asked again. It was her duty to be persistent.

Victoria, suddenly remembering to lower her voice, because she finally glanced down at her son, stood there bobbing and weaving, and twirling a short strand of her hair into a tiny pinwheel curl. "Oh, I said yes. Darn it." She said it with a look of cheesy compromise on her face. And where Buck was concerned, Jubi took note, that it wasn't a new look. It was the kind of look that proclaimed, *Well, you know we gotta have a man, don'tcha! Don't be stupid.*

"Oh," was all Jubi could say, for she had already mastered the "every woman needs a man, no matter what" lesson. She wasn't surprised about Victoria's decision. She hadn't moved much, and she didn't feel like talking much or hashing over the nuances of these latest events.

Victoria gave an exhale that said, "Well, that's that. Might as well get the baby and go home." But when she moved in close to Jubi and the playpen, she stopped short to inspect the side of Jubi's face. Her cheek was a rainbow swirl of purple and maroon on a gingersnap canvas.

"Jubilee, what happened to your face, girl?"

Jubi made a quick move to turn her cheek in the opposite direction. "What?"

Victoria turned Jubi back around and pulled her
hand down away from her face. "That," Victoria said
slowly. "It's a handprint. Why you got a handprint on
the side of your face? And it's all red and stuff."

Jubi's mind raced to put together an explanation,
but she came up empty. She just stood there. The seconds screamed.

"Girl, you done got slapped?" Victoria said. "Your
daddy slapped you?" She was looking around and asking, "He's here? I didn't see his car. What happened?
What'd he hit you for?" She was trying not to chuckle
over Jubi getting a beating over something or another.
And she tried to stay focused, because this was now the
latest juicy news in the room. She wanted the details.

Jubi couldn't think straight. She replied, "No," when
she meant to say, "Yeah," and let Victoria assume that
her parents were there. But an awkward, guilty expression remained fixed on her face, and she avoided direct
eye contact. It made her look suspicious, and to make
matters worse, her eyes now threatened to tear up
again, which would give everything away.

Just the same, Victoria, standing there assessing the
situation, smelled a rat. "What's up, girl?" she asked,
though it didn't sound like a question. Victoria abandoned the task of packing up her baby and vacating the
premises. She grabbed Jubi's hand, spied some discol-
oration there too, and pulled her down on the couch.
Jubi winced. She wanted to run, escape. Perhaps she
could roll under the couch and stay there like a runaway slave. But it was the second time that night she
was trapped.

"Well, I had somebody over tonight." Jubi said it, but
she didn't look her in the face.

"Say what?"

"Yeah," Jubi said. The fake smile was back. "My boy-friend," she added in a rush, because she didn't want to sound too slutty.

There was a pause. Jubi couldn't read Victoria's expression. She wasn't smiling, just looking. Was she mad because the baby had been there? Or mad because her parents weren't home? Mad because it was a boy? What?

Jubi rushed to explain. "The baby was fine. He's a church boy. Everything was all right. And he didn't stay long. I . . . I didn't know he was coming over. Victoria, please don't tell. Please?"

"A boy, huh?" Victoria said, strangely intrigued, lacking an ounce of motherly concern about anything. "So baby girl gotta have a man, too, huh?" She chuck-led. "Well," she said, "I guess there's a lot of that goin' around. We guess, huh?"

Jubi's heart pounded a mile a minute. She wondered if her fear was visible. She tried to mask the fear. It was hard. Victoria, finishing her chuckle, looked at her face again.

"But seriously," she said, "how'd you get that red print on your face, huh?"

The question was met by a brief silence.

Jubi feared that a lie wasn't gonna cut it, but she had to cough up something. She broke eye contact and pulled herself up off the couch, saying, "Oh we were playin' around with the baby and stuff. And Trouble's fake airplane caught me in the face."

"Trouble! What'd you say?"

Jubi was devastated that his name had slipped out. But it was out. "Yeah." She gave a fake chuckle. "Ty," she added and screamed inside because she couldn't think of anything but the truth. "That's just his nickname. It don't mean nothin'." She laughed it off. "He's cool and everything."

"Yeah?" Victoria said to Jubi, looking suspicious, but when she stared down at her sleeping baby for a second, and he looked okay, she seemed to swallow the whole account. "Yeah? Well, I don't know if I'd want anyone named Trouble." She laughed. "Is he cute?"

"Yep," was all Jubi said.

"Tall?"

"Yep," Jubi answered, noticing that the stranger's voice inside her had cut her answer short. She looked at the blank wall where Trouble had her pinned against her will.

"So what else y'all do, huh?" Victoria was playful and proud of her little protégé.

Now Jubi seemed ready to just ad-lib—whatever it took to get this conversation over with, whatever Victoria wanted to hear. "Well," she said coyly, "well, we kissed a little."

"Yeah? And what else?"

Jubi's body tensed up. Her stomach turned. A crooked smile on her face, she did her best to play it off. "We kissed a little. Watched *Columbo*. Then he went home," she said. "He's a good church boy," she added for extra measure. Then a scary thought made her plead again, "But please don't tell anybody, please."

Thoroughly delighted that all her life lessons had rubbed off just fine on her student, Victoria was back to the business of picking up her sleeping bundle and angling the repacked diaper bag onto her shoulder. On her way out, she said, "Awww, don't worry, girl. Your little secret is safe with me." Jubi breathed a sigh of relief. "But y'all cool it on that playful rough stuff. You know?"

No, Jubi didn't know. "Huh?" she huffed, clueless.

"You know what I mean. That stuff can lead to some other stuff you might not be ready for. You know," Victoria said. She was out the front door by that time. "I'll pick up the playpen tomorrow. We'll talk, maybe go to the mall or something. Okay?" she said, heading across the lawn. "You gonna be all right," were her final words of wisdom before she headed to her own abode. She had stayed too long as it was. Buck was waiting in her bed. She wouldn't have come to pick up the baby at all if she didn't just have to hash out her new news, hot off the press. She needed to make herself feel okay about it.

"Yeah. See ya later," Jubi said. She closed the front door. She locked it. Those bothersome tears sprung up. A new Jubi headed up the stairs to bed, and to hell for lying, deceiving, and committing a shameless act. The old Jubi was gone for good.

The final days of June 1987 came and went, but Jubi's menstrual cycle did not. Trouble's presence seemed constant, but his flesh seemed to have come and gone. Ty "Trouble" Custis never called again. And Jubi overheard various side conversations at church and learned that the boy wonder had left town for some athletic program and maybe went away to school. Trouble's busy-bee parents were still around, buzzing around all through church service. Jubi hated seeing his father, because he was a Trouble replica. She went out of her way not to catch glimpses of him, but sadly, sometimes it was unavoidable. The trauma she'd endured supplied her impetus every Sunday to fake a fight or cause an obstruction so she wouldn't have to go to church. It never worked. It only caused Jubi, Esther, and James to arrive at the praise and worship hour feeling drained and extra needy. It was getting harder and harder for James and Esther to paint on their happy faces. Sometimes the battle with Jubi raged on right up to the church door.

They'd no sooner hit the sanctuary than Jubi would bolt in the opposite direction. Esther, determined to get her in the sanctuary, would run after her.

"Just where are you going, young lady?" Esther would do the whisper-yell while she grabbed her daughter's arm.

"To the fellowship hall," Jubi would whisper-yell back, trying to break free of the hold, accrue witnesses, and keep it moving.

"Oh no, you're not. You're gonna sit in that sanctuary, and you're gonna listen to what Pastor's got to say." Esther would swing Jubi around, trying her best to smile at the members gazing at the Sunday morning melee.

"Ohhh, Mama!" Jubi would retort in protest, like she was being dragged to the guillotine. And so went the new Stone Sunday ritual. Sometimes Esther prevailed. Sometimes Jubi managed to get away clean. But the battle of wills endured and would have no end. Jubi's creativity when arguing was as boundless as the range of her beautiful singing voice. Choir rehearsals presented a problem, as well.

August scooted by. The end of the Labor Day holiday meant the back-to-school bell. When mid-September rolled in without a sign of a rich red flow, Jubi got it. She had to face it. She was pregnant.

What else could it be? She'd lie awake in the middle of the night and think curious thoughts, like when she erroneously thought that kissing a boy got a girl pregnant. She thought of how, now, she knew better. Since the start of school, if she wasn't at school or wasn't forced to go to church, she would remain shut up in her bedroom, thinking. She socialized with friends at school, but only enough so that she didn't seem strange to those around her. She hadn't the strength or the desire for much else. She also needed to keep connections open in order to keep up with homework assignments for the days she skipped school. She kept up with that only when she felt like it. But for the most part, whatever friendships she'd cultivated at school or at church eventually died due to lack of nourishment. Teenagers moved on. It was easier that way, it seemed.

But Jubi still adored Victoria. She'd spend more time there. She still babysat for her and Buck too. Buck seemed nice and friendly, and relatable, like maybe he had some kids of his own around somewhere. "Hey, Jubi girl," he'd said to Jubi, with a big laugh and a smile. His cinnamon smile was bright when he wasn't drunk. Buck, a tall, thick, heavyset man with muscular limbs like Popeye's, was drunk a lot, though. But he always looked happy to see Jubi. He loved to talk to her.

"So how's school goin'?" Buck would ask like a parent.

"Fine," Jubi would answer, being the usual teenage vague.

"Good. Good. You make sure you get all you can outta those teachers of yours."

"Okay. I will."

"Yeah," Buck would say every time they'd have that same conversation. "This world is a rough-and-tumble place without a good education."

"I know, Mr. Buck," Jubi would retort. She could see he liked being called mister.

"You'd better listen to me, naw," Buck would advise her. But sometimes it looked like he was convincing other people besides her. Maybe he wished he could go back in time to convince his younger self.

Jubi took note that the look Buck gave her was different from the look he gave Victoria. And she based her respect on him for that fact, alone. His look was as far removed as could be from the dirty-old-man looks she clearly got from other men and boys. The new Jubi had X-ray vision. And that was a good thing.

But when Buck was all sauced up, he roamed around, looking for a fight. Victoria always seemed to be his target. Victoria was a beautiful woman. She couldn't help being an object of interest to male passersby, and, it seemed, she couldn't help flirting. It was her way. But maybe that wasn't always what caused Buck to attack her. Who knew? He and Victoria would get to arguing, and it often spilled out onto the front lawn. He'd beat her up, then scurry off before the cops came. He'd be gone for a couple of weeks, as if to let her bruises, black eyes, forehead knots, and her memory heal, and then he'd be back—love renewed. Victoria's mother couldn't stand him. Jubi had heard her tell Esther so. When they'd fight, Victoria's mother would come over and snatch the baby out of harm's way. She'd whisk him away in her car. But she always brought him back. Then things would gradually get back to normal, until the next blowup. This roller coaster that was their life felt normal, Jubi noted. *Must be what all couples do,* was Jubi's thought. *Except my mom and dad, but that's 'cause they're old and churchified, and not the norm,* she'd reckon.

Victoria put up with Buck. "I do it because I love him," she'd say. That was how she explained it to Jubi when they talked. Victoria had a lot of wisdom about things, Jubi noted, a lot. Maybe if she hung around Victoria long enough, some wisdom about what to do about her growing problem would drop from Victoria's lips. *Maybe I'll come right out and ask her what to do,*

Jubi thought to herself while lying on her canopy bed one day.

One frigid October morning, Jubi had had a particularly rough time getting up. "I'm sick, Ma!" she hollered in the direction of the hallway. She sat on the bed's edge, feeling drug-addicted tired and nauseated, and not knowing why.

"C'mon, girl, put some octane in it," Esther called out from her bedroom. Having arrived home not too long ago from her nightshift, she had started taking off her nurse's uniform but stopped midway when she realized that she'd probably need to take Jubi to school to get her there on time. Jubi usually walked or took the bus down at the corner. "Get ready. I'll take you to school," Esther called out.

"Okay. Thanks, Mom," Jubi returned, wishing that this was a day when her mother and father both had the day shift. If that were the case, Esther and James would have left for work long ago. On mornings when she felt sick and grungy or when sadness overwhelmed her, she would mill about until her parents cleared out, and then she'd lie back down. Jubi had skipping school down to a science.

Her mother waited in the living room. She stood at the piano and dug around in her purse for something and nothing to pass time. She didn't feel like another early morning fight with her daughter, so she decided not to try to hurry her up.

Jubi was almost ready, primping her unruly brown hair one last time, and thinking about how she never wanted to see food again. Especially since most of what she ate ended up in the toilet, anyway. *Why is that?* she thought. Her clothes were getting tight too. That was another revelation. In another two months, she wouldn't be able to fasten the buttons on anything. Instead, she'd become pretty handy at holding everything together with rubber bands, threading them through buttonholes and securely wrapping them around buttons. At home, she took to wearing baggy sweats and big T-shirts. At school, she kept her coat on all day. Nobody seemed to notice, care, or question her.

Mother and daughter hit the door and walked to the car, which happened to be parked in front of Victoria's front lawn. Jubi stopped short, surprised at what she saw.

"Hey, Mom," she said, astonished. "Look over here," and she pointed to a spot a few feet in front of her.

"Well, I'll be darn," Esther said, the sight bringing her to a halt as well. There in front of them both was a frantic gray squirrel standing on its hind legs, using its front paws as if they were a pair of hands. The squirrel was busy prying open the cellophane wrapper on a slice of Kraft cheese. The squirrel was so focused on its treat that it failed to scurry away at the approach of two inquisitive human beings.

When Esther and Jubi continued on a few more steps to the car, there in the gutter was a stray cat, which also failed to look up because it was determined to scratch open a box of Birds Eye frozen peas. Maybe he preferred vegetables. Near one of Esther's front tires, another stray cat scratched and meowed at a cellophane-wrapped package of raw chicken. *Have these animals been to the grocery store?* Jubi joked to herself. She and her mother stood there laughing and staring at the sight.

The answer to Jubi's question was no, but later both Esther and Jubi found out that Buck had indeed been to the grocery store, and apparently, he had bought the groceries with his money, which must have been a fluke. So, sometime during the night or in the wee

hours of the morning, during another ruckus, he felt
fully obliged to throw the groceries out into the street
before he made his usual getaway.

That was the last time anybody heard tell of Mr.
Buck or laid an eyeball on him. Esther helped Victoria
nurse a serious gash on her head that day because she
refused to go get treatment at a hospital. "Hospitals
ask too many questions," Victoria snapped at Esther,
forgetting that she was a nurse. She made an effort to
sweeten her indictment of Esther's chosen profession
with a look of respect. Esther knew what she meant.
She hadn't taken offense.

It was thoroughly unspoken, but everyone could
see that Victoria was brokenhearted and embarrassed
about Buck for a long while. Her mother didn't bother
to bring the baby back for a couple of weeks, not until
Halloween. After that last fight, Victoria began to suffer
headaches, migraines. It was another thing she pushed
under the rug, refusing to seek treatment. Really, the
total truth was that she just didn't care for hospitals,
period. But often she'd have to call in sick at work and
lie still under the bedcovers in total darkness. Jubi
would come over and watch her little boy when that
happened. It happened quite a bit.

Esther, of course, did the grocery shopping for the
Stone family. And just around Halloween time, for
some reason, she noticed that the supply of sanitary
napkins had not been depleted like it should have been.
A strange notion hit her. It made her remember the
second special talk—which had been aborted so many
times. One afternoon she bothered to knock on Jubi's
bedroom door.

"Yeah?" Jubi called out. She was lying there, staring
at the autumn-colored tips of the trees swaying outside
her window.

"It's me, dear. I'm coming in."

Jubi rushed to spread some books and notebooks and other things on her bed. She had them right on the floor beneath her for just such a time as this. And she draped the comforter, which was bunched up, across her belly. "Okay," she called out.

"Hey, girl," Esther said, walking in slowly, kind of surveying the room, kind of not. Overall, she noticed that there seemed not to be much fight in Jubi. That was the way it had been lately, except where going to church was concerned. At present, she was just happy about it. But still, a question about it all surfaced in her mind. "You feeling all right?" Esther asked, surveying her baby's face. *It always looks sad these days,* she noted silently.

Seemingly dumbfounded, Jubi said, "Yeah. I'm okay. You okay?"

"Well, you know, I'm a little tired," Esther said, sitting down on the bed. "Working, working, working. And you know the big church celebration is coming up soon. We're burnin' that mortgage." At that remark, Jubi winced and fought to control it. "So how's school?" Esther went on to say. "Everything okay there?"

"Yeah. We got a test coming up soon in algebra," Jubi said. She was lying. She really didn't know what was coming up in any of her classes at the moment, nor did she care. But it sounded good. The new Jubi was proud of her growing skill at lying.

Esther asked her next questions gingerly, because she wasn't yet quite sure where she was going with them. Anything that even remotely involved sex or pregnancy was just too ludicrous to consider. "Your stomach feeling okay? Cramps and such? You know you're in the thick of puberty now." Then to give her questions legitimacy, she added, "All kinds of things are happening to your body." She was proud of herself for coming up with such a good segue. She kept at it. "Your period doing what it's supposed to do, is it?"

Jubi tried her best not to flinch or give anything away. "Well, yeah," she said. "I guess so. What is it supposed to do?" She kind of chuckled.

Esther chuckled too and said, "It's supposed to show up, for one thing. And hang around for a certain amount of days, you know." She was being clever. Bravely, she looked at her daughter. "Yours behaving itself?"

"Oh, Mom, you're so funny," Jubi said. "I guess so. It's good." She looked away and thumbed through one of her textbooks.

"Oh," Esther said. "'Cause I thought I hadn't seen any of your napkins being used. That's all."

Jubi shifted onto her side, suddenly conscious of strange goings-on in her stomach. There was a monster inside her wreaking havoc. The new laid-back Jubi calmly said, "No. No. Everything's fine, far as I know."

"Huh," Esther said, looking at her but letting it go at that. Silence moved in for a few seconds, and then Esther changed gears. "Hey, sweetie, you wanna watch a movie together?"

Jubi shot the idea down. "Naw," she said as if she was deliberating, but she wasn't.

"You sure? I could tell Daddy to pick up a video on his way home," Esther said, perky and overworking her efforts to bond with her daughter.

"Naw."

"Wanna come down and watch TV? I think *Cosby* is on tonight. How about it?" Esther said. Now she was begging for some quality time.

Jubi finally left her textbook alone to look at her mom but still refused the invitation. "I don't think

so, Mom. I'm a little tired," she said. "And I've gotta
study." Study—that would always be her trump card.

"Oh, maybe you're coming down with something. I
could call and make an appointment with Dr. David-
son," Esther said, concerned.

Jubi's innards were on fire with fear, and she was on
red alert, but she was getting good at acting and lying.
The new Jubi, the stranger that now resided within
her, helped her to play it calm on the surface. Without
so much as a flickering eyebrow, she said, "Naw, you
don't have to. I'll feel better soon. I think I've been
through the worst of it, anyhow."

Now the silence had them both studying each other.
Jubi acknowledged in her thoughts that if she were
not this new Jubi, this monster on its way to hell,
she'd like nothing better than to be cuddled up in
her mother's arms, cracking up over something those
comical Huxtable kids did. Or maybe she could use her
strength to yell out, "Mama, help me. Please!" Maybe
her mother wouldn't spit on her in disgust for the sin
she'd committed. Maybe her mother would wrap her
in her arms, protect her, fix her, press her head on her
shoulder, and make everything all right. Maybe she
could even turn back the hands of time. But Jubi said
nothing. Her lips could not part themselves.

Esther looked at her daughter, continuing to lovingly
stroke her hair, reminiscing silently about the days
when Jubi's favorite thing was to rummage through
her jewelry box and pretend to be a princess. She wondered where those days had gone to, and why they'd
left. Later, much, much later, she'd wonder why she
had allowed herself, a health professional at that, to
remain in the dark like she had. Why hadn't she probed
further, like a good mother was supposed to do? Why
hadn't she discussed anything with James? They dis-

cussed everything, almost. And then came this. She'd kept him in the dark, and it was a mistake. And how had pride, or perhaps just plain old stupefied denial, worked to nearly cost her, her daughter's life? Was that really the price she was willing to pay? Was it? Decades apart, both Esther and Jubi would experience a revelation about the road each one of them took, and about the secrets they had intended to carry to their graves. But at the moment, however, silence took over.

Since Esther lacked the nerve to challenge, and Jubi the will to divulge all and seek help, their conversation was over, because it had nowhere else to go. Esther gave Jubi's hair one last soft, loving stroke. She leaned over and kissed Jubi's forehead. It was a gesture that was supposed to convey "Lemme know if something's wrong." Esther got up and removed herself not only from the room but also from her troubling thoughts.

A few days later, Jubi took to wrapping up sanitary napkins in old newspapers and disposing of them accordingly. Her goal was to adjust the level of the household supply. Some were clean. Some were laced with ketchup and Tabasco sauce for added insurance. She'd totally missed her mother's inference by way of a gentle forehead kiss. But her mother's little talk did indeed ignite in Jubi a definite call to action. Finally, Jubi knew she could no longer accept that her body and mind were just having a misunderstanding, that wishful thinking was all it took to make a budding truth nonexistent. It was time to face reality. *I gotta get rid of this thing,* she thought. *I gotta do something.*

Chapter Seven

Hope Aborted

With a new Saturday afternoon dawning, Jubi was hanging out at Victoria's again, playing with Victoria's son and talking. They were looking at a rerun of *I Love Lucy*. Lucy was pregnant and was trying to wiggle out of a big easy chair. Kind of out of the blue, Jubi asked a question. Or maybe it was more like she presented a scenario.

There's a girl at school," Jubi said, like she wasn't building up to anything much, "who is pregnant."

"Yeah?" Victoria said. She was sitting on the couch next to Jubi. Her little boy was sitting between her legs, twitching and squirming, while she cornrowed his hair. A big jar of blue Afro Sheen hair grease was the only thing between them.

"Yeah, only she doesn't wanna have it."

"And she told you that?" Victoria asked, her full attention on Jubi, who was pretending to be interested in what was happening on the TV.

"Yeah, well, we're kind of close. She's my best friend," Jubi said. That last part made her twitch a little. Victoria was all ears. Jubi could feel it. "She was wondering . . ."

"Wondering what?"

Jubi turned to face her mentor, a serious look on her face. Victoria held a wad of her son's thick, bushy hair that she'd separated into three pieces. She stopped braiding and absentmindedly rested her wrists on his head. The boy was thankful for the reprieve. Victoria was thinking and resting a lot these days. She tired easily and didn't go out to parties, like she used to before Buck left, and she rarely finished any task without a rest in the middle. She turned to face Jubi and was silent for a moment. Maybe she was studying Jubi's face; maybe she wasn't.

"She was wondering how she could get rid of it. That's all," Jubi said and looked back in the direction of the television. The sitcom had moved on.

Victoria did likewise. She resumed her hair pulling, twisting, and braiding, even though her eyes hurt and her vision kept getting fuzzy. "Well, I had a girlfriend in that fix one time," she said.

"Yeah?" Jubi said, still being nonchalant. "Well, what happened?"

"Castor oil," Victoria said.

Jubi turned to face Victoria. She looked stunned. "Castor what?"

Victoria was quite the picture of wisdom. "Castor oil," she repeated. "It's a tonic you take. It comes in a tiny bottle, and you get it at the drugstore."

"And that got rid of it?" Jubi asked, incredulous.

"Yep," Victoria said. Her little boy's complaints had turned into cries for help now. "Cleaned her right out."

"Just like that?" Jubi said it like she'd just found a pot of gold, even though she didn't mean to.

"Works like a charm," Victoria said. "So go tell your best friend that."

"I will," Jubi said. And that was that. Instead of morning classes that Monday, Jubi knew a trip to the drugstore would be in order.

***

All Monday afternoon, Jubi checked, nursed, and rechecked the tiny little bottle of castor oil she'd purchased. She'd been forced to ask the pharmacist about its whereabouts in the store, and she'd been terrified that her secret was stamped on her forehead. But the busy pharmacist had barely looked at Jubi and had simply pointed the way to her freedom. She couldn't wait to get the bottle home, to the safe confines of her bedroom. Or maybe she'd consume it in the safety and privacy of the bathroom. She'd do it in one big gulp, she fantasized. *I wonder how it will come out?* She wondered too about the evidence of her pain and sin growing inside her. She wondered about it, but it wasn't a big worry. Sin was supposed to come out. She knew that for sure now. Would it magically disappear, just like it had appeared? She did know this, though: when it left, finally, she could move on with her life.

Well, she stood in her bedroom, in front of her dresser mirror, and carefully loosened the cap on the bottle. She took a deep, brave breath, thinking, *Good-bye and good riddance,* then turned the bottle up to her mouth, intending to swig the entire contents for good measure. But quite abruptly, Jubi found out that there was a little something Victoria had failed to divulge. The stuff was vile, hugely and grossly vile. Jubi swigged, gulped, gagged, and then spit out the portion that had got into her mouth. She spit it right on her pink and white throw rug. The castor oil tasted so terrible that while coughing and gagging for the twenty to twenty-five minutes, she had no concern for the fluffy rug. That would emerge when she concerned herself with cleaning up and covering her tracks. For now, she begged the wad of gum she'd stuffed in her mouth to take the taste away. She thought, *Oh my goodness*! *How am I going to get this down?* A fresh idea struck her, and she went to the kitchen for a chaser.

Mixing the castor oil with something tasty sounded like the perfect solution. This time she'd take it a tablespoon at a time. Jubi had purchased two bottles of the stuff, and was committed to consuming it until the thing inside her evaporated. But another problem arose. She poured the castor oil with care on top a puddle of Coca-Cola in a small bowl. The castor oil wadded up and sat next to the caffeinated puddle. She tried it with apple sauce. She loved apple sauce, but it did nothing to camouflage the dreadful taste and consistency. Soon she discovered that castor oil just wouldn't mix with anything. So now it was time to just be brave. So down the hatch went the castor oil. It was horrible. But the worst part was that apart from strange cramps and rumblings in her stomach, nothing seemed to happen at all. The castor oil idea was finally aborted.

It was mid-November, right before Thanksgiving. Forest Unity's evening service, which would feature the church's mortgage burning celebration, promised to be a grand one. The church was packed with members of both the Bible Deliverance Church of God and Forest Unity Memorial Church of Baltimore. Christian dignitaries and community leaders were in the house of God. All were anxious and excited to hear the guest preacher of the hour. It was the Reverend Daniel J. Harris, or Li'l Rev, as folks liked to call him.

Reverend Harris was the Bible Deliverance Church of God's famed protégé son. He was a rising star in the community. And he was arguably the handsomest young preacher, and since he was still up for grabs, every young woman dreamed of making him her trophy husband. He knew how to preach the Word too. The Forest Unity and Bible Deliverance choirs were set to show off. To pay off a mortgage, especially in the face of a declining membership, was indeed something to give praise about. And with Li'l Rev raising everyone's emotions to a feverish spiritual pitch, the day would be remembered as a historic one for all. Jubi would etch that day in her memory for very different reasons.

For the Stones, and for everyone else crowding into and milling about the church's foyer, this was the second lengthy church service of the day. Jubi had lost her battle to skip the morning service, mainly because her choir had to sing, and while she'd been determined not to be tortured a second time, her parents insisted she attend the evening service. The Stones had arrived at the church after filling their bellies with fried chicken dinners and peach cobbler, which had been served at the local church-community hub, Miss Annie's Soul Food Kitchen. That had happened during the break between services. So maybe their satisfied bellies accounted for the silence in the car during the ride over. Maybe not. Not even the radio had played, because the channels that played religious music had quit for the day. Esther and James didn't mind listening to R & B music or even a little jazz in the car during the week, but on Sundays they put their foot down.

Standing in the parking lot, James had kissed his wife. Then he had given Jubi a light squeeze and had reached for a kiss. She'd playfully avoided it. "Daddy, we're in the public," she'd said. He'd made a stupid face to make her laugh, and then he'd scurried into the church to take his place on the deacons' row. Esther and Jubi had followed suit at a slower pace, both with their church faces on. But their playful countenance had evaporated, they were both on guard, Pitted against each other, they both laced up their armor. The going-to-church war had started.

Stepping into the hustle and bustle of the foyer, where the meet and greet was in full swing, Jubi managed to win the sanctuary battle by making a beeline for the ladies' room. It was in the opposite direction of the sanctuary. Now, let the record show that it wasn't the first time Jubi used this ploy. And sometimes it worked; sometimes it didn't. But this time, in a crowded foyer, it looked promising. Esther was in hot pursuit of Jubi when First Lady Beola Wicker, observing the battle maneuvers, intervened. She commandeered Esther's attention.

"Sister Esther, how you doing this fine evening?" Beola asked. "You tired yet, girl?" She chuckled because she had cracked herself up. As she spoke, though, her look was direct, as if her words carried a double meaning. And while she spoke, she cheerfully and gently pulled Esther's arm in the direction away from the bathroom. As Esther began to decipher Beola's double meaning, she realized she was now headed for the sanctuary, and away from Jubi.

Esther was caught completely off her guard. It had been her plan to force Jubi inside the sanctuary to witness this glorious celebration, to enjoy it, and to appreciate and understand it as the fruit of all her labor. This evening was the justification for all those church meetings she had had to attend, for all the times she had fussed at Jubi to get dinner on the table, for all the times she had needed to abandon her personal duties as homemaker and mother. Esther was dead set on her mission's success. An added bonus would be the great preaching Jubi would take in, and from someone so vibrant and young. "See what good ministry can do? See where a life led totally in Jesus can lead you?" She imagined herself saying this to her daughter later, as they hugged, huddled together on the couch, like they used to do. They would go over it all lovingly and would agree.

It would be a grand teachable moment. *Perhaps God will even see to it to clear up whatever Jubi's opposition is to going to church,* she had imagined and prayed before church. *This could solve everything. I know it.* Esther had fantasized well about it. Oh, the burst of expectation was almost more than Esther's befuddled heart could take. *But faith without works is dead. And a believer, even a baby believer, must stay close to the vine.* Esther would come to understand this in the literal sense. It would be her staunch advice to her daughter as soon as she could manage it.

Well, Beola had a hold on Esther's arm, and it broke Esther's focus. Jostled, Esther rushed to paint on her happy church face. "Uh, oh, I'm fine, fine," she said. Her voice sounded a little cheesy. "Running late this evening," she said, frazzled. She tried unsuccessfully to give a lighthearted chuckle. "How are you, Sister Beola?" Esther surprised herself by letting the first lady lead her away without a struggle from the bathroom door.

As they strolled arm in arm like schoolkids toward the church's foyer, Beola leaned in and whispered, "Esther, let her go. You got her to church naw. You and Deacon Stone always do. Y'all are doin' the right thing. Let God take over."

Esther was mortified, speechless. She glared at her friend. The glare crumbled into a look of defeat, then mutated into a look of agreement. "You know, B," she whispered, "I just don't know what—"

Beola cut in. "You doin' right. You doin' as much as you can." Beola looked direct at Esther. "Esther," the first lady stressed, "You got her here." She let a second lapse to allow her words to soak in. Then she worked to lighten the mood. "Lord, have mercy! You know that age. You can't do nothin' with it." Beola spiced her words with a laugh.

Both of them could hear the Forest Unity men's choir ministering with excellence in the sanctuary. The sound was strong and sweet at the same time. The Bible Deliverance Church of God's combined choir would be up next. Soon Reverend Harris would take over the pulpit. The evening service would be hot, both in terms of the temperature and the spiritual climax. The sexton would toy with the idea of flipping the switch on the air conditioner. The debt retirement service would end four hours after it began. And it would be unforgettable. Ten visitors would walk down the aisle to join the church, which was a coup.

Beola's laugh eased the lines in Esther's face, as well as the tight rope knotting in her head and stomach. Esther conceded the fight. "Yes, indeedy. I wouldn't wish parenting a child this age on nobody," she said and laughed. The sound of her own laughter sounded strange to Esther's ears, but at least the laugh and her smile were real.

Still arm in arm, they continued their walk to the sanctuary.

"C'mon, girl, let's go on in. Enjoy yourself. God's got it," Beola said, coaching her friend. "And ain't you on the program to introduce Li'l Rev?" Beola asked. She was teasing now, calling Reverend Harris, Li'l Rev.

The burst of a chuckle escaped Esther. She couldn't help it. The only word she could get out was, "Yep."

The two were smiling and communing like the old cherished friends and cohorts in the FISHH Ministry that they were. Beola joked, "Huh, I know you don't wanna miss introducing that hunk of a man." The devilish comment had them suppressing all-out laughter this time. Hitting the back row of the sanctuary, the two friends gathered their composure and headed for their appointed places in the service. By the end of that grand service, Forest Unity Memorial Church would be owned outright by its congregation, free and clear.

Jubi hid in bathroom stall for the first few moments. She was bracing herself for the confrontation she knew was coming. But none came. Slowly, she unlatched the stall door and stepped out, surprised to find herself alone. She exhaled a sigh of relief as she cautiously ventured toward the bathroom door. She stopped short when she spied her reflection in the long, invasive mirror above the row of sinks. The new Jubi stopped her cold. Rage set in. Then hurt. Then fear. Then questioning. How'd this happen to me? she asked silently. She stared at her reflection, desperately searching, but no answer came. Tears surfaced.

Of late, she had noticed how uncontrollable tearing up had become. It was getting to be a reoccurring annoyance. And there was other stuff she'd noticed too. One minute she could forget her secret hell. She'd be watching TV, laughing at something she saw, feeling normal, and then her fate would slap her in the face. And it would slap her hard, without warning, just like Trouble had done. In an instant, she'd be imprisoned inside a plume of despair. She could not forecast, she had noticed, the arrival of her wide range of emotions or control them. And she was insanely jealous of every young girl she saw, from toddlers to teens. She'd watch a baby girl playing with toys in her stroller or holding on to her mother's neck simply for pleasure and security, and the sight would make her head and her heart plead, *Why can't that be me? Why can't I start all over again?* Sometimes the yearning felt unbearable. *Oh, God, get me out of this body, please! This can't be happening to me. Why'd you let this happen to me?*

Standing in the bathroom, held captive by her own image, she swiftly lost control of her emotions again. She couldn't even revel in her triumphant battle waged against her mother. Despair was coming. Jubi prayed that no one would come in the bathroom and catch her falling apart like this. Again, she was at the mercy of fate. She fastened both hands over her mouth to entrap the full-blown wail that her body fought to push out. There was no stopping the flood coming from her eyes. As soon as she could feel herself quieting down, she grabbed a wad of paper towels to dry her drowning face. Her eyes were as red as overripe apples and felt just as worn. She could do nothing about that, she decided. Jubi had to vacate the ladies' room, because the law of averages with regard to someone bursting in worked against her. Her only defense was to hide somewhere secluded until the end of service and hope she would woman-up.

Carefully exiting the ladies' room, she careened dead into Will Promise. He had come out of the men's room next door and was very happy to see her. *What a break!* was his thought.

"Hey, hey, hey, girl, where you running to?" Will asked. His easy smile was as big and toothy as ever. But then it was common knowledge that he had no control of it. It always blossomed full.

"Hey," Jubi said with her head down. Her left hand clutched her little patent leather purse that matched her kitten-heel shoes. Her right hand was attached to a wad of overused paper towels, like gum stuck to the bottom of a shoe. She focused on making her second getaway of the day.

"Hey. Whoa," Will said, blocking her path to freedom. "Wait a minute, girl. You can't say no more than that?" he joked. Then he saw her face. His smile evaporated. He remained in her path. "What's this? What's going on? What happened, Jubi?"

Jubi dragged herself along the hall, trying to get away like a cornered roach, and she kept her head down. But the jig was up, and Will kept after her. He grabbed her shoulders, kind of pinned her to the wall. He had her perfectly cornered.

"Don't you have to get up there and play drums or something?" Jubi asked. Her voice was weak, but rude.

"No," Will responded quickly. "That was this morning, remember? What's wrong, Jubi? Why are you crying?"

When he said the word *crying,* Jubi felt another wail coming on, and her sweet gingersnap face looked like it too. By this time, she had managed to free herself from his hold and reach the exit door, scraping the wall as she went. She fought to say, "Nothing. Nothing's wrong. Just leave me alone, okay?" Go . . ."

"C'mon," he said, serious like, taking charge. Jubi looked up, surprised. She didn't know if she'd ever seen him act serious or not. "C'mon," he said again, leading her out the door to the church's playground. He didn't have a coat on, but he didn't act like he was cold. He was just concerned about the girl he had had a crush on all this time.

When they hit the air, Jubi's wail came, full strength. Will, all of sixteen to her fourteen, held her in his arms and said nothing for the next five minutes. They were alone in the cool open air. Jubi struggled to regain some semblance of composure. She reached inward to figure out just how she would explain this, cover her tracks. That was mostly what she did these days, cover her tracks.

Will stepped back a bit to examine her. She wiped her face and dabbed at her eyes both to stall for time and to clean herself up, but as far as alibis were concerned, she came up blank about what to do or say next.

Softly, he asked, "What's going on, Jubi? I know you've been acting strange for a while now." He paused and studied her face. "You don't talk to nobody anymore. What's up?" he asked in a whisper. "You can tell me. It's all right," he assured her. "You had a fight with your parents? Somebody said something to you? What?" He wouldn't take his gaze off her. And somehow it forced her into a web of truth.

"I'm in trouble," she whispered.

"What?"

"Trouble," she said, flinching when she said the word *trouble,* looking away from Will to keep him from seeing it. And she was sniffling and blowing her nose. "Something bad happened, and now I'm in trouble," she heard herself say.

Will still had a hold of her again. He appeared puzzled. "Well, why don't you tell somebody about it? Tell your parents, maybe. Deacon Stone is cool," he said. He added that last comment to make up for the lame statement "Tell your parents." "I know there's somebody who can help," he said.

Jubi broke away from him. With a blank stare, she said, "Nobody can help me. Somebody took something from me, and I'm in trouble. And that's the way it is."

"Well, maybe we could go tell Reverend Wicker or somebody like that, maybe—"

Frantic, Jubi cut him off. "No!" she shouted. "No, no, no. Please, just stay out of this. Please, Will. Nobody can help me. Nobody!" She looked up at him directly for the first time. "And you don't know anything about anything. You're just some dumb old church boy." She tried to shoo him away. "Just, just go play your drums, okay?"

Will grabbed hold of her again. If he was cut by her remarks, he failed to show it. His concern for her had only intensified. "Calm down," he said. "Calm down. I won't. I'm not going away." He tried to smile that easy smile of his, but the situation felt like life and death. "I don't know anything because you haven't told me anything, Jubi. You haven't told me anything. Now who hurt you? What did he take?"

Jubi froze and stared at him. For her, time stopped when Will said, "He." Now she couldn't remember what she'd actually said. She couldn't trace the conversation. Had more slipped from her mouth than she'd intended? Her thoughts raged. *You said, "He." What in the world?*

"Just please, please don't tell anyone," Jubi pleaded, ignoring his questions. "Please don't tell."

"Tell what, Jubi?" Will asked.

His look at her was dead on and motionless. It promised to drive her crazy; she couldn't read it at all. Her thoughts raced. *What do you know? Who talked? Did Trouble tell you? He bragged, I bet. Oh my God. Nobody can know this, nobody! Oh my God.* Her thoughts threatened to overwhelm her and provoke a monsoon of tears again. Her constant cloak of shame choked her unforgivingly. It squeezed and squeezed. *Please, God, I wanna be dead.* Jubi's body fell limp in Will's arms. Her inner thoughts turned into frail words. She couldn't be more out of control of things. "No. Nobody. Nobody." She was pleading but not making sense. Still, he seemed to keep up.

"Nobody what, Jubi? Nobody hurt you? Or nobody can help you? What's your trouble, Jubi, huh?"

"Just don't tell. Okay? All right? Just don't tell no-body." She was weeping and pleading.

"Okay," he said. "Okay. I won't. I promise." He held her close. And their words were over.

He held her, and his embrace was snug and gentle at the same time, she noticed, like her daddy's embraces. She wanted to let herself feel safe, but knew she didn't deserve it. Because she was full of sin. He kissed her on the cheek and smoothed her brown curls, caught in an uncomfortable breeze. She didn't deserve it. She didn't expect it, but she let herself enjoy it, because hopefully, she'd be dead soon. And at that moment a bond was forged.

Will led her back inside, and Jubi let him. They settled in an intimate corner of the fellowship hall. Her tears and her dread had vanished, at least for a time. He made no more effort to press her on her hurt. He gave no indication as to whether he had figured it out or not, or knew anything at all. And they talked small talk, silly talk about school and church, both making believe that what had happened had never happened. Jubi didn't know how Will was managing such a feat, but she knew that she was getting better and better at make-believe every day.

Esther and James, along with a flood of worshippers, found their way eventually into the fellowship hall, where they hoped they'd find Jubi. The place was busy, with hungry church folks lining up for the ample feast being offered.

James smiled when he saw Jubi and beckoned her over. "C'mon, girl. You ready?"

"Yeah," a smiling Jubi said, and she got up to make her way to her father. When she reached his arms, she looked back toward Will, who was watching. She waved a quick good-bye, and Will's smile ballooned.

His eyes conveyed his good-bye. And for at least a moment, Jubi's sorrow was gone, and she could act happy.

After that encounter with Will, though, Jubi still didn't cotton to going to church, because the Trouble replica still hovered around the church grounds, but at least because of Will's presence, choir rehearsal wasn't that bad. Besides, a new solution was slowly emerging, one that was even better than getting that thing out of her, somehow. She wouldn't worry about facing her shame or shaming her parents or even the church. Death was imminent. *It has to be,* she thought over and over again in the solitude of her bedroom. And it was the perfect solution too. Jubi was so pleased and so relieved. *Boy, it's great to be happy about something again,* she thought. *Happy.* And what a break, because it had come to her just like that.

About a month had past. It was December. Christmas was coming. *I've gotta speed this thing up,* was Jubi's thought. She'd been taking a couple of pills out of the medicine bottles she found in her parents' medicine cabinet. Just a couple of pills every now and then. The only prescription pills she was sure about were the muscle relaxers her mother had for her back. The medicinal use of every other bottle of pills she stole from was a mystery, but it didn't much matter to her. She just wanted to fall asleep and not wake up. The problem was that all she really ever did was fall asleep. She kept waking up. And she was terribly sluggish and drowsy all the time. Daily functioning had grown harder and harder, she noticed. All she wanted to do was sleep.

Class work and homework were hard to do, and that was when she went to class. She became ever more thankful for the weeks when both her mother and her father worked the day shift. She had their work schedules committed to memory, and she cleverly stayed abreast of any sudden changes. The days of when she could skip school outright were precious. Nowadays going to church was more than just an irritant. Getting ready to go to church or instigating the battles not to go had become harder. She didn't have the strength. Jubi soon ceased waging these battles not to go to church. They were just too hard. Luckily, knowing that she didn't have long to go, she found churchgoing much more tolerable. *I won't have to put up with this for much longer*, she'd tell herself.

Her parents took the new, agreeable Jubi as a triumph, and as a sign of maturity on her part. *Thank goodness*, they both thought. Trying to act normal was hard. But Jubi worked her hardest at that, because keeping her shameful sin under cover was a major motivator. Oh, everyone would find out after she was dead, she knew. *But at least I'll be dead,* she thought. *What a relief.* She had grown fond of fantasizing about it.

Jubi was sure she'd be dead because before Christmas break she ventured into the school's library, deciding to investigate her growing symptoms. And actually, that was the first real ray of hope that she stumbled upon. She looked up her symptoms—her cramps, her bleeding off and on, her increased nausea, and other discomforts—and she found the perfect name for what ailed her. As she sat at the long black desk, her finger trailed the tiny black words on the pages of the encyclopedia she'd chosen, and there it was. Ectopic pregnancy. Its recorded symptoms revealed much.

Jubi read intently as the library and all its roving occupants vanished from her awareness. *An ectopic pregnancy develops outside a woman's uterus.* And while she took the word *uterus* to mean her stomach, there was more explanation to behold. Jubi glossed over the next few sentences. Then one caught her eye. *The products of this conception are abnormal and cannot develop. It cannot turn into a normal pregnancy. No fetus will grow.* She paused to look up the meaning of *fetus,* then rushed right back to the description of this ailment.

In the description, she spied the phrases *very dangerous, the artery ruptures,* and *heavy bleeding,* and then she saw the happy word *death. It's the leading cause of pregnancy-related deaths,* she read. *Finally,* she thought, *there is a God.* There was more, but she stopped skimming and reading after that. She had learned all she needed to know. With that revelation, she stopped trying to overdose on drugs undercover. She ceased her bouts of starvation, and anything else she could think of. Once she had even hurled herself down her staircase. Now Jubi knew she needed only to wait for the death promised to her.

Three nights after New Year's Eve, Jubi saw a second ray of hope. She was sitting on the couch, half dozing, half watching *The Facts of Life,* when her stomach began to ache. *Cramps,* she thought at first. *No big deal.* Of late, they seemed to happen a bit more, but nothing ever came of it. These days her body was doing all sorts of things with all the pills and crap she had ingested. *So what?* she thought for the first hour.

The hospital was short staffed that night, and Esther had to pull a double shift. The day shift turned into the three-to-eleven shift. James was away for a week at a conference for lab researchers. It was quite a big deal

that his supervisor had included him on the trip. He
sensed that it was a sign of an imminent promotion.
Esther was glad that Jubi was acting more like her old
self again, and that was good. Still, she hated leaving
her alone like that for such a long period of time. But
she'd asked Victoria to peek in on her. That was the
norm, anyway.

That night Jubi's cramps began to worsen. And she
noticed, sitting there on the couch, that every time the
cramps came, they evolved into a strong throbbing,
then subsided, and then went away completely. But
somehow as soon as she reassured herself that all this
was a passing thing, they'd come back. *My goodness,*
was her thought. She massaged her stomach slowly.
Her ribs felt a little sore, she noticed. *Maybe I should
get some water,* she thought. Her pain hit with a vengeance. It prompted another thought. *Maybe I have to
go to the bathroom.*

Jubi stood up, turned the TV off. She was no longer
interested, anyway. She climbed upstairs as best she
could and headed for the bathroom. Standing in the
hallway, she felt a pop inside, and a sudden gush of
fluid rushed out of her. Stunned and confused, she
looked down to discover it was mostly blood mixed
with another liquid. *Water?* she wondered. But it was
a fountain, flowing in the middle of the floor. She had
to think quick. She thought, *Cover-up. I've got to clean
this up.*

She hurried to the bathroom and sat on the toilet,
hoping that the gushing would stop. The plan was to
let it stop, then get up, get the mop or something, and
clean all that mess up before her mother got home.
But it didn't. It didn't even seem to slow down. She
sat there, realizing that there was a very obvious blood
trail leading from the hallway to the bathroom. She

thought and thought, trying to come up with a plan. Intermittently, the cramps resurfaced, each time with a vengeance. It really hampered her thought process and her ability to come up with a plan.

When the most recent wave of pain subsided, she finally realized what this all was. "Oh," she said to no one but herself. "It's happening. It's happening. How stupid I am. I'm dying." But her thoughts remained on covering her tracks. It was habit. The bleeding just refused to stop. Another thing she thought, *Forget it. It's around nine o'clock, I think. I'll just go lie down. And be dead when Mama gets home.* The idea brought relief.

More cramps hit. After she removed herself from the toilet, doubled over, she made her way to her bedroom. She was a mess, but she fell onto her bed, belly up. The awareness that there was a blood trail from the upstairs hallway to the bathroom, across the toilet, and into her bedroom, where it ended like a ragged trail of bread crumbs, pierced her, but it just couldn't be helped.

Chapter Eight

Death

It was around ten o'clock, perhaps, and Jubi, a bloody, wet mess, lay on her canopy bed, weak and yearning for sleep. No slumber, not even final slumber, would come. There was no position that brought her body any relief. She shifted to her right side, getting twisted up in her robe and nightgown. The cramps would hit and level her flat. Her body aches sent her to try her left side, then to lie flat again. It was a ballet of cascading pain and the discovery that it had repeat performances, of which she couldn't plan for or manage. It seemed to have a mind of its own, and it went on in the darkness of her bedroom for hours. Her forehead was drenched with sweat. She had discovered that quick, short puffs of breath and exhalations helped divert some of the pain, and she hoped that maybe she could keep that up until her death.

A different kind of panic set in when Jubi heard the distant opening of the front door. It was her mother, home from her shift. "Oh my God," Jubi whispered as she tracked her mother's sounds and movements downstairs. "God, please kill me! Kill me!" she pleaded. Angry, she said, "Why won't you answer any of my prayers? Why do you hate me so much?" Jubi could hear her mother trudging up the stairs.

To say that Esther was dog-tired that night would have been an understatement. She pulled her aging body up the stairs, tugged on the mahogany banister for assistance. Reaching the top of the stairs, she thought she smelled an odor. It wasn't exactly foul, she noted slowly, but it seemed oddly reminiscent of hospital smells—and, sadly, of her childhood and younger womanhood. And the multicolored brown and burnt orange carpet, she noted, felt clumpy under her feet. It was slightly discolored, maybe. Maybe not. *Oh goodness,* she sighed inwardly. *I've been at that hospital so long, I've brought it home with me.*

Esther walked past the bathroom, and in her peripheral vision she noticed some disarray. Perhaps she noticed the blood draped over the toilet, splashed on the side of the tub, and dripped on the black-and-white tile. Perhaps she didn't. But she kept walking toward Jubi's room to check on Jubi—as she did every night she came home late.

Jubi heard her coming. Thankful that her reoccurring cramps had decided to subside, she held her body still. Her mother's silhouette stood in the doorway. "Hi," Jubi said, trying to sound normal, hoping that it would keep her mother from entering the room. Thankfully, her mother neither entered the room nor reached for the light switch.

Esther stopped short, noting that the hospital smell was strong inside the room. "So you're still awake, huh?" she said, not moving.

"Well, I wasn't, but I heard you come in," Jubi said groggy like. Faking. She saw the shadow of her mother's arm move upward. "Don't cut on the lights," she said in a rush. "I'm . . . I'm trying to get back to sleep," she said, regrouping. Relief came when she saw her mother's arm shadow move back down to her side.

Esther couldn't quite get why she was being so coop-erative with Jubi and why she couldn't command her feet to enter Jubi's bedroom, because she felt an incli-nation to do it, or why she couldn't just be on her way down the hall. "What's going on?" Esther asked Jubi, still standing in the doorway.

"Huh? I'm all right," Jubi said, hopeful that the ques-tion didn't have some kind of double meaning. "I'm sleepy. That's all. Night, Mom. Okay?"

The child was telling the parent what to do, Esther noted, but tired and filled with a sense of foreboding, she didn't feel like finding anything wrong that night. So she said, "Good night. See you in the morning. School tomorrow, you know. It's Monday."

"I know," Jubi answered in a low voice, confident that she'd never see the sun rise.

Esther went into her room, took off her uniform, put on her nightgown, and fell into bed. She broke her habit of going into the bathroom to take a quick shower first, or at least to wash the make-up off her face. But that was just what happened.

Jubi listened intently until she was convinced she heard silence. It brought a strange sense of relief. But then the pain hit. This time it was major. She cupped her mouth with both hands to keep from yelling. She had no tears, but whimpers, here and there, did escape her throat. *When will this all end?* It was her most burning question, because it occurred to her like clock-work until the wee hours.

It was now a strong wave of pain that attacked her mercilessly, then moved, then returned. She cupped her mouth and whimpered. She tossed and turned—when she could. Without warning a hideous pain belt-ed her so hard, her body convulsed and her lower half excreted a clumpy, wet blob of something. She reached down and pulled it out. Clutching a piece of it, she held it up close to her eyes in the darkness and saw that it looked like a piece of liver. Her mother loved to cook liver, and she hated to eat it. Jubi's body convulsed again, her vagina ripping open by itself.

The pain was nondescript in her mind at this point. Her innards moved, battled, and pushed matter out without her assistance. It happened in the darkness of her bedroom, amid the mounted shelves that held her dolls. It happened amid her teen-idol posters on her walls, amid her discarded textbooks and book bag, strewn here and there. And it happened in the presence of her pink Princess phone, which had careened to the floor because of her sudden movement. Jubi reached down between her legs to feel two clumps of tiny toes. Forgetting the original plan for death, she screamed hysterically for her mother.

Esther was in a dead sleep, but she wrenched her back when she was jolted awake by Jubi's screams. For a brief couple of seconds the primal screams sounded familiar. She was dazed and confused, but still there was that innate built-in alarm for when a baby cried out for its mother. There were no intelligible words, just screams coming from Jubi's bedroom. The web of sleep finally broke. Esther jumped out of bed. She shouted to no one, "Jubi?"

Esther felt like she was rushing at the time, but in hindsight, she decided that everything happened in slow motion. There was screaming, screaming, screaming coming from her daughter's bedroom. James was gone. *Why isn't he here?* was her thought. And she couldn't get down the hall fast enough even though she felt like she was rushing. In fact, she could feel herself drenched in dread, unable to run. *Why can't I run?* She wondered why she couldn't move swiftly like she did when she had to at work, when she was helping a distressed patient. And she couldn't talk, either. In her flesh, she wanted to yell out, "I'm coming!" *Wouldn't a mother do that?* she thought. There were many strange thoughts in this grand strange moment. She reached her daughter's bedroom door and stopped. She flicked on the lights.

The light revealed a horrifying scene. Blood was everywhere. The hospital smell was pervasive. A mass of afterbirth lay at Jubi's knees and on her belly. Jubi's soiled nightgown was up just enough to reveal two tiny feet attached to two tiny legs. They looked like they belonged to one of Jubi's favorite doll babies. Except that they weren't brown or peach or even the color of a gingersnap cookie. They were colorless, raw, with pink and blue veins visible throughout. And they were stiff, lifeless. Esther's eye traveled up the scene to Jubi's face. She was silent now. Her eyes were closed. Jubi had the look of pain and fear painted on her face. Whether life was behind her eyelids, Esther did not know. Her first impulse was to faint. Just drop to the floor. But she couldn't. There was no time for such relief.

In a giant step, Esther knelt down at her baby's side, feeling her daughter's dead arms for a pulse, lifting her eyelids for signs of life. "Oh, please. Oh, please. Oh, please. God, I'm sorry for everything I've done," she said to her maker as she picked up the Princess phone, slapped its receiver down on its base to revive its dial tone. She needed to call for an ambulance. Monday morning had arrived, but Jubi would not be going to school on that day. Esther wanted to hold her baby in her arms, but she refrained from moving Jubi's body. There were still signs of life, and Esther wanted to keep it that way. But she held Jubi's hand to keep it warm, while not looking at her lower half . . . on purpose.

Esther heard the sirens come into play. In fact, she was sure she heard two sets of sirens competing with one another. She gently released her daughter's hand and hospital-rushed herself to the front door. She was starting to get her wits about her now. When she opened the front door, two men had already popped out of an ambulance and were carrying a stretcher with a blanket on it.

"Where, ma'am?" one of the men said when he reached the front door.

"Upstairs, please," Esther heard herself say as she pointed. She peeked out the door and quickly spotted Will standing out on Victoria's front lawn and a duplicate ambulance scene in front of Victoria's door. The police were there too.

Will caught sight of Jubi's mother and wondered what was happening. But he had his hands full and his focus was elsewhere as he described how he was leaving his house, heading for school as usual. "And I found Ms. Victoria lying unconscious in her walkway." The back of her head was bleeding, and there was a stream of blood coming from her ear. How uncanny that both ambulances would speed off at nearly the same time.

Esther shut the front door and followed the men upstairs. They spied the scene, and if they were floored by what they saw, they didn't let on. Poker-faced, the men stood at opposite ends of the twin bed and yanked the top sheet off its mattress. It was almost off, anyway, from when Jubi had clutched it during her burst of labor pains and desperation. On the count of three, they lifted Jubi and her half-discarded matter, all wrapped in the sheet, onto the gurney. They strapped her securely. There were some quick questions that mortified Esther, because she couldn't answer them.

"How old is your daughter, Mrs. Stone?"

"Fourteen," Esther said. She could answer that.

"How far along was your daughter?"

Esther couldn't answer that. "I . . . I didn't know she was pregnant," she was forced to say. "I . . . I didn't even know she had been with a boy." Her eyes teared up. Her strong voice cracked.

The two men looked at each other, then began searching for vitals. Then one of them said on the way out with Jubi, "We'll take good care of her. Don't worry. This is not a unique case."

Case! Esther screamed in her head, offended. *My daughter ain't no case. She's a good girl. And we're good parents. We ain't no case!* Out loud, she had no argument. She walked swiftly behind them, silent. They would be headed, Esther already knew, to Providence Hospital, where she worked. And she didn't want thoughts of embarrassment to enter her head, but they got in, anyway. *This will be all over the hospital an hour after we get there.* It shamed her to worry about a thing like that at a time like this, but she did. Esther jumped in her car and followed close behind the ambulance. As she drove, another thought assaulted her. *How, oh, how in the world am I gonna break this to James?*

At the hospital, Esther rushed behind the paramedics, who raced Jubi toward a restricted area for patients. At one point, one man raced on ahead with Jubi, using the gurney to burst through a pair of steel-plated double doors. And, *swish*, Jubilee was gone from sight. The other paramedic stopped Esther from going any farther.

"I'm sorry, ma'am, but you can't go there," he said it in a patient way, cognizant of how she felt. But he said it firmly, meaning that there was no negotiating room. Esther understood, but she gave it a good try, anyway.

"But I work here," she replied, trying to reason with him.

The young man took a breath and said, "I know. But not in this instance." The fact that he had recognized her startled her. He went on, "They'll take good care of her and let you know something as soon as they can."

Esther huffed, feeling defeated.

The paramedic added, "I promise. Please go have a seat over there."

She looked at him like the notion of her taking a seat or taking it easy was ludicrous. But she gave in and turned around just in time to see Victoria being wheeled in, her frantic parents in tow. Esther was full of questions about that too. Victoria didn't look conscious, and her parents were in such a tizzy, they never even saw Esther standing there on the sidelines of their peril.

When Jubi came to, she was disappointed. She found herself in a strange bed in what looked like a sterile hospital room. An orchid-colored doctor stood over her. He had a meticulously trimmed salt-and-pepper mustache that connected to sideburns that connected to his full head of wavy salt-and-pepper hair. A peach-colored nurse stood attentively beside him; she was a middle-aged blonde and looked older than the doctor. Jubi guessed that she was a bit younger than her mother, who was fifty-one. They stood there staring at her, void of smiles. They had been talking about her, Jubi assumed, but had canned it when her eyes opened.

"Well, hello, young lady," the doctor said without introducing himself. The nurse just stared. He pulled back the sheet to reveal the thick, heavy mass Jubi felt between her legs. In her haze, and in the immediate moment, she'd forgotten about it. Her look was blank, because she had expected to be dead. "Well, young lady, what do you think about all this, huh?" the doctor said. His voice lacked compassion. "So what did you think? It was gonna disappear?" Now he was downright nasty.

Jubi's eyes were stuck on the creases of his unfriendly face. But she had no voice, no wherewithal to respond. It was a rhetorical question, anyway.

In one stroke of determination that held no mercy, only purpose, the doctor grabbed hold of the tiny legs and pulled. Jubi's voice came back. She screamed and clasped the bed rails for protection and found that her wrists were tied to the rails. The nurse, like clockwork, reached behind, grabbed a gray basin, and held it in position just at the time the doctor freed the stiff dead corpse from Jubi's loins. With disgust, the doctor dropped it in the basin. Jubi's voice went silent at the point of extraction, but the pain lingered. And she heard the stiff tiny bundle of death make a plunking sound as it disappeared beneath the basin's rim. It never occurred to her to crane her neck to see if it had a head, or to ask whether it was a girl thing or a boy thing. And no one ever, ever said. Her inability to think straight at that moment would emerge as a major regret later on.

The doctor gave some instructions to the nurse, and they were off. And Jubi lay still, feeling something wet trickling onto the huge pad beneath her. If there was pain or discomfort, it remained her private business, because no one ever came in to inquire. She laid there feeling empty, yet still feeling full of sin and shame. How was that? she wondered later.

On day two, she woke up. The first thing she noted was that her wrists were free, though she couldn't recall when that had happened. It was afternoon, and she found her daddy sitting at her bedside. Esther had called him that infamous wee hour, and he had taken the next plane home that morning. At the sight of him, tears plummeted down the sides of her cheeks.

"How are you feeling, gingersnap?" he said, making an effort to be playful. But that made it worse in her head. She'd been soiled, contaminated, she knew. But now worst of all, her daddy knew it. She was nobody's little gingersnap anymore. Jubi cried silent tears. She had no words. "How you feelin'?" he asked again. This time he was serious.

"Fine," she heard the Jubi stranger say. But she failed to look him in the eye.

He repositioned himself a bit, uncomfortable, cleared his throat, then got right to the point. "Jubi," he said directly, "who did this to you? Who was it?"

She took her time to speak. "Nobody," she said, looking at her bedsheets.

"Naw, Jubi. Somebody! You didn't do this to yourself. And I wanna know who."

Jubi didn't know it, but an enraged James had swept her bedroom with the prowess of a seasoned detective. He had searched for clues that would lead him to the slithering reptile who had taken advantage of his daughter. He had also questioned the neighborhood kids to find out what they knew.

"Have you seen anyone you don't know hanging around our house?" he'd asked a group of neighbor kids, who were a bit disjointed by such questioning from a grown-up.

"Did you know Jubi had a boyfriend?" he'd come right out and asked a neighbor girl who walked to school with Jubi, he knew. Well, she used to. It seemed that their friendship and interactions had kind of ended.

James would have had a good talk with Victoria, to find out what she knew, if he could have. So far, his investigation had led nowhere. But he was quite confident that he'd find out something, especially if he talked to Victoria, because Jubi loved her so. Jubi hung on her every word, he knew. And Victoria was such a nice young woman; both Esther and James were in agreement about that. Surely if there was ever anything Jubi felt she couldn't share with her parents, being able to share with another responsible adult was a good thing.

Jubi snuck a look at her father amid the awkward silence that descended and saw an angry gleam in his eye. It was a look she had not seen in him ever. He'd come right out and asked the question, and it conjured up visions of her daddy being arrested for killing Trouble and his stupid parents, or worse. One of them might hurt her father, she thought. She couldn't tell. She just couldn't. And it was all her fault, anyway. *He'll find that out, and everything will get worse,* she thought—if that were possible. *He'll know I'm a whore!* Jubi stayed silent. The quiet in the room choked them both.

James's anger subsided when he detected the sorrow and fright in his daughter's eyes. He stood up, stroked her shoulder, and leaned over to kiss her on the forehead. He whispered, "You're protecting him, and he's not worth it. But I love you, baby. And ain't nothing gonna ever change that." She looked away from him again and felt the urge to cry, but she was empty.

Jubi's hospital stay amounted to seven days. There were no visitors, she noted, which made sense in her mind. *People only come to see people who deserve to be sick.* Doctors and nurses came in and went out. Orderlies, she supposed, dressed in mint-green tunics and matching slacks, wheeled her here and wheeled her there. The doctors cleaned her out, stitched her up, and she took into her veins IVs of saline fluid and two pints of blood. The blood donation came from her father.

The news of what had happened hit the hospital airwaves, just as Esther knew it would. Of course, her church friend and coworker at Providence, Peggy Gentry, learned what had happened, but Esther hadn't been the one to tell her. Peggy got it from the hospital pipeline, like everyone else. They were both on shift when Peggy found out. Immediately, she went to Esther and embraced her. Esther teared up at the touch. Her weary body released its tension into her friend's arms. Walking around, pretending not to notice the strange glares and snickers or not to catch the snippets of hurried whispers around her, was daunting.

"Esther, keep strong," Peggy said, pulling her into a nearby waiting room that was, thankfully, empty. "How is Jubi?" she asked, glossing over the fine point that she had not heard about what happened from Esther.

"She's coming along," Esther said. She glossed over Jubi's condition as well. "The doctor said she'll be all right in time. Nothing was permanently damaged, they think, and she should be able to have babies later, when she wants to." That last part, about having babies, kind of caught in her throat when she said it, for she realized again that her baby girl had actually been pregnant. She had actually had premarital sex. Peggy correctly intuited her friend's revelation, and her shame, for Esther was such a proud woman. She grabbed Esther and pulled her into her arms again.

"Look," Peggy said. She stepped back to look Esther in the eye. "This isn't your fault. And, sadly, this isn't an isolated case."

"Yeah, but it's not supposed to happen to us," Esther confessed. "We didn't just give birth to this child. We prayed her in," she said. Her voice was laced with a cocktail of disappointment and anger.

"It's a challenge to raise kids in this world today. They got so much comin' at them. I know! I'm a parent too! And we're fighting this world to raise 'em right . . . keep 'em safe. The devil's after our children."

Esther just listened. She agreed about the part that the devil was after her good Christian-reared child. But, for her, the jury was still out on the carnage not being her fault. Her hindsight of certain events blamed her, directly. *How could I have fallen asleep at the wheel?* she thought. Out loud, she had no further comment on Peggy's take on parenthood or the devil. She just stood there, motionless, listening to her friend, trying to digest it.

"You want me to look in on her? Peggy asked sincerely. "See how she's doing?"

To that, Esther mustered up a quick "No." She hadn't thought it through, but for some reason, she just didn't want anyone seeing Jubi in that sad way. She just didn't.

Since many who worked at the hospital also went to Forest Unity, the incredible news spread there too, like a dry brushfire. When it got to Reverend Wicker— relayed to him by Beola—he stopped everything and made a call. James picked up the phone.

"Deacon Stone?" Reverend Wicker replied when he heard his deacon say hello. "James?" the reverend continued, wanting to be less formal.

"Yes, Pastor. How are you doing?" James said.

"The question is, how are you doing, James? And how is our little Jubi?"

"Well, she's as fine as can be expected," James said "She's healing nicely . . . physically. But in her spirit . . ." James trailed off, then gathered enough resolve to finish his point. "She's not talking much, and she's not eating, and she's not telling us how this all happened."

"Well, uh-huh," Reverend Wicker responded, not at all surprised about what he'd heard. He thought it all over. "Well, you know, these kids . . . ," he said. Then he rethought what he was going to say. "The girl was scared. You know, she got in over her head with things and was afraid to tell it."

"I know," James agreed, but he was thinking about how there had to be much more to it than that.

"I don't know, James. We do everything to let our children know they can come to us, but sometimes, they just don't. Too much fear sets in. Or they just decide to rely on the wrong worldly counsel. Lord knows, it's out there, all around them, for them to get."

"But this was awful, Pastor," James said. "Jubi nearly lost her life."

"I know. I heard. Look, let the child know that we love her. The church loves her. Let her know that she can come to us. And none of this mess changes that," the reverend said. He licked his thumb and pointer finger and began thumbing through his calendar. "Look, I'm coming over there to see her," he said, deciding he'd drop by the very next morning. "Can Jubi receive visitors?" he asked.

James had been sitting at the kitchen table, eating a meat-loaf dinner with all the fixings, which Esther had prepared for him, when he flicked the bright yellow receiver off the wall kitchen phone. It was mounted on the wall just above his head and possessed a long spiral cord so that conversations could be conducted throughout the kitchen. Esther was still in the kitchen too, washing pots and pans, making herself a soapy, silent eavesdropper.

"Yes, Pastor, she can have visitors," James said, thankful, but not surprised. The Reverend Charles A. Wicker, Jr., served all his congregation well, just like his daddy had done before him.

Esther heard that last comment, and panic set in. She quickly turned to face James and started waving her hands and shaking her head no.

James looked at her, befuddled. He stopped talking and pressed the receiver to his chest. "What?" he asked her.

"No! Tell him no!" she said in a loud whisper. "She can't have visitors."

"But . . . but I thought she could," James said. He put the receiver back to his face and said, "Oh, Pastor, sorry. Can you hold on a moment? Thanks, okay." And the receiver went back across his heart. He looked at Esther, confused, and repeated, "But I thought she could? I don't see why she can't."

"Well, no, she can't," Esther whispered back. "Not yet. You're mistaken." She kept her eye on him until his facial expression conveyed acceptance of this conflicting news. She watched him correct himself in the phone's receiver.

"Oh, well, no, Pastor, she's not ready for visitors yet. My dear wife here is correcting me," James said.

With things straightened out and safe, Esther went back to washing pots and pans. James and Reverend Wicker discussed some more stuff, such as duties for the deacon board. The reverend prayed over the phone with him, and then the conversation was over. The church, by way of word of mouth, would pass on the new news that Jubi was recuperating well, but that she could not receive visitors. Everyone understood. Folks who interacted with Jubi on a regular basis, like the choir director, Sister Cherry, the Sunday school teacher, and her young choir mates would decide to wait patiently to put their arms around her and reassure her that she was not alone in anything.

For now, though, they'd show their love by showering Jubi with get well cards, some handmade, from the kiddie Sunday school class. There'd be no discussion about the specifics of what happened. That was too sticky an issue. But she'd know that if she wanted to start a dialogue, they were willing and ready. Sister Cherry and the Sunday school teacher decided to collect all the good wishes, the sealed notes, the colored-in bunny rabbits with bandaged heads and thermometers sticking out of their mouths and such, put them in a box, and wrap it prettily. Sister Cherry dropped by the Stones' house on the same evening of Reverend Wicker's phone call.

When the doorbell bellowed, Esther yelled out, "I'll get it." So James never bothered to get up and go to the door.

The choir director, also a church friend of Esther's, greeted her with the beautifully wrapped package. "How you doin', Sister Esther?" Sister Cherry said. Her brow was wrinkled with concern. "How's our little Jubi? She handling all this as best she can?" Sister Cherry asked earnestly. But it gave Esther pause because it skirted a fine line to her. "Look," Sister Cherry continued, because she either didn't detect the line skirting or ignored it, "Jubi's not alone in this. Our children are up against a lot in this world."

"Uh-huh," Esther uttered, being careful not to invite conversation. She didn't feel like talking about it, about anything. There was another awkward pause between the two church friends.

"Well." Sister Cherry said after realizing she was standing there, frozen, holding a box, "the choirs and the Sunday school family, especially all the kids, wanted Jubi to know that we're praying for her." She brushed some imaginary dust off the top of the package before she could bring herself to relinquish it, as it had been birthed with so much care and concern. She handed it over, saying with a smile, "Jubi should have fun going over all the things the children made."

Esther thought that the word *fun* was a curious one to use in a conversation about this dreadful situation, but she commanded her face not to show it. "Thank you so much, Sister Cherry," Esther said. "I'll be sure Jubi gets it." Esther's smile was crooked in the way a smile was when somebody was embarrassed.

Still, either not detecting Esther's discomfort or choosing not to detect it, Sister Cherry offered a genuine hug. Esther felt it, and she received it. She needed a hug; maybe she even wanted to collapse into it. But she held herself up. And she did not invite Sister Cherry in to chat. Esther closed the door, thinking, *I'll give this to her when she gets home.* She made her way upstairs and stashed the beautifully wrapped box on an upper shelf on her side of the bedroom closet. She wanted to keep it safe.

Will, who had contributed a private note to the box of good wishes, planned to wait patiently, as well. But his aim was to embrace Jubi. And he very much planned to get to the bottom of it all. He had an idea, and he knew he'd keep her secret when she confirmed it. Maybe some payback, he supposed, could be meted out to the guilty party. All that happened around day three of Jubi's stay in the hospital.

Victoria was unconscious when they brought her to Providence Hospital. For three days, her mother and father kept a vigil at her bedside. They vacated their post, taking turns, only when they had to take care of their grandson. Or take him to day care. Or pick him up. Or drop him off at a neighbor's house, a longtime friend turned trusted babysitter. The diagnosis was an aneurysm, and there was a tremendous swelling in her brain. Her parents wanted a clear-cut list of reasons why this happened.

"What in the world could have caused this?" her father had asked Victoria's doctors, with anger and frustration in his voice. The doctors were sympathetic, but vague. No satisfactory answers emerged. Victoria's parents pressed hard for an explanation the first night, but quickly it became apparent that all the doctors' focus needed to be directed at possible remedies. "Well, just how do you plan to bring her back to us?" her mother had asked through tears. The doctors were vague again. And the days mounted in intensive care.

"I'm sorry . . . no flowers, stuffed animals, or food," called out the head nurse, craning her neck from her seat at a bustling nurses' station. "I'm so sorry," she repeated to Victoria's father, this time with a bit of patience in her voice.

The comment stopped him short, and his eyes grew dull hearing of it all. On his way back to his vigil at the hospital, he had decided that a lovely bouquet of pink roses seemed like such a grand idea. Victoria loved when menfolk brought her flowers, trinkets, and things, especially her favorite man of all time, her daddy. When he was meticulously picking out and purchasing the flowers, he'd had a flashback that made him feel good.

He'd come home from work, waiting with anticipation to see his little girl pop out of nowhere to greet him at the door. Her smile and her eyes were big with happiness, and she gleefully welcomed the one she loved most. And her little life was big.

"Daddyyy! Hi, Daddy!" she'd yelled out, with her arms spread wide, ready for him to lift her up like a spaceship headed for the heavens. She'd beam at being held in his big, strong arms.

Her hair was always neatly parted and combed into two perfect Afro puff balls. They looked like huge Mickey Mouse ears. As soon as her little feet touched the floor, she'd jump up and down, saying, "Daddy, whaddya bring me? Whaddya bring me?" faithfully knowing that he had not come home empty handed.

He'd reach into his pocket and pull out something. Most times it was of little monetary value—penny candy, a box of animal crackers, a tiny toy bracelet. Sometimes, if it was summer, he'd drop coins into the cream-colored palm of her waiting hand, because the ice cream truck was on its way. They both somehow understood that the value of the gift wasn't the point. Then she'd ask, "Daddy, did you think about me today?"

"Yes, pumpkin." His response always came with a smile and a kiss on her cheek. "I thought about you all day." His wife would come in the room, smiling, hugging them both, and it always completed the scene.

After being stopped at the nurses' station, Victoria's father, feeling deflated, walked back into the lobby, approached a row of elevators, and dropped the beautiful bouquet of flowers in the trash. Then he hurried to be with his wife and daughter.

For three or four days the only signs of life were the rhythmic beeping of the machines that stood in for her breathing, eating, and excreting, and the sorrowful, twisted look of pain spread across her once very beautiful face. Victoria really was a vibrant, breathing, voluptuous Barbie doll. Yes, she had some progressive ideas. She embraced them as she rolled with the punches after disappointing her parents when she became an unwed mother. But she also reached for the tradition-al—that became clear when something kept her com-ing back to church. She was young and healthy, and she had all the time in the world to work out her ideology. But, for some reason, all that ended somewhere in the wee hours of that fateful Monday morn. Victoria never regained consciousness. Victoria died that Friday. She was twenty-six years old.

Before Jubi left the hospital, the rude doctor who had yanked the life and death right out of her loins said to Esther, right in front of Jubi, "Now that you know she's having sex, better put her on birth control pills."

Esther stood frozen, neither agreeing nor disagree-ing.

He smirked when he said, "I'll write out a prescrip-tion. You'll get it when she's discharged tomorrow. He paused, in thought. "And I'll send you home with some samples so she can get started on them right away. Okay?"

Jubi didn't say anything, either. She sat upright and still on the edge of the hospital bed like she was just an-other inanimate object, like the sheets and the blanket and the pillow. But inside she felt mortified, embar-rassed, and ashamed. Her thought was, *So now they think I'm some kind of sex fiend. I'm a whore. Better get me on those pills fast, 'cause I might get right ta humpin' as soon as I get home.*

If there was anything merciful about this moment, it was the fact that her father was not in the hospital room to hear this. He had gone to clear up matters concerning the hospital bill and their health insurance particulars, and to go fetch the car and bring it around front. He'd be ready to receive Jubi when she was wheeled to the curb in a wheelchair by the floor nurse, who was another workplace acquaintance of both Esther and James.

Her anger and hurt grew. The poison it emanated contaminated her soul. Jubi was angry at the doctor, at her mother for believing what the doctor had insinuated, and at herself, because the whole bloody thing was all her fault in the first place. Her only solace in all this was that at least there was one person on this earth who knew she wasn't a whore. One person who knew the whole deal and would never accuse her or condemn her to hell. *Thank God, I have one person I can trust. She's the only person I can really talk to . . . who trusts me. I can't wait to get out of here to see Victoria and tell her what happened. She's probably wondering where I've been all this time.* These thoughts consoled Jubi the night before she knew she would be discharged.

The three of them were quiet during the ride home from the hospital. The car radio played R & B oldies, but the volume was faint. If you breathed loudly, you couldn't hear the music. Jubi chalked up the silence to shame. For an entire week nobody had asked her what happened. Nobody except her father that one time, and she felt fairly confident that he wouldn't do that again. She assumed the silence was due to her whorish act. But perhaps it wasn't.

When they all walked into the house, they were overcome by a sense of a slow-motion dread. Jubi felt that the house was different. It had a different air about it. Even so, all she wanted to do was to disappear into her room, while at the same time being aware that she wasn't quite sure about seeing her room again. Would it be as she'd left it—a bloody mess? Would it feel like a tomb? A casket? She should have died there, but she'd been viciously betrayed by God. Or would it be a nice bedroom, crisp and clean, void of any hint of death? The one thing she was sure of was that it was her only refuge, her only escape, and she couldn't wait to head there.

"Lemme take your coat, baby," her daddy said softly and politely, like he was talking to a stranger. He took Esther's too and hung them up, his included, in the foyer closet.

Jubi headed in the direction of the stairs, but Esther caught her. "Not yet, baby. Not yet," Esther said, grabbing Jubi's hand and pulling her to the couch. It was strange, but Jubi could have sworn it was the first time she had felt her mother's touch since this whole thing happened. Stunned, she did not balk, but just obeyed. Esther sat down near her daughter. James came in and sat down on the coffee table, looking directly at Jubi.

Here it comes, Jubi thought. *The inquisition.* She felt barricaded and bare. She was helpless, and she couldn't come up with a single game plan, besides pleading the fifth and repeating the now infamous "I don't know," which was the thing she said the night it happened and she failed to die. And it wouldn't matter what they asked, she told herself. If she could muster up words, her answer would always be, "I don't know."

"Jubi, darling." Her father spoke slowly, but directly. "On the same morning . . ." He paused to readjust his emotions. He gathered his strength to say what he needed to say. "On the same morning that the ambulance took you to the hospital, Victoria got sick." He stopped again, to give that time to sink in. "Another ambulance had to take Victoria to the hospital."

Jubi's strategizing fizzled as she slowly realized that this conversation must not be about her. Her expression changed from defensive to puzzled to blank. "What's wrong, Daddy?" Jubi said in a frail voice. She felt her mother's arm tightened around her. She didn't acknowledge it, but she was thankful for it. "How is she? You mean, she was in the hospital the same time I was there?" Jubi thought more about it, then grew angry. "You mean, she was there, and you guys didn't even tell me?" She tried to loosen her mother's arm, but her mother would not have it. "How could you do that, Daddy? I mean—"

James cut in. And his comment cut into Jubi's anger. "Listen to me, baby. This is serious," he said. "It turns out Victoria was sick. Real sick, Jubi. And nobody knew that. Victoria was unconscious the entire time she was there. You couldn't have visited her."

"But you could have told me, Daddy. You could have let me—"

"Jubi." James demanded her attention and her silence. "Victoria died."

"What? What?" Jubi said. Her body deflated onto her mother's bosom, and now she directed her questions to Esther. "What? Mama, is that true?" Jubi surrendered to a sorrow, and her voice was unrecognizable even to her. With all she'd been through, she had never felt such bewilderment.

"Yes, baby girl," Esther confirmed. "Victoria passed away Friday night. We're sorry, baby, but you were healing. We just couldn't tell you then. We couldn't."

Jubi wanted to be angry, but an insurmountable feeling of loss took over. *Oh my gosh,* she'd come to think later. *I prayed and prayed for death, and, God, you sent it next door. Is this my fault too?*

Answers about Victoria's aneurysm, speculation
about what or who had caused it, would come up
later—way later. But in the moment, there weren't
any more words on the subject. Jubi's tears gushed.
Her sorrowful cries were primal again. Jubi burrowed
herself in her mother's arms and sobbed—perhaps
about everything. She cried in her mother's arms until
she was hollow and felt like dust. James got the two of
them a blanket. Jubi collapsed and slept there.

Victoria's home-going service took place at Forest
Unity Memorial Church. James, in his capacity as deacon, acted as the go-between to assure everything went
smoothly. Victoria wasn't a member of the church, but
she had become a frequent visitor, and folks had gotten
used to seeing her. They had taken pleasure in wooing
her to join. And she had taken pleasure in it too; she
had often shared that fact with Esther. Everyone at the
church was saddened by the sudden, seemingly sense-
less loss.

Victoria's parents and baby boy, and some extended
family members, whom Jubi had neither seen before
nor heard tell of, crowded in the first seven rows of the
sanctuary. They listened intently to Reverend Wicker's
sermon about mortality. "No one knows the time or
the hour," he preached, "so the thing to do now is to get
your house in order." Three of Victoria's relatives, Jubi
noted, came to the altar.

Thankful, Reverend Wicker said to them for all to
hear, "God is pleased with you today. And so is your
beloved Victoria. Weep no more for her." He said it
with a warm smile on his face, and he paused to let
both the smile and the message soak in. "I know for a
fact that she accepted our Jesus Christ as her personal

Lord and Savior. And today our sweet Victoria resides in victory!"

Esther and Victoria's mother were seated at least eight rows apart, and thankfully, neither could see the other's facial expression, because both of them had reached the same conclusion. It had to do with the particulars of a dream that Esther had shared with Victoria's mother months earlier. The message of the dream was that sweet, searching Victoria would indeed get the final victory one day soon. But at the time, neither of them had thought that her victory would translate into an untimely earthly death. Esther and Victoria's mother would stumble upon one another years later in the mall. They would agree to have lunch, and they would confirm that they both had misunderstood the message of the dream. They would agree that the dream revealed Victoria's early passing and her victory of eternal life.

When the Stone family came home from the funeral, Jubi went straight to her room, retrieved the little round disk of tiny pink pills she had stowed away in her underwear bureau drawer. She ran back downstairs and threw the pills in the kitchen trash can. After returning to her bedroom, Jubi cried—for herself and for sweet Victoria.

Gradually, things grew normal in the Stone house, meaning that no more tough questions were asked. School and work schedules resumed. But the word about what had happened had climbed up and down the high school grapevine, and the seemingly shy, quiet Jubi suddenly earned valuable street cred. Because she was the girl who everyone knew for sure had had sex. She had a secret boyfriend, and she had had the cojones to do something about the problem that resulted. Now, suddenly, Jubi was in with the in crowd. But the in crowd was also the no-good crowd. Hanging with them, she learned their savvy ways and street hipness. "That band of thugs," as Esther called them during a fight with Jubi, taught her about smoking weed and partying. And when Jubi offered up her abode as a perfect truancy hideout—while her parents worked the day shift—well, she attained legendary in-crowd status. And she liked it.

Church attendance and church work worked their way back into the Stones' lives. Peggy and Beola, the FISHH Ministry, and many of the church members fell over themselves to embrace Esther and James. They whispered scriptures of love and endurance. They prayed without ceasing and planted words of encouragement in their ears. They worked hard to reassure them that they were loved and that they were family. Reverend Wicker preached a fiery sermon on the first Sunday they all returned to church, about judgment and how "that was God's job, and no one else's." He bellowed it to the rafters. The congregation threw up a cloak of "Amens."

But both James and Esther had their church faces plastered on—several layers thick, it seemed. Somehow their tremendous need to be uplifted and ministered to, and even taught during this trying time, retreated behind false pride. They sat on their respective pews— Esther and Jubi in the congregation, James on deacons' row—stone-faced. So what do you do when all good efforts are rebuked?

At home Jubi put up resistance about going to church when she felt strong enough. Whenever she could, she escaped to the church's fellowship hall. The sight of Will was a bright spot here and there, but she wouldn't let him talk about anything of substance. She wouldn't let him pry, challenge her, or dig deep about her new friends, who commanded her attention. If he insisted, she'd threaten to deprive him of her company. She could do that now because she had a slew of friends who angled to be around her. The new attention, and her new seedy activities, made her arrogant, nasty, and disrespectful at home and aloof at church. *Those sorry-behind church kids are so corny, so sad, so stupid,* she'd tell herself, laughing in her head, *they don't even know how to have real fun.*

Jubi was smart enough to attend school just enough to keep the scent off, and to pass her classes and exams that needed passing. She muddled her way through high school, and by her senior year, she was reintroduced to her sexual allure, her ability to attract the opposite sex. *But this time,* she thought, *I'm gonna call the shots.* Soon after Jubi barely graduated from high school, she disappeared from the daily lives of her weary and aging parents.

During a fight about how disrespectful Jubi had become, because she had started staying out late and coming home in the wee hours of the morning, Esther said something like, "Well, if you can't live by our rules, then . . ." And that was that. The gift was gone.

Chapter Nine

Behind Closed Doors

1993 . . .

Will and Jubi skidded from the curb like they were running late for an appointment. Will drove around the city for about ten to fifteen minutes, appearing to be aimless. Neither of them said anything. They let the radio do all the talking, the singing, the joking. Soon it was clear to Jubi that they were headed to Druid Hill Park. Which was fine, in a settling kind of way, she thought. The day was still nice and sunny, she noted, but evening hadn't quite come in yet. It hadn't come it to cloak all things sinful, yet. And for what they were going to be doing, she thought, they were going to need some cover. She'd manage, though. It wasn't a real big problem for her.

"Hey, look," Jubi said, breaking the silence. "You know, I ain't got no problem with it, but if you wanna go to a motel or something, I . . ." She paused, then re-started. "I could take a shower and all. You know, clean up a bit." Then she took her gaze off him and looked out the passenger-side window. "Huh! But if it ain't no problem for you, it ain't no problem for me," she said. She lied.

Will Promise never took his eyes off the road. And he didn't respond. But he did make a U-turn off the main Druid Hill Park drag and head back to Route 83. Now they were headed to East Baltimore. He knew of an out-of-the-way motel over there. Jubi remained silent and correctly tracked his moves. But now, however, she was feeling both relief and disgust at the same time. Because when this transaction went down, it would signal to her that her very last connection to anything pure and wholesome was over. She'd be bona fide grade A sewer sludge.

They powered up to a one-level, sprawled-out motel surrounded by burned-out, boarded-up buildings. Seedy dudes and gathers of slutty-looking ladies communed on nearly every corner, and it was clear that this motel knew its purpose and its clientele. Will parked in front of one of the motel room doors. It was about three doors away from the main office.

He turned off the engine, looked at Jubi, and smiled. He smiled like he couldn't help it, and said, "Wait here for a minute." He got out of the car, turned, and said, "And lock the car door till I come back." During their forty-minute ride, Jubi noted, that was the only thing he said.

"Okay," Jubi said and followed orders. That was what she'd be taking from here on out, she knew. Orders. She'd be filling requests and faking that she liked it, lived for it. It was a job, and an increasingly revolting adventure. But by now, it was also her routine. *Why are men like that?* she often thought. *Not only do they like to screw your body, but they want to screw your mind too.*

When Will returned, he had a door key in his hand. He walked up to the passenger side and motioned for Jubi to unlock the door. "C'mon," he said. He opened the car door for her. She followed orders. "We're in luck," he joked. "We got the room right in front of the car. How 'bout that?" he said as he led her inside. He closed the door, locked it, double bolting the two of them in the room.

The tiny room was outfitted with an awful, musty 1960s-style decor, and it looked like the dingy, moldy-looking rug and the worn-out bed and nightstand had been there just that long. The blue beaded bedspread had lost all its little crocheted beads. And they would find out that the television did not own any clear pictures. Will watched Jubi as she moved toward the bed and plopped down, not appearing to be disgusted at all. He stood there and studied her face. When she became aware of his gaze, she looked down at her knees.

He sat down beside her and moved to hold her waist. That was when she jumped up and said, "Well, I'ma go check out the bathroom. Okay?"

"Okay," he said, making an up-and-down sweep of her body with his eyes.

"You gonna be here when I get back?" she asked, kind of joking, kind of not. Because she suddenly realized that this whole thing could be just a cruel prank for the neighborhood fellas—to drive her out to nowhere and leave her stranded.

Or, on second thought, and even worse, because it had happened a number of times before, maybe it was a case of one guy doing the setup and two or three others showing up to cash in on the deal. When that happened, she would always be clear on the fact that if she didn't comply, her life would be in definite peril. Even if she did comply, her life was not that far from jeopardy, like the time when some druggies thought it was hilarious to throw flaming matches on her exposed private parts. They did it just for the fun of watching her dodge, plead, and scream. They kept it up until police sirens caused them to quit and scatter like rats.

But on the regular, beyond the dread, the vomit, and the fearful reality of physical pain, she'd resign herself to thinking, *So what?*

But those were the horrible instances that had swarmed around in her head earlier, during her fight with Esther. They had surfaced, especially when she yelled out, "You don't know nothin' about me—what I'm goin' through!" Why, oh, why, couldn't I have held on to that bracelet? was her current thought. She replayed the part of the fight when she declared to her mother, "Your God can't do nothin' for me." It was replaying in her head when she gave Will a crippled grin just before she shut the bathroom door.

He kept his gaze on her until she disappeared. It was funny, he later remarked about that day, that she wondered if he'd still be there when she got out of the bathroom, or if he'd still be there alone, and not with his boys. He wondered if she'd climb out of the bathroom window and run away. None of their doubts materialized.

The bathroom was creepy, like you didn't want your naked feet to touch the floor. Towels were at a premium, so Jubi used toilet paper to line the floor. The fix wasn't foolproof, but it would have to do. Finally, in the shower, she let the spray of hot water beat down on her body and her nerves. And for a few minutes she managed to let herself feel good. She soaped and rinsed, and soaped and rinsed a second time. The tiny bathroom fogged quickly from the steam. Afterward, she dried her feet as best she could to keep the toilet paper from sticking and stood over the sink.

Rubbing the bathroom mirror clear of steam, she spied her reflection but didn't want to. The image that eyed her back was emotionless and that of a stranger. So she ignored it. Her only concern at this point was to figure out how to brush her teeth. Jubi had no tooth-brush and no toothpaste. With her finger positioned under the warm running water from the sink's spigot, she brushed her teeth as best she could with her bare finger. She thought, *Well, this will have to do.*

Twenty minutes later Jubi stepped out of the bath-room, wrapped in a thin white bath towel. It wouldn't have fit her all around if she hadn't been so skinny. She found Will sitting on the bed, shifting his attention between the television and a radio that was attached to the end table, trying to get the victory out of either of them. Her appearance made him stop what he was doing. He smiled. His undivided attention was all hers.

"Come here," he said softly.

Jubi moved a little but didn't step toward him. She stood there holding her towel together and said, "You got some money, right?" She was trying to keep it busi-ness.

He smiled, watching this strange Jubi play tough. "Yeah." He reached into his pocket, pulled out some bills, and brandished them before her eyes, then threw them atop the nightstand. "Yeah, I got some money," he said. "Is that what you want? Come over here and get it." She joined him on the bed. Her eyes moved back and forth between Will's person and the money lying there freely for the taking.

Jubi's towel was tucked tight, but it wasn't impos-sible to remove, if Will decided to make his move, she noted. *But why do you still have your clothes on?* she wondered. He pulled her gently into his arms. *Why does this feel so good?* was her next question. Her question, said out loud, was, "So what do you want first?" She talked to him like he was a john. She hated it, but she needed to get this thing going. She needed to get back to Ambro.

Will didn't respond audibly. He kissed her, starting on her cheek, then moving to her mouth. It was a
soft, long kiss, and he didn't let up until he could feel
her open up and respond. Jubi's body felt like mush.
To keep her strength, her business resolve, she'd steal
a glimpse of the money on the table. But when she
looked back at him, silent, lazy-eyed, and sensual, her
body converted to mush again. Will had the longest
curly eyelashes, she noted. They were cute when he was
a young boy, and they were still cute. Except now they
were also alluring. *Dang it!* she thought.

All the two of them could hear was their breathing.
He pulled back, studied her, rubbed her bare shoulders, massaged her back, then kissed her face again,
migrating to her lips. He took his time, and she let him.
She also noticed how a good fifteen minutes had to
have gone by, and he never made a move to disrobe her
or himself. It was like she knew where this was going,
but on the other hand, she didn't know. But she did
understand how it felt like an eternity of pleasure. And
after what she'd been through, fighting her parents,
losing the bracelet, it felt like relief even. So she just
gave up and let it happen.

Finally, he spoke. "So what do you wanna do, Jubi?"

She found that she loved it when he spoke her name.
Probably always had. But she wasn't quite sure how
to answer that question—not from him, anyway. If
it came from some old run-of-the-mill, dirty john, of
course she knew how to answer. "Whatever you want
me to do, Big Daddy," she'd whisper like she liked it. It
was all a crappy game, she knew. But what in the world
was Will asking? She thought, *Are we gaming each
other?* She asked herself inside, *Or do you really, really wanna know what I wanna do?*

His kissing her, now it was down on her shoulders even, and his gentle, yet strong hands massaging her back allowed her to fantasize about the outlandish. *God, you feel good.* She let her mind and her heart go there. Genuinely wanting him in that way, or maybe at least wanting the safe feeling of his touch after all these years of having sex, was actually a virgin feeling for her. She only knew to trust her father's touch, though she hadn't felt that in a while and doubted if she ever would again. After Trouble, she'd figured out that sex— her body—was just a useful tool, a cash register. It was something that women could use when they needed something tangible from a man. It was better than money, and it was everlasting.

"So what you holdin' on to it for?" one of her old high school chums said to her when she was acting funny about giving in to Ambro back in the day. "Shoot, that dude's got money, and he wants to give it to you," her friend observed with a dry laugh. "You actin' like you gonna run out!" She laughed that upper-hand laugh. "Shoot, Jubi," she said, nudging her in the direction of Ambro, a tall, muscular, superflyish-looking brother with a stringy Jheri curl hairdo.

"What?" Jubi said to her friend.

"What you mean, what? Quit hoggin' it like you gonna run out. You got more." She whispered, laughing heartily.

"Run out of what?" Jubi said. She knew, but she wanted to hear her girl say it.

"You know what I mean, girl—that gold you got down between your legs. Now, get over there and talk to the man. Let him know he got what you want too."

The two girlfriends stood in the midst of a dimly lit, smoky, underarm-stuffy basement, at some renegade party thrown by someone from the old in-crowd crew. Ambro, after having an intimate slow-grind dance with a reluctant Jubi, now stood in the far corner of the room, keeping his eye on the thing he wanted—her. He held on to a clear plastic cup of something in one hand and seductively pulled drags off his joint with the other hand. He was trying to style for her benefit.

"Shoot, girl," Jubi's friend said, keeping up her troublesome nudging, "he's old. He got some money and some get high, and he wants to give it to us, if you act right."

Later that night, Jubi and her girl, Ambro, and some other shady-eyed dude left the basement party and ended up at Ambro's cold-water flat on Pressman Street, off of North Avenue. Actually, it was a big, once beautiful three-story plantation-style house diced up into flats. When you walked up the front steps, it was easy to pretend you were in a fairy tale, but reality punched hard.

After a good round of drinking and pot smoking, Jubi's friend and the other guy disappeared into the bathroom or somewhere. Jubi gave in to Ambro, right there on a mattress he had on the floor. Afterward, sometime around dawn, Ambro put her and her girl in a cab, generously threw an ample amount of money in her lap, and sent them home. The sun rose on the revelation of Jubi getting home after an all-nighter again. She and her parents got into one heck of a fight. Jubi stomped out, walked a couple doors down to her friend's house. She didn't answer the door. Bewildered and mad, still in last night's clothes, Jubi walked to the corner bus stop, trying to map out her next move. Before that happened, a cab sailed by, she hailed it, and the next thing she knew, she was standing at Ambro's front door. He looked glad to take her in.

"Get on in here, baby girl," he said with a yellow smile. "I knew you'd be back for some more." She walked into his welcoming arms, and into a hell where sex was a very useful tool.

"So, c'mon," Jubi said, enjoying Will's kisses with her eyes closed. "Let's do it, all right? Take off your clothes, man." They had to be twenty or thirty minutes into this foreplay. And Jubi snuck a reassuring peek into Will's lap. He was ready.

Slowly, Will reared back just enough to look Jubi in her eyes. "Is that what you think I want?" He didn't appear dreamy-eyed anymore. He looked serious, maybe sad, even. "You think I want you?"

"Yes," Jubi answered and reached to pull his T-shirt off, but he resisted. She was confused by his reaction. His movements said one thing, but his body said something else. "I know you want to," she said.

"No, I don't," he said.

Jubi looked down into his lap, laughed, and said, "Yes. Yes, you do. So what's the holdup, huh?"

Will backed all the way away from her and struggled to say, "No, I don't, Jubi. Not like this." He stood up and walked around her, behind her back, and repeated, "Not like this." Will sighed. Jubi caught it just as she turned around to face him. She was still tightly clad in nothing but her towel. "I just wanted to see how far you'd go."

Humiliated, confused, and ashamed because she still wanted that money lying innocently on the nightstand, her eyes teared up. She shouted, "So what did you bring me here for? Huh? What kind of game you playin'?"

"Not every man wants you for sex, Jubi."

"Yes, they do," Jubi said, tears dropping from her cheeks. "What are you? Some kind of—"

"No," Will cut in.

"Oh, then," Jubi said sarcastically, "oh, then you some kind of churchy saint. Huh?"

"No, Jubi." His voice sounded tired. He was tired about what he'd been hearing about her all these years. "You and me had something special a long time ago. And I just had to get your attention." He walked the length of the tiny room and threw up his hands and said, "The opportunity just came up, that's all."

Jubi's hurt and confusion strangely turned into some kind of jealousy. She said, "Oh, I know you ain't gonna tell me that you're some kind of a saint over there in that school you goin' to. I heard some stuff about you too." She charged and threw out a venomous "Saint Will."

He neither confirmed it nor denied it. He plopped back down on the bed and forced her into his strong arms again. She fought him for a moment but then surrendered. She was pissed off that it felt good. "Jubi, is it such a surprise how I feel about you? That, maybe, you feel the same way about me too?" She was crying audibly now. "I can't stand to see you like this. This isn't you," Will said. "Jubi, this isn't even you."

"Stop it, Will."

"I mean it, Jubi. You're gonna die out there if you don't stop." He tried to pull her up to look at her. She wouldn't let him.

"Stop your jokes. This isn't funny," she said, sucking up her tears, trying to put a stop to them.

"This ain't no joke. Jubi, you're gonna die if you don't get your act together," he said. "If you try, I'll help you. For real."

Jubi broke from him, still drying her eyes, still wrapped in her thin white towel. The thought of sex, it seemed, for both of them somehow vanished into thin air. She stood up and made a declaration in the middle of the room. "It's too late," she said, wounded, but full of resolve. "Will, it's way too late. You don't know. And you don't know me."

"But it's never too late."

"It's too late!" Jubi shouted and disappeared into the bathroom. She slammed the door.

It was funny, in a kind of unfunny way, she thought as she snatched off the towel and threw it in the bathtub, how her life was full of déjà vu moments. Here she was once again, forced to make a grandstand exit without a clue about where she was going or how she was going to get there. Jubi threw her dirty underwear in the bathroom trash can and buried them under a tiny mound of toilet paper. "Those are done," she whispered to no one, to her own dismay. She put on her bra, pulled on her dingy jeans, and covered up in her stained sweatshirt, sweat socks, and tennis shoes.

Jubi reappeared in the motel room, fully clothed, to find Will standing in the middle of the floor. When he saw that she was dressed, he grabbed for his keys.

"Jubi—" he said, but she cut him off as she fidgeted, then went for her jacket.

"Ah, you think you could give me a lift outta here?" she asked, looking down at the rug.

"Yeah. Yeah," Will said. "Where you wanna go?"

Jubi now had her eye on the nightstand holding the money. "Can you take me up around North Avenue?" she asked.

Will saw her eyeing the money; he was disgusted and worn out, because he felt that he'd given it his best shot. "Take it," he said. "Just try not to kill yourself with it."

Without words, she jumped at the money and grabbed it like it was a life preserver. She balled it up, unable to look him in his face, and stuffed it in her pocket. Later, she'd find out that he'd given her 150 dollars. But she wouldn't find that out until after Ambro beat her good for being out from under his thumb for so long. He snatched the wad of bills out of her pocket and counted it out loud in front of her. But she was touched, though, about what Will had done. And she was ashamed for letting this thought pass through her mind. *That's nice, but I bet I could have gotten a lot more with that bracelet.*

In the car, filled with suffocating silence, except for the radio, Will said to Jubi, "And try not to let him kill ya for it." But she knew what was in store for her.

Jubi also observed how Will seemed to know just where he was going, without her direction. When he traveled down North Avenue and got to the corner of the block where Ambro lived, she rushed to say, "Let me out right here. Please."

Will obliged. He slowed down, pulled over, and turned to look at her, maybe look at her for one last time. She returned his gaze but kept her silence. Will reached over and kissed her on the forehead. "Not all men," he said. "Not all men." Then he added, "Take care of yourself, Jubi. Okay?"

"'Kay," she said softly, ashamed to look at him, and pushed herself out of the car. She stood there and watched it fade into a wavy sea of brake lights and moving traffic. Then she turned and headed up the block, on her way to Ambro's flat.

Chapter Ten

The Book of Esther Stone, Part I

Lancaster County, Virginia, 1950 . . .

The spastic yells, grunts, and pleas for earned grace and mercy bellowed throughout the house. They boomeranged off its pale yellow cinder-block walls. Loud breathing and heavy panting contracted the air. The sounds even seemed to follow Esther's two older brothers, charged with shooing all their younger siblings out of the house like scattering dust bunnies and across the road to the neighbor's abode until things could settle down. Esther was fourteen years old at the time, standing in the midst of what was to shape her future—her career, her gift.

Esther's job was to stay close and at the ready for whatever she was instructed to do to help her mother bring her latest baby sibling into the world.

"Keep that water coming fresh, chile," her aunt Laura said. That meant as soon as the basin of water was tinged pink or bloodred, it had to be thrown out and replenished. And if the task meant a sprint to the cement well, out by the side of the house, then she'd do it. During the stabbing contractions, which seemed to go on forever, Aunt Laura instructed, "Get a clean rag. Dab it 'cross your mama's forehead." Another roving command was, "C'mere, naw. When I roll her this way, you git under there quick and grab that bloody sheet out from under her. There, naw. Good. That's right. That's right. Use that towel to dab that up. Naw put that clean one on. Okay. Okay. Hurry, chile. Move it!"

Esther obeyed. Keep in mind that children were much older for their age back then. But mostly, by this go-round, Esther really didn't need much instruction. She had learned to think for herself, and she had done this from age ten. But this birth was a tough one.

Esther had experienced a whole range of her mother's birthing screams and such on four previous occasions, but this round wretched up even more intense. There were seven children in the Bailey home. If the incoming baby made it, that would make eight Baileys. The sounds of her mother and the sight of an unusual measure of flowing dark maroon blood shook Esther's nerves to the core, and it was the first of three pivotal life experiences she'd never forget in her young life. They would define her.

"Hurry up, chile!" Aunt Laura shouted. She stuck a note in Esther's hand, hugged her, and twirled her around toward the front door. "We gonna need some extra help with this one," she said.

The moonlight created a shiny eggshell crown over Esther's thick brown braids, which she always wore greased with Dixie Peach Pomade and roped around her head. She darted out into the night to scurry across the road to the white neighbors who were already holding down the fort for all her siblings. But they were friendly and giving, almost to their detriment, and well known for such. Esther needed them to call the doctor. They were the only household for miles with a phone.

Esther huffed and puffed her way to the neighbors as fast as she could; road dust and pebbles invaded her shoes as she ran. Clear across the road, and while she was banging on the neighbors' front door, her mother's screams remained stuffed in her ears. But before long, she was forced to return home, minus the note that explained the emergency, and minus the sought-after news that the doctor was on his way.

"It's Sunday. And it's too late for me to go traipsin' out at all times of the night," Doc Crocker had said on the phone. "Besides, colored babies been comin' into the world without my aid all this time," he'd told the neighbor lady, who had stood there, visible to Esther, with a growing crumpled-up smile. "This one will get here too, no doubt," he'd concluded, talking so loud into the receiver, Esther heard every word he said. Right before the doctor hung up the phone, he said, "Hey, you tell Charlie that if he comes up here to play checkers again, tell 'im I'ma beat 'im again, just like I did last time." He let loose a roaring laugh, then said, "Bye naw. Y'all go to bed naw. Quit messin' round wit' them coloreds like you keep doin'." And he was gone. The room was filled with an awkward silence that choked Esther.

Doc Crocker was the only doctor in the little town, ironically called Lively. The town was a tiny, insignificant speck on the map of Lancaster County. And the Crocker family either owned or had a say over every bit of it. The Crockers owned the one modest food/general store. They ran the only bank the town had, and the only post office too. If colored citizens got mail from relatives who lived up north, they were handed their mail after it had been sloppily tampered with, because a Crocker postal clerk needed to make sure that no outsider was about to stir up any trouble. A Crocker was the school superintendent for both the white and the colored schools. And the town sheriff, who was voted in, was always a Crocker.

In the southern tip of Lancaster County, every colored person knew how stepping out of one's place could cause you to disappear from this world without much fanfare or consequence at all. Their out-of-town relatives, especially northerners, or *Yankees*—the Crockers spat that out of their mouths like it was worn-out chewing tobacco—well, out-of-town traveling coloreds also knew that if they violated the fifteen-mile speed limit while driving through Montross, the town just before Lively, circumstances could turn tortuous and/or deadly in a matter of minutes. "It was a nigga trap," some folk liked to joke. So colored drivers worked hard not to give the police cause for a flag down.

And back in Lively, old Doc Crocker was proud of how well kept his doctor's office was, with its scrubbed-down separate-but-equal waiting rooms, which were comfortable for his white and colored patients.

Esther's good neighbor had hung up the phone, and Esther had hung her head low, with her eyes aimed at the woman's shoes, while she did it. There'd been a hug and an "I'm sorry" from the neighbor, meaning she had done all she could. And that had been followed by Esther's swift bolt for the front door. She was forced to return home, minus any helpful news.

Esther's mama, everyone called her Mama Adele, would bring in her eighth child, an eight-pound baby boy, during the wee hours of a Monday morning, and Esther would firmly step into the shoes of assisting midwife. Mama Adele was a midwife to every other colored woman in Lively, as well as in two other nearby towns. The nearest colored hospital was in Richmond, and that was about an hour and a half away.

Esther was the oldest girl and a proud assistant mother to Mama Adele. But she loved it. She mimicked her mama's moves and decisions in every way. Esther more than loved her mother, who loved, protected, and reared her brood with an iron hand. Esther idolized her mother. She watched her dress. She watched her cook and keep house, and she learned. Esther dutifully watched how her mother ruled the house cleverly behind her daddy's back. Mama Adele always honored her husband and gave him his props up front, though.

And Mac Bailey, as folks called him, especially the ladies, was indeed a real man too. He was tall and lanky, poured in smooth chocolate brown skin. But it was his tight, well-defined body that was evidence of how hard he worked. Mac Bailey took care of his house, his children, and his wife. He took pride in that fact. Being a provider was how he showed his love at home.

Soon, Esther's two older brothers disappeared from the daily in-house grind to work from sunup to sundown with their daddy. Mac Bailey worked in a Hanover sawmill factory in the next town, and that was why Mama Adele had to step in when it came to the daily operations of the house and the rearing of the kids. She also brought in a little money too, midwifing, and sometimes tending to somebody's ailment or tending to a wound when somebody got hurt. Everyone knew that she was the one who could nurse you out of it.

Mac Bailey didn't do much talking around the house, either, and he never argued. "That's a waste of a good person's time," he always used to say right before he said nothing at all and walked away, if ever there was a disagreement brewing between him and Mama Adele. So silently, all the children knew that whatever word their mama put down, well, that word was bond. Whether or not she and Mac had made some kind of pact behind closed doors, nobody knew . . . but, well, if they had, it remained a well-kept secret even after Mac

Bailey's death. When he died, he and Mama Adele had been married more than fifty years.

All the Bailey children had chores. And they did them without being run after or spanked. Esther was Mama Adele's little assistant, making sure everything got carried out to her mama's perfection. And it did. Mama Adele kept a clean and orderly one-story cinderblock house. The front yard was supposed to be green, but it wasn't. But it was so endearing how, right up to her death three years after Mac passed, Mama Adele nursed the sickly growth of a little peach tree she'd planted in the middle of her balding grass yard. She'd planted it just before, Esther recalled, the kids knew that their mother was in the family way with that last baby boy. It was hilarious how if she saw a car come into her yard, about to mow the baby tree down, she would go running outside, waving, warning, and protecting it.

And rules were rules. The Baileys had a strong Christian foundation. They kept to themselves but loved their neighbors and helped out whomever they could. They forgave those who trespassed against them, lived to earn their eternal crown, and they believed in turning the other cheek—except for the time when Mama Adele found out that a sinner woman, a former schoolmate, had eyes for her husband. Ms. Shirley was her name, and everybody in Lively knew that she was part of the colored ilk that wasn't God-fearing or churchgoing.

Well, the question would go down—and become legendary—about what in the world, on one fine Sunday morning, had gotten into Ms. Shirley, besides some bad liquor, perhaps, to make her drive into Mama Adele's front yard, run over her precious peach tree beginnings, and stake a claim for Mac Bailey. That was a question to which no one would ever know the answer. Esther would recall it and laugh about it many decades later. But there was one thing for sure: What went down after Ms. Shirley rushed her high yellow self out of the car—that was an account etched into the annals of Lively history forever. It was a story recounted by the white and the colored.

On Sunday every Bailey went to church. And on that legendary Sunday morning, just like all the ones before and all the ones after, Esther helped Mama Adele get the little ones ready. When all the kids were cleaned, Vaseline greased—patent leather shoes, included— dressed, and prepped, they were sent to the family room couch to sit mannerly by themselves until their parents scooped them up to head for the church house.

On Sunday children were definitely seen and not heard. Some other rules, by the way, were that you did not question God and you did not question your parents about God. If God said it was wrong, it was wrong. If God said it was right, then it was right. And that good teaching came down from on high, from the good pastor.

"Amen, Church?" the pastor would send down loudly from his pulpit.

And the church gave back a firm "Amen!"

Back to the front yard affair . . . the children were all sitting patiently on the couch, facing the front living room window and careful not to come undone. Esther emerged first, followed by Mama Adele and Mac Bailey. They all heard a car screech to a halt in their dirt driveway, a car door open and slam shut, and a declaration made. At the sight of all that, Mama Adele was already headed past the screen door, aiming to protect her peach tree bush.

But before she could gain traction, there was Ms. Shirley, standing in the front yard, dressed in all her nightclubbish finery, yelling, "C'mon outta there, Mac Bailey. I'm tired of this. . . ." She said a curse word, and all the kids heard it plain and clear. With all the prior commotion, they had scurried to the front window with their bottom jaws dropped and their eyes about to pop out of their sockets. But the profanity, and on a Sunday too, induced a chorus of snickers. Esther recalled that it was at that moment she lost sight of her daddy, but her mama was in full view.

Mama Adele carefully put her Bible and her black patent leather purse down on the porch steps. She kicked off her black patent leather pumps right there and walked up to the woman calling for her husband. As she approached Ms. Shirley, Esther couldn't hear all her mother was saying, but she thought she heard some scripture. While that was going on, Ms. Shirley had some more to say.

"Yeah, that's right, you hefty b. . . ." She coughed up another profane word. "That's my man. He needs to be out here, and I'm tired of waitin'!" Then she looked past Mama Adele, toward the house, and yelled, "C'mon outta there, Big Daddy! I said I'm tired of . . ." Poor, poor Ms. Shirley, for those words were the last intelligible words she'd be able to say for at least the next six to eight weeks.

Mama Adele gave the first push. The second push she gave slammed Ms. Shirley up against her own car. Mama Adele brought her upright again by a handful of Ms. Shirley's shiny, black, curly wig hat. Ms. Shirley screamed and offered a hard swing, but it was wild and struck only air. Mama Adele let her go quick, then grabbed another clump of wig hat curls to steady Ms. Shirley and carefully aimed the dead-on slap Ms.

Shirley took across the face. Had there been music and smiles, one could have mistaken the movements for jitterbugging. When Ms. Shirley fell to the dirt, the wig hat was still in Mama Adele's hand, along with a couple of Ms. Shirley's cornrows, which were hidden underneath. It gave all-the-way live meaning to the phrase *I'll snatch you bald.*

All the baby Baileys stood at the window, pushing and shoving, crying, and screaming for their mother's safety. "Stop, Mommy, stop! Come back! Come back!" they wailed, but that was useless.

The two oldest brothers and Esther held the little ones at bay while they rooted for their mother. They understood the scene plainly, and there was a total absence of fear, because, clearly, Mama Adele had the situation in check.

Ms. Shirley was now sprawled out in a sandy dirt patch that should have been green. The dirt patch now trailed pinkish, and harbored a few of her teeth. She tried to get to her feet. Her mouth was full of dirt and profane dirty words, literally, as she had the nerve to cry out for Mac Bailey to come to her rescue. But he was nowhere to be found. Esther insisted later that she was sure she heard her mama recite some scripture as she pounced on the harlot woman while she lay faceup and helpless. Mama Adele could ball a fist up at anyone who threatened her children, her marriage, or who bad-mouthed her pastor. That was the exception to the turn-the-other-cheek rule. And, Ms. Shirley, Esther overheard her mother say to her Aunt Laura, "she had it coming to her."

Ms. Shirley got her jaw broken on that day, her nose too. And as she struggled up from the ground to get into her car, her nightclub dress was filthy and ripped. Her complete bra was showing, which produced a gleam in the eyes of the junior Baileys. She was shoeless, with her pretty polished pink toes completely busted out of her jagged stockings. Ms. Shirley strained to open her car door to make her exit. Like Lot's wife, she dared not look back for fear of learning another lesson about trying to steal another woman's husband. While she bellowed and cried and struggled to open her car door, Mama Adele dusted herself off and said loudly, yet in a controlled manner, "Now, hurry up home before your black eyes close shut."

The events of the rest of the day, Esther said whenever she told the story, were a blur, but she believed that once the ruckus was over, Mama Adele cleaned herself up, and the family went on to church. They didn't miss a Sunday of churchgoing.

The year was 1950. And down through the next few years, as far as the Bailey household was concerned, routine was routine. The Baileys remained God-fearing. They kept to themselves, yet they remained proud but cognizant of society's social hazards for colored people. Not until the latter part of the 1950s would the house enjoy indoor plumbing. And in the town of Lively, while the rest of the world moved, invented, and challenged, not much progressed.

In 1951 Congress ratified the Twenty-Second Amendment, which said that no president could be in office for more than two terms. And that if a former president had already been elected twice, he or she could not run for that office again ever. In 1952 Eisenhower and Nixon bragged of their November victory. In 1953 DNA, the blueprint for life, was discovered by American scientists. In 1954 somebody won the argument to add the "under God" part to the Pledge of Allegiance. In 1954 there was *Brown vs. the Board of Education*—which declared segregation in schools to be unlawful, though you couldn't tell it in Lively, Virginia, or throughout much of the commonwealth. And in 1954 Esther Bailey turned eighteen years old, and that was the year in which she fell in love for the first time.

From age fourteen to eighteen, Esther grew into a beautiful young girl. Her hue was olive and her skin was smooth like her mother's. She filled out, inheriting her mother's womanly curves. But if she attracted the attention or looks of church boys or schoolboys, she didn't notice or care. Not until a new boy showed up at church. One delightful summer Sunday, after church school let out, he smiled at her and said hello in a soft, polite way. And in her heart that was all she wrote.

Emmett Dorsey was twenty-one years old and a head taller than Esther. He was the color of buttercream and freckle-faced. His smile was bold and bright, but that was because, some said, he was from up north—New York—and up north a colored boy could be bold and bright with ease. Emmett was related to one of the families in the church, and the story went that he'd perhaps got into some kind of trouble—just some light stuff—and somebody decided that he needed to spend his summer down south until things cooled off. He was a nice boy. Emmett was friendly and inquisitive about the way his people had to manage their lives down south just to get along.

"Whaddaya mean, I can't try on the jacket?" he said a little too roughly in a clothing store in Richmond. Emmett had gone on a little shopping trip with his uncle. His uncle pulled him back gently, while the irritated salesclerk stuck his pointer finger in the air, indicating a sign that read: COLORED. YOU TRY IT. YOU BUY IT!

It always stopped him short to see the FOR COLORED ONLY and the FOR WHITES ONLY signs posted at the entrances to public bathrooms or chained to public water fountains. Emmett had to get the rules told to him a couple of times, along with the proper ways of fighting back or at least standing your ground with your dignity intact.

"Unc, how can you all just walk by that water fountain like it ain't nothin'?" Emmett asked his uncle while on that very same shopping trip. He was perturbed and fast growing too angry at the way colored folk seemed not to notice the righteous indignation of it. In fact, he felt they all looked just fine about it. "I mean, Unc, I mean no disrespect and all that, but y'all a bunch of lackeys down here."

Emmett's uncle did take offense at his young, hot-headed nephew's disrespect, but it was his innocence and social ignorance mouthing off, and it needed to be addressed. "They see it," his uncle said mildly. "We all see it," he said while they walked to Crocker's General Store on another day when Emmett brought it up.

Before they got to the store, they passed a FOR WHITES ONLY water fountain. "You know what, Unc? I'm a little thirsty," Emmett said, smirking. "I think I'ma take a drink." And he bebopped, cool like, toward the water fountain.

His uncle rushed to his side and pulled him back. The move attracted looks from curious passersby. Emmett's uncle stood skin-to-skin close, then crushed Emmett's forearm using muscles that Emmett was shocked to realize the old man had. It stunned him, made him stiff like a statue. They were eye to eye now, and though his uncle wore a smile for the onlookers, his clenched teeth sent a serious message to Emmett.

His uncle said smoothly, "Boy, you want me to bust your head open right now? Or do you want those good ole boys over there to do it?" His uncle directed his stare to a group of interested men loitering on the general store porch. Emmett's uncle paused and glared. "'Cause the difference is that I might not kill ya." Then he added, "They'll help you out simply because it's Friday, and they ain't got nothin' else better to do." His uncle finally let go of his arm and said, "Now, when things calm down, you and me can talk about all this later." His uncle let a nanosecond or two whisk by to let his nephew absorb what he'd said. Emmett had never been so still and silent. "You understand me, boy?" the uncle asked. Emmett nodded in affirmation. The uncle backed up a little and loosened his emotional Holy Grail grip. "You ready to go on in naw?" he said that in a normal tone and with a real smile.

"Yeah. Yeah, Unc," Emmett responded. He wore a new awareness upon his face. But who knew at the time how long it would last? The two, the Southern uncle and his Northern nephew, moved on through the afternoon, aware of the insult around them but looking unaware. The whole strategy that both Emmett's uncle and the preacher told him later was "to keep your wits about you, think first so you can learn how to live to fight another day."

A couple of Sundays went by before Emmett managed to find himself in the right place at the right moment to approach Esther. But she had stood out to his eye on the first Sunday that he arrived at the church. She was cute, and it seemed to him like she didn't know it. She acted like a little girl instead of a budding young woman who knew what she had to offer a boy. He liked that. *Being banished to this hick town ain't gonna be so bad, after all.* Those were his first thoughts when he laid eyes on the sweet, soft-spoken girl with bombshell curves. He rushed to get her name from his cousins, and the whole rundown on her family.

"Hey, Esther," Emmett said. They had been let out of the church during the time in between church school and the start of the church service. The summer morning was bright and warm. The day was rounding out perfectly. He snuck up behind her. His peppermint-scented breath tickled her cheek. But he was careful not to brush up against any part of her person. For such a move would have been too forward in Lively.

Esther was startled at the sudden awareness of him. And when she would look back on that day, she'd know without a doubt that it was the first time she had ever been that close to a boy who was not her brother or father. And she never, ever forgot the feeling. Standing there, stunned, she said nothing for a few seconds. Then her olive cheeks blushed, and she smiled. Finally, she said hello back.

The two moved into an easy conversation about nothing. Esther pretended not to know who he was or his name, but she knew both. Even if she wasn't taken by his handsomeness, Lively was a small town, and it was nearly impossible not to get the goods on newcomers and visitors. For the month of July, Emmett and Esther's only contact was at church services and the church revival. They forged a friendship quickly. Easily. Fondness was just around the corner. One day in early August Emmett stepped up his boldness to come and call on her at the Bailey home. Mama Adele was watchful but tickled. Mac Bailey was watchful. That was his baby girl. And Emmett was acutely aware of that. His summer experience down south had matured him greatly. He was learning to see what was visible to the eye and what wasn't.

By late August Emmett and Esther had graduated to dating. They were going to movies and whatnot. On a date at a drive-in diner in the next town, owned by a colored family, they sat huddled together in Emmett's uncle's car. To them both, heaven didn't seem so far away.

"When did you say you had to go back to New York?" Esther asked. She said it like it hadn't been on her mind for days. Like she hadn't practiced how she planned to let the concern come out of her mouth. There was a long pause. The two of them were twisted up in each other as tightly as they could be, with clothes on, and were fixated on the moonlight peering through the windshield of his uncle's 1950 secondhand Ford station wagon.

"I don't know," Emmett said, but he was thinking. "Maybe next month." Then he looked at her with his bedroom eyes and said, "Or maybe never—if there is something real to keep me here."

That statement caused them to untwist themselves, because now a serious conversation was brewing. "What do you mean, Emmett?" Esther asked. But she had an idea. They'd danced around the topic before. "I mean, whaddaya saying now? You're sayin' that you're ready to live here now? In Lively?" Her tone was not mushy, but incredulous.

"Well, no, not Lively." He knew he had to fess up to that nonsense. "But maybe Richmond," he said, looking her straight in her face. And then he said it. Up till now, he'd been stopping short. "Esther, I love you."

"What?" Her heart was melting like butter in a warmed-up skillet. She wanted to say more, to say the same, but instead she said, "What?" a second time.

"You heard me. I love you. I do. I wanna be with you always. I've been thinkin' it all over, and I'm sure of it." Emmett turned, put his hands on the steering wheel, and gripped it for strength, because he meant what he said. "So what do you want to do about it? How about get married or something? How 'bout it?" Silence moved in, because he had turned off the radio, which had served as an excellent mood modifier. Love songs had abounded. But now the talk had been bumped up a notch. So Emmett had turned the radio off.

"I love you too," Esther said softly. She had mixed feelings, though, because she knew he would never succumb to living in Lively or Richmond, or in the South, period. And she had been nowhere else. She had never even thought about moving away from her family. In a few weeks love had sprung up, and so had insurmountable problems. But it was a packaged deal.

She said, "I love you too. And, of course, I'd marry you. But . . ."

A broad smile was painted on Emmett's buttercream face. His sense of triumph was apparent on more than his face. It had spread to his loins. "Well, let's do it, then. Let's get married. And who cares where we live?" He let a moment slip by. "Look," he said, "you can come home with me. To New York. You'd love it up there. Yeah, yeah, let's do that." He said it like it was settled.

If it were possible for Esther to be irritated and gloriously happy all in the same bushel of moments, then that was exactly what happened. "Look, you act like New York is some kind of promised land for colored people, but I bet it ain't."

Emmett was forced to concede that she was right. "Naw, it ain't. I'm sorry if I'm always making it seem like that, but I do feel like it's better than here." His expression twisted up, like a skunk had walked by.

Esther ignored that last part of his statement and said, "Well, then, tell me. Tell me how colored people are livin' up there—in the promised land." She smirked. Her eyes were still on his. Maybe secretly, she wanted to hear some good news. Maybe not.

"Look, baby. New York is just my home. That's all. And, no, it ain't no promised land. Up there, colored folks gotta fight for everything they get too." He turned and looked at her. "And sometimes, they even fight each other."

"What are you talking about?" Esther asked. Hearing him about to give proof that all wasn't perfect, up north, intrigued her.

"Well, look. You ever heard of the paper bag test?"

"No."

"Yeah. Well, sometimes the so-called elite colored won't mix with the poorer coloreds. And they're places up there too where we can work but can't play, like some of the fancy nightclubs. And we can't just live anywhere we want, either."

"No. Say it ain't so." Esther was being facetious now. "But what about this paper bag thing?"

Emmett gave her a quirky look, playfully acknowledging her tone. He continued. "Okay. I'll tell you." He sighed like he was revealing the dirty laundry about the place he loved. "There are some colored clubs up in Harlem that you can only get into if you pass the paper bag test, or unless you're real famous and stuff."

"What are you talkin' about?"

"They hold a brown paper bag up like this," he said, holding up a bag that had once held his dinner and pressing it up against his wrist. "And if your complexion is the same color or lighter than the paper bag, well, then, they let you in. But if it ain't, well . . ."

Esther burst out in laughter. "Nawww, you gotta be kiddin'!"

Emmett started laughing too at the sad, naked silliness of it all. "Yeah, yeah. I ain't kidding."

The two sat there, thinking, letting the lighthearted moment linger before the mood turned serious again.

Emmett said, "I love you, Esther. I mean it."

"I love you too." She let him kiss her, patiently, to confirm it. The feeling that his kiss created in her was no longer a new one.

"So we gettin' married, right?" he said.

"I guess so," Esther managed to say in between passionate kisses and hugs.

"And we can figure out where we can live later, right?" Emmett said breathlessly. His hands moved about Esther's body like he had four of them.

"I guess so," Esther said, welcoming and combatting his two sets of arms and hands. She even wondered while they kissed how in the world he had managed to turn the radio back on while caressing her. He had had to turn the car back on and everything to do it.

"Well, then," Emmett said directly in her ear. His full lips juiced her earlobe. And he could sense that she liked it. "Let's make it official."

"You mean set a date?" she whispered back, panting and negotiating his many hands.

"Girl, you know what I mean. You love me, right?"

"Yeah, I love you, Emmett. But I love not going to hell too. And I just can't right now." Somehow she summoned up the resolve to push him away, and he let her.

"Okay, okay, girl," Emmett said as he heaved in a breath, tried to calm down the evidence of his emotion, and returned to his neutral corner behind the steering wheel. The lovefest was over. "But I do love you, Esther Bailey. And that's for real," he sighed.

"Yes," she said in agreement. But it was her virginity that prevented her proving it, as he put it. And she wanted to keep it. Mama Adele had said to hold on to it for dear life.

"Okay," Emmett said, pulling out of the diner's parking space and then the lot. "Lemme take you home now."

"Okay."

And live to fight another day, was Emmett's parting thought at that moment.

There were more dates, more occasions when Emmett said, "Well then, show me your love, Esther. You're a woman naw," as Emmett put it. He declared it more and more convincingly each time they were alone together.

But they did grow in love. In both their hearts, they were going to get married and create a life together. It was a given. Emmett put the love motion before her strongly at every opportunity. He put it to her right up until the starry night when she said, "Yes."

Chapter Eleven

The Book of Esther Stone, Part II

"I got something to tell ya," Emmett said.

"Yeah? What?" Esther said. The two were sitting on the couch in the Baileys' family room. It was post–family time, post–huge Sunday dinner.

"Yeah," Emmett said.

Emmett and Esther faced each other now, and they looked as though they were the only two people in the room. But they weren't. The younger Bailey siblings, now school age, milled about the room, walking in and out, laughing, snickering, trying to catch them in an embrace or catch them kissing. When they weren't doing that, they roughhoused throughout the front room and thoroughly enjoyed the nuisance they made of themselves. However, the focus between the two lovers could not be shattered. It sealed them in an invisible casing.

"I joined the Army."

Her eyes bugged. "You did what?"

"Yeah, well, you know, I kind of had to," he worked hard to say. "My number came up, and . . ." He wasn't finished.

"What?" she said to him, sure she couldn't have heard him right. Then she whipped around and snapped at the little nuisances. "Hush up. Sit down. Would you guys get outta here!" Her irritation had cracked the seal of her focus.

Mama Adele overheard the ruckus—on purpose—from the kitchen. She called out, "You kids all right out there?"

"Yes, Mama."

Emmett grabbed hold of her hand and said, "C'mon. Let's go get a soda or somethin'."

"'Kay," Esther said. She let Emmett pull her up from the couch. And before the screen door hit its wooden frame, Esther yelled in, "We goin' out, Mama."

Mama Adele chuckled and called out, "Okay, I knew ya would." But the last part of that hit only air.

A couple of weeks prior, Emmett had been summoned back home to Harlem for some reason. Esther didn't know why, though Emmett had told her his mother needed him for something. The whole thing was vague and mysterious to Esther. And she was convinced that he was never coming back. It was his way of escaping, she decided on her own, and she cried her eyes out for seven straight days after he left. They loved each other. *But I just couldn't give in*, she thought. She went through it over and over in her mind. *I couldn't! It ain't right. Somebody would know. God would know.* Her mind and her conviction tortured her, she felt. And that didn't feel right, either. And what if I got pregnant? she asked herself more than once. *Oh my Jesus, Mama would be crushed. And Daddy would kill Emmett.* That last mixture of scenarios always ended the debate—both in her head, and with Emmett in the midst of their passionate, sensual wrestling matches.

"You want Mac Bailey to put his shotgun to your head?" Esther would say, kind of in jest, kind of not. Emmett would chuckled, but then he'd always stop to pull himself together and rev up the car. Sometimes she took the softer route. "Please, Emmett, stop. Stop asking me," she'd say, breathless. "I can't, Emmett. This ain't right—not yet. We gettin' married, ain't we?"

To that, Emmett always said, "Well, yeah, girl. You know we gettin' married."

"Well, then," Esther would say, reasoning as best she could, "then let's just hurry up."

During her days of crying and feeling heart weak, she came to the sad realization that she had lost Emmett for good. That big, cute city boy probably wasn't used to waiting on girls to prove their love. And his abrupt departure because of some strange emergency was her proof that time had run out on this poor old, hick-town girl who didn't know how to be a woman. But Emmett did return. In fact, he was actually gone for only seven days, and his first stop back in Lively was Sunday morning church service, and Esther's arms.

Emmett was glad to grab Esther and get away from the Bailey house racket. He and Esther rode to the drive-in diner. They enjoyed their sodas. Esther enjoyed his kisses and tender caresses. And she told herself that she didn't want to lose him.

He loosened his embrace to look at her, think of the right grouping of words to assure her about him joining the Army. "Esther. Don't worry. The Army is a good thing," he said. "It's our ticket outta here."

She listened and studied his pretty buttercream face and his full beige lips in motion. She was also on the lookout for anything that he wasn't saying.

"Baby, we'll get married as soon as I get finished with boot camp. Okay? I'll have some money in my pocket, and I can pay for everything. We can get us a little place too."

"'Kay," she said and smiled, and she kissed him. And he supped on it like it was fresh fruit. But behind her eyes, she wondered how she would manage being away from her family—away from her mother.

Emmett said to her in a soft tone, "You and Mama Adele can plan it. The wedding." His cheeks blushed pinkish when he divulged, "I already asked your daddy for your hand."

Esther shrieked with delight and hugged him around his neck tight.

His laughter was joyful. "They think I'm out here askin' ya right now," he said. He powered up the car and backed it away from the diner and onto the road.

"Where we goin'?" she asked.

"For a ride," he said.

Evening had moved in, but the summer sun hadn't thought about giving up yet. It was still light outside. The roadside was lush green, fertile, and beautiful. The air invading the rolled-down windows boasted scents of freshly cut grass. When Emmett came to a stop, they were parked behind the sawmill in the next town. Esther was aware of the Hanover Sawmill Factory, of course. It was where her father and her brothers worked, though she hadn't been there since she was a little schoolgirl.

"Wow," she said. "Haven't been here in a while."

"You haven't been *here* ever," Emmett said, feeling proud about his clever turn of phrase. He turned off the ignition and moved to take Esther into his full embrace. She accepted, knowing that the game of tug-of-war was about to begin.

"I love you, Esther."

"I love you too, Emmett," she said and went right to her question. "When do you have to go?"

He pulled back and took a second before he spoke. "Tuesday," he said.

Everything stopped. Tears flooded Esther's eyes. "But today is Sunday!" Esther moved to open the car door to eject herself without a single forethought about where she was ejecting herself to. But she jumped out, anyway.

Emmett jumped out and sprinted around the head-lights to catch her in his arms. Her tears were full blown now. He held her tight and reached into his pocket. He was good at multitasking. Emmett pulled out a ring. It halted her escape to nowhere. Gently, Emmett took hold of her trembling hand. In spite of all the housework and midwifing, her hand felt soft and fragile. And he took hold of it gently, like he was afraid it would break. When Esther recalled all this later, she said that it was like it happened in slow motion. Slowly, he slipped the modest engagement ring on her finger.

"I got it while I was gone," he said.

She had no words, but her new tears were happy. And there were no more words between them. Emmett stepped back just a little and took Esther's hand to lead her around to the backseat car door. Soon they'd be skin to skin—as best as they could manage—bursting inside one another's love and a ringed promise of mar-ried life together.

Esther returned home that evening a new woman—in secret. The whole Bailey house was abuzz, though, about the impending nuptials. Everyone laughed and giggled about how everybody knew that Emmett was going to pop the question except Esther. She would be the first of the Bailey brood to get hitched.

Emmett was sent to Fort Jackson in South Carolina for basic training. He learned how to be a soldier but was terribly frustrated and angered to learn that his main duty would be latrine maintenance. He was hav-ing some serious trouble picking and choosing his bat-tles, like his uncle had tried to teach him. He got into several scuffles with his fellow colored comrades, and it served to extend what should have been an eight-week basic training into twelve weeks and longer. He kept getting pushed back for punishment. Emmett's emotional respites, though, came in the letters he wrote to Esther and the sweet-smelling ones she sent back. Those letters made his face shine. "But it was too bad that he couldn't let that carry him to victory," Esther would remark many years later, when she was strong enough to explain what happened.

Three days before he was supposed to graduate, get leave, and return to his beloved Esther to marry, so they could begin their new lives together, Emmett challenged the color line in a nightclub just outside of camp. Upon his exit, a couple of white soldiers conspired to teach him a lesson.

The actual account of Private Emmett Dorsey's death that was sent to his home, along with his body inside of a flag-draped coffin, was vague. Esther was nearly inconsolable. She and Mama Adele went up to New York for the funeral. It was actually the first time Esther met Emmett's mother, and his mother was sweet to her and acted like she had been waiting to accept her into the family.

A week after Emmett's death, Esther received a precious love letter from Emmett. In it he joked, "By the time you get this letter, we'll be married, finally." He wrote about how he couldn't wait. She cried until her ribs hurt when she read it; then she got mad and set it ablaze. Later, she was sorry she hadn't kept it. But what was done was done.

Something else had been done, Esther knew. She was pregnant with Emmett's child. Her period never showed up after that fateful Sunday at the sawmill before Emmett's departure. She had plenty of experience tracking the changes in her body, because she'd played assistant midwife to Mama Adele at an early age. On the bus ride back to Lively from New York, Esther divulged her secret to her mother. She had already prayed for God's forgiveness. Now it was time to face her mother. She was thankful that the bus from Richmond to the general store in Lively wasn't crowded. She and her mother sat in the back, and there was no one close around.

"Mama?"

"Yeah, chile?"

"Emmett and I loved each other."

Mama Adele chuckled a bit, a kind of unfunny chuckle. "I know that, chile. Where you think I been all this time?" She took her child into her arms at that point. "And no, I don't know why these sad, terrible things happen, Esther." Mama Adele sighed. "I just know that for us that's still among the living, well, we just gotta keep on living. And doing our best, 'cause that's the way God wants it." It was sound advice, Esther knew, and she'd heard it from her mother her entire life.

"Mama," Esther said as she started to tear up and sniffle. Mama Adele produced a tissue from somewhere and wiped her daughter's face. Esther pulled herself upright and decided to be a woman about it. She looked her mother right in her face. "Mama," she said, "I'm sorry, Mama, but Emmett and I loved each other." She paused a moment to catch her breath. "We were gonna get married, and . . ."

"Sweetheart, I know that. And I'm sorry too about the way things happened and all, but you—"

"Mama, I'm in the family way." She paused and heard her mother's silence. "Mama, Emmett and I . . . He's gone, but we're going to have a baby."

Only the engine noises from the big old Greyhound bus and the whistle and whoosh of escaping air from its windows were audible for a notable measure of time before Mama Adele put her daughter back into her arms and said with a sigh, "I thought so, chile. I didn't want to, but I thought so."

Esther's first thought was surprise, but then the surprise evaporated. Not much else was said, nothing about that, anyway, during their ride home.

The day of their return was a Friday. That night, when the house had settled down and all had gone to bed, Mama Adele came into Esther's room. She wasn't asleep, just lying there, staring at the paint cracks in the ceiling, feeling widowed before she had even gotten the chance to be married.

"Esther, baby," Mama Adele said, closing the door behind her and moving in to sit on her oldest daughter's bed. "I see you're not asleep. And, you poor child, I do understand why." She took a moment to straighten the bed linens and to give Esther a gentle stroke on her cheek. "But this sad situation has gone on long enough, and we've got to move fast to get you back to normal," she explained.

Esther looked up. She sat up some and said, "Mama, please. Just give me some time. I'll be all right." She touched her bed linens, the part where her stomach was positioned underneath. "At least I've got Emmett's baby. I've got that, ya know. And I know we'll be all . . ."

Mama Adele leaned in with compassion, but aiming to give her daughter some hard, cold facts of life—as she saw it. She leaned in and said, "Oh, baby. You know you can't keep that seed. You can't have no baby with no Daddy to give it. You can't raise a seed, I tell ya, with no husband!"

"What?" Esther was dumbfounded.

"God don't want you havin' no baby with no husband. It ain't right," Mama Adele said compassionately. "That's a sin, gal. You know that."

"I know, Mama," Esther argued. "I know. I said I was sorry. And I asked God for forgiveness long ago for . . . for . . ." She looked away when she said, "For being with Emmett in the sinful way."

"Yes, chile. Okay. And I know the Lord's ready to forgive, but you' talkin' about heapin' a second wrong on top of the first one."

Esther was confused now. "Well, well, Mama, no. Of course, that's not what I'm tryin' to do, but . . ."

"Well, good, then," Mama Adele said with strength. "You understand, then." In her mind, the problem was on its way to being resolved. "It's goin' to take us a day, maybe two, to get everything ready." Putting the matter to serious thought, as if she hadn't already done so before she even came into Esther's bedroom, she said, "Ella Woods over in Montross is experienced at this." She looked over at Esther and said, "I've never done this, you know. Not this particular thing." Then she was back to thinking and planning out loud when she added, "Your Aunt Laura will come and help out. She'll be a big help, and she always keeps her mouth shut. I know she will for her own blood."

"Help out with what?" Esther asked with urgency and confusion.

"Oh, baby, Esther," Mama Adele said, "you do know what I'm talkin' about." She sighed out of the frustration of having to actually say it. She didn't like doing that, because the devil got into things when you said them so he could hear. Every Christian knew that the devil couldn't invade your thoughts. Mama Adele continued, "We got ta get that seed out of you, darlin'. You know that." Her breath rushed out of her nostrils. "Esther," she added, clarifying matters, "you can't have no baby out of wedlock. You can't have no illegitimate child!"

Oh my God! Esther's thoughts screamed in her mind as her bottom jaw dropped. She turned from her mother's face and projected her fright onto the pale yellow cinder-block wall in front of her. She failed to get up the nerve to say anything. Her innards flushed warm, and she could have sworn she felt the inside of her stomach twitch. But just where did the fright in her head and heart reside? She searched. Did it exist in the part where she wanted Emmett's seed to grow so it could be in her waiting arms? Or did it exist in the shame she felt over giving birth and being unmarried and being full of sin? And that was the dilemma that silenced her voice.

Her head was swimming, making her dizzy and sick to her stomach. *Am I full of sin?* she asked her self silently. *Or am I full of Emmett's love—our baby?* There was one thing, Esther was sure of: never in her eighteen years had she disobeyed or even questioned her mother. Mama Adele always knew what was best for everyone in her world. Esther had never gone against her mother's direction. She opened her mouth to say, "No. No. I'm not doing anything to get Emmett's seed out of me." Well, at least she shouted it in her head. But the actual words never got beyond her mouth. They never hit the air. She felt mute and helpless.

Mama Adele was getting up from Esther's bedside now. With all the preliminaries set, she was heading to the door. She touched the doorknob but didn't turn it. She said to Esther, "I hate to do this on a Sunday and all, but Sunday, after dinner, we'll just tell your father we goin' out to check on a baby comin' into this world. And you, me, and yo' Aunt Laura will head on up to Ella's to go 'head and get this thing done." She stood for a second to let it sink in for them both, then said, "Okay?" But she didn't wait for affirmation of the plans. She opened the door and made her way out.

Enclosed in total darkness, Esther tried her best to allow sleep to take her away from what had just happened. She was terrified.

Ella Woods's wooden house was little more than a dilapidated shack. And the house sat way back off a one-lane dirt road/driveway. With a slow, careful drive up to the house, one could drive oneself right out of the 1950s and into at least one or two decades prior to that. Ella was a woman who looked to be about in her fifties, maybe, and she was the color of toast, perfectly made. And though her face was defined by hard-life lines, there were traces of a once attractive woman. Rumor had it that Ella was quirky and had a stack of money by doing what she did. But she kept it hidden, some thought, in mason jars buried out back behind her house. And she never spent her money on nothing she felt wasn't a bare necessity. For fifty dollars, cash money, you could come to Ella's full of sin and leave empty. She had a brisk business.

In Ella's younger days, she had had four husbands; all of them died within five years of married life. That fact sparked the rumor about her having a white liver. Esther never knew why such a saying existed, but it went that if a woman married multiple times and all her husbands died off quick, then that woman was said to have a white liver. And maybe the reason why Ella Woods hadn't yet caught ahold of a fifth husband was that she was now about three hundred pounds, but only five foot four, and smelled of an equal mix of female B.O. and chewing tobacco. Much of this Ella background info, Esther had accrued as she sat in the backseat of Mama Adele's car during the ride up to Montross. Mama Adele and Aunt Laura chatted the entire way there. Esther was silent and out-of-body dazed.

Ella's front yard looked like a forest. Her front and back rooms were a mess too. The doors were open, so anyone could see. She had a third room in which she did all her medical procedures. Ella didn't look, act, or talk much like she had been to elementary school, but the fact was that she had made it right through to formal nurse's training. She just didn't finish. She got married to husband number one instead.

Well, her third-room operating room, such as it was, wasn't as badly disarrayed as the others. The bed appeared to have clean sheets on it. There was a nightstand next to it that held a beautiful antique blue and white basin with a matching water pitcher inside of it. That evening, right on into the wee hours of that Monday morning, it got plenty of use. The wooden chest of drawers was where she pulled out clean towels and washcloths. The top drawer was where she fetched shiny steel-looking surgical instruments. She'd gotten them from that nursing school she went to up in Baltimore.

"She probably stole them," Mama Adele had said one time to Aunt Laura. It was at another time, after she had to make a visit to Ella's. "That's probably another reason why she didn't finish up there." The two women, busy at bringing in a sweet little baby girl for one of Mama Adele's steady clients, had chuckled at the remark. Esther had been there, assisting. She had heard it, but she didn't know this Ella they spoke of, so it was white noise at the time. She'd been busy being seen, useful, but not heard.

It was funny to Esther at the moment—that is, if anything could be funny while lying in a strange bed, waiting to get the life yanked out of you—that that snippet of verbiage got called up in her memory right at that time. But it did.

The top of the chest of drawers was crowded with liquor bottles filled to various capacities. There were white bottles of rubbing alcohol standing there too. When Esther, Mama Adele, and Aunt Laura arrived, Ella was proud to give a tour for Esther's benefit, she assumed.

"Esther, chile," Ella said, pointing, "you go on in there, take off your clothes, and get on in that bed there." She added, "Cover yourself up with the sheet over there," and she pointed to the line of neatly folded sheets across the end of the bed. All the sheets were crisp looking and white, Esther noted. Ella, Mama Adele, and Aunt Laura sat in the front room and chatted while Esther went on in slowly to follow those instructions. The night was hot. All the screened-in windows, three of them, were open. Esther later said she'd never forget the sound of the crickets that night. They seemed louder and busier than usual, perhaps urging her to climb out of one of those windows and escape.

All four women were in the room now. Three on their feet, milling about; Esther naked, shaking, and nervous beneath the sheet she clutched. Her eyes followed their every movement. Ella walked over to her, sat at her bedside with a bottle of white lightning in her hand, and a full paper cup. "Here," she said. "Drink this down. It will help the numbin'."

Esther heard her but never budged. She didn't even look like she was thinking about budging or complying with any further instructions to be uttered that evening. Mama Adele came to the rescue. She sat on the bed and pulled her baby up into her lap. Then she took the paper cup full of booze from Ella's hand.

"C'mon, baby," Mama Adele said with patience in her voice. "You gotta do this."

Esther looked at the cup, held almost to her chin now, but failed to move. She twisted her face like what was inside of it smelled awful.

"I know. I know," Mama Adele said. "I don't like no liquor, either." She shook her head and added, "I don't condone it, baby. But you gotta drink it this time. It'll make things easier for ya."

Esther finally released the sheet with one hand and carefully took hold of the cup. She moved it to her lips and took a sip, shut her eyes, then took a gulp. After she swallowed, it was like she had to come up for oxygen. "Yuck!" she said. "It tastes like rubbing alcohol. How in the world do people drink this stuff for fun?"

Mama Adele chuckled. "Keep drinkin', baby, till you got enough of it down ya."

Esther's face contorted. She experienced coughing jags in between gulps. Her stomach innards convulsed, rippled, and jiggled. About three or four more gulps and she stopped. "Here," she said, giving the cup back to her mother.

"Okay. Okay, baby girl," Esther's mother said as she took the cup. "I guess that's enough for now."

Ella had some other kind of numbing medicine that she mumbled about. Esther laid back down, flat, watching her. She tensed up every time the woman came close to her, but it wasn't long before all that liquor took effect. The room started swaying. Esther's eyes were hazing over, and she really couldn't make out what Ella was saying. And she was losing track of time. One of the last things she remembered was finding her voice. She felt herself rear up to say, "Mama, I don't wanna do this. I don't. Mama . . ."

She felt her mother gently persuading her to yield and go back to a lying position, and stroking her hair, which was damp with sweat. "Okay. Okay. There now, Esther, honey," Mama Adele soothed. "It'll be over before you know it. The body's good about gettin' rid of things that don't belong there."

"Mama, I don't want—"

"Hush, chile. Shh."

Time was indeed lost for Esther. She recalled screaming horridly, but she couldn't recall at what point her screams happened. She couldn't even recall if the screams were audible or just in her head. In what must have been in the early hours of Monday morning, a funny smell abounded. It was a mix of rubbing alcohol, blood, liquor, and womanhood.

When full consciousness popped her eyes open, she found herself soaked with blood. Blood seemed to be everywhere. A searing pain, in repetitive throbs, rushed into her back and pelvic area. It moved in with such determination, she couldn't feel if she had legs or not. Esther tried but couldn't lift herself up. She burst out in screams and cries, and this time there was no doubt that her desperation was audible, because all three women, her mother first, rushed to her side. For seconds, Esther could not recall why there was such pain, only that there *was* pain.

Reality dawned, and questions filled her mind. *Where am I? What's happened to me? Mama?* Then the questions became clearer. *Oh my God, can you help me? What? Is my Emmett gone?* That last thought brought her in full view of the situation. She hollered and cried, and her cries were primal, with purpose now. Inside her chest, her howls broke the sound barrier, but her body was weak, and nearly bloodless it seemed. So to everyone else, she sounded like a pitiful, wounded kitten, too weak to fight. Esther's horrible, pointless cries persisted as she clutched her mother—the one whom she now hated. But she had no one else to cling to.

They returned home in the late afternoon that Monday. Mama Adele and Aunt Laura put Esther right to bed. The older boys and their father were still at work. Esther slumbered off and on for at least three more days. She rose up only when her mother either helped her to the bathroom or brought her food. Mama Adele explained to Mac Bailey and the family that Esther had come down with something because she was so weak from grieving over the death of Emmett.

In the fall of 1955 the Baileys would spring for a used black-and-white television set. They bought it from a pawn shop in Richmond. It was Mama Adele's insistent wish, because she said that the house could use some fresh cheer and distraction. Emmett's death still loomed in the air, and Esther's smile and energy were just simply gone. She seemed different, somehow, everyone remarked in her absence, because she kept to her bedroom most of the time.

In November of 1956 the television purchase proved timely, because *The Nat King Cole Show* aired—setting a landmark as the first ever network television series hosted by a colored entertainer. The groundbreaking show lasted only for thirteen months, though. NBC tried feverishly to get sponsors for the show, but advertisers stayed away as they were too afraid of offending their Southern customers. The network foot the bill for the year the show was on. Reportedly, Nat King Cole himself remarked, "Madison Avenue is afraid of the dark." Also, in November of 1956 Esther—even though about thirteen months prior she could not imagine being away from her home, her family, or her mother's rule—left home. Esther Bailey settled in Baltimore. She never returned to Lively, Virginia, not even for a visit. She also never uttered a word to anyone about the sorrow that led up to her departure.

Chapter Twelve

Sick and Tired

During Jubi's teen years, of course, Esther and James loved on their baby girl something fierce, but they couldn't help growing old and out of touch with her world. "When Jubi was sixteen or so, she started hanging around a scummy crowd at school. Then she started skipping school," Esther said, sniffling and testifying again to her fellow church members in the FISHH Ministry.

The monthly meeting happened to come right after Esther and James's rescue of the sapphire bracelet, a horrible scene. Easter was on the horizon, and the meeting's agenda was a discussion of how to best minister to bereaved families during the upcoming holiday season. The ministry also wanted to raise monies to give out holiday food baskets to the needy and make festive Easter baskets for the kindergarteners at Ashburton Elementary, up on Hilton Road. But if the FISHH acronym truly stood for "Fellowship, Intercession, Study, and Healing Hurts," then the time-out to minister to its own was justified.

"I mean, she just stopped living right." Esther looked up to give eye contact to one of her beloved church members. Really, all were well versed in Esther's saga. With sorrow and surprise, she said, "It was her senior year. And she barely finished high school." Esther looked down again into her fresh tissue, which one of the church members had handed to her, and said, "We should have done something, I guess, but we didn't even see it coming. That's when all the real hell broke loose." Her brewing anger grew visible on her face. "That's when our daughter fell into the hands of the sure-'nuf devil." Beola was sitting to the right of Esther, holding her hand, issuing moral support. Her other close friend, and coworker, Peggy, was sitting to her left, doling out the fresh tissues and the "Amens."

"That's when our Jubilee fell into the nasty affections of a no-good Negro," Esther said. "Excuse me, y'all, but I mean what I say. That no-good Negro named Ambro." She twisted her lip up when she said the man's name.

Ambro was thirty years old and was estranged from his much older wife and their three kids. He was a no-good S.O. Boob. That was how James referred to him. "Straight from the pit of hell," James declared to anyone who would listen. Somewhere along the line, Ambro had traded whatever self-respect he had for the handouts of strangers, mostly women, who thought his tired, wiry frame and high yella face was something good to look at.

Ambro's looks were reminiscent of the drug-pusher guy in that seventies movie *Super Fly*. Oh, he must have been fine at one point in his life—Esther gave him that much. "But those days were long gone by the time he came around to mess up Jubi's life," she always declared. When Mr. Look-So-Good turned into a womanizing slug, he was nothing but the devil incarnate in Esther's eyes. He might as well have shown up on her front doorstep wearing a red bodysuit with a pointy red tail and holding a rusty pitchfork.

Now, Ambro might not have had a working neuron in his brain, and he might not have had principles or a pot to piss in, but there were a few things he did have. He had Jubi's mind and soul. Jubi was a bottomless pit for everything that fool wanted to teach her. He spoon-fed her his crappy outlook on life, and she lapped it up like a stray kitten placed in front of a bowl of sweet milk.

Ambro taught her sex and some tricks. He refined her weed smoking. He taught her how to snort cocaine and even introduced her to heroin. Then he taught her how to steal and connive to get the drugs they needed. Ambro taught her skin poppin', arm veins, wrist veins, back-of-the-knee veins, and ankle veins. He caused Jubi's budding hourglass figure to shrivel. Her skin just hung off her fragile five-foot-six-inch frame, ashy and brittle. Her eyes were sunken in and had dark circles. Her face was gaunt, and her cheeks were drawn in.

When she was a little girl, Jubi's brown locks, which she got from her mother, crowned her delicate heart-shaped face with glory. Esther kept her silky hair curled in big, pretty, shiny Shirley Temple loops, and she garnished them with expensive bows. In the blink of an eye, it seemed, all that was gone. On any given day, you could spy Jubi dragging herself down the street, her hair standing all over her head, looking like a used-up Brillo pad.

Jubi was missing out on that special time in every girl's life when she transitioned into womanhood with grace. That was a time when sweet and sexy coexisted in the same body, and Mother Nature put up her warning sign that said LOOK BUT DON'T TOUCH UNTIL THIS BUD HAS FULLY BLOOMED. Jubi's innocence had dissolved quickly due to her hard experience. She'd skipped that irretrievable step in her youth. But that didn't matter to Ambro. To him, she was cotton candy on a stick, and he enjoyed tearing off and devouring every bite of her. He loved to crow about it to his friends. "Oh yeah, she'll do whatever I say," he bragged to his boys.

To the naked eye, it seemed like Jubi had broken her parents' heart in a thousand pieces. After all, they were nice middle-class black folk who worked hard all week, attended church every Sunday. Bible study was every Wednesday at Forest Unity Memorial Church, and they never missed a lesson. Like most parents, they loved their child, and their prayers for Jubi had no end. So what went wrong?

Nobody could figure it out, either. Close confidants tossed around possibilities with Esther and James, and behind their backs. Had they been neglectful to Jubi in some way? Was the trouble justified due to some wrong they'd done in their early lives? Was Jubi merely a bad seed? Could something this horrible befall blameless, God-fearing people just like that—for no reason? Such random misfortune made everybody nervous.

Esther held on to the belief that everything that happened to Christians—be it good or bad—had to be rooted in some kind of divine purpose for their lives. And if things were going to pan out right, if they were going to pass the test, then they had to keep believing and praying that they would. She didn't think it strange that it took her so long to marry or to have Jubi, for she knew her past. Secretly, she knew that it was tangible proof of God's forgiveness. He had forgiven her and given her a second chance after she gave herself to her precious Emmett, unmarried, and allowed the destruction of their seed.

Esther thought it divine that her name, Bailey, had changed to Stone when she married James. She felt it had special significance. The Bible scripture, 1 Peter 2:4–10, talked about a living stone. Even though that stone was tossed, it turned out to be the most important one of all. It also talked about God's chosen people being brought out of darkness and into the marvelous light. So Esther believed that her Jubi would come around, if she could just stand firm in her faith. Esther's favorite scripture was the one that said, "Faith without works is dead."

In her family's trial, her heart said that her work was her faith. Her work was also her steadfast praying and her unconditional love for her only child. And she was absolute in her belief that it was Jubi's birthright to have a successful life—not failure. Esther was insistent that all this messy stuff happening now was simply from traveling along a cobblestoned path in her journey, a path that would end. "The devil just got a temporary stronghold on our baby's life, that's all," Esther and James declared whenever the subject came up around them. "If she didn't have such a heavy calling on her life, the devil wouldn't be after her so hard," they'd assert. But Esther was tired.

In the meantime, they kept on praying without ceasing for their precious baby girl to come around. By that time, Jubi had been in the pure wilderness going on three years. And the waiting was hard. But the fact was that Esther and James were used to waiting. On their jobs, they waited for equal pay and recognition. They had waited for true love to come their way, and they had waited for the birth of Jubi—especially Esther. So if they could wait for all that, they could wait for Jubi's turnaround.

However, there was some wisdom to be gained during all that waiting. Right up to the sapphire bracelet drama, they had learned how to deal with their daughter's flesh while they waited for the deliverance of her spirit. They had learned to kick their guilt to the curb, mostly, especially since they knew they had done their best at rearing her. Guilt, they'd learned in Bible study, was a useless emotion that didn't fix anything. They had also learned to put all their valuables—their portable, pawnable stuff—out of sight whenever Jubi came to visit. They had realized that it wasn't their precious little ginger-hued baby who was robbing them blind. Well, it wasn't *really* her. It was the demon-spirit drugs that possessed her. Such pearls of wisdom would help them to survive until the victory, which they were sure was on the way, arrived.

By the time Jubi was seventeen and a half, it was normal for her to spend nights, weekends, and even weeks away from home. Esther and James wouldn't know where their daughter was. Finally, they learned to stop calling the police every time she dropped out of sight. They soon learned to accept the hard, cruel fact that she was with Ambro. Whenever the police did drag her home, she'd just go right back to him, anyway. They finally realized Jubi had to come home of her own free will.

Whenever Jubi was forced home, special delivery by the police, as soon as she hit the front door, the shouting began. Then the police had to come out for that. The drama always played out the same way, with Esther crying, James exploding, and Jubi storming out again, knocking over everything in her path. That time when Esther and Jubi went to blows in the living room, they broke two lamps and the legs off the coffee table, and knocked over the TV before James could get between them. It was a devastating low for Esther. She fasted for nearly thirty days after.

On one particular Saturday night, Esther prayed especially hard for a breakthrough. She remembered her heart was feeling extra heavy, like someone had poured sand into it. Esther was fifty-seven years old by then, and the struggle to keep her baby alive had already pounded ten extra years into her heart. Esther had grown weary from knowing all the things Jubi could have been but wasn't. In her early school years, Jubi was an exceptional student. She always got it and took it to a new level—until the devil got her. Now Jubi was gaining on her twentieth birthday, and Esther struggled not to lose hope. She clung to the notion that her daughter was still young enough to get her act together. With God, Jubi could do anything. Esther had to believe that.

Well, on that night, Esther gingerly crouched down on her knees to pray. Her knees pained her, and she leaned on the edge of her bed for support and then stretched her body flat on the floor. Esther was so tired, she almost fell down.

"Lorrrrd," Esther cried out, "just like I knew you'd always give me this child, I know you ain't gonna let the devil take her from me. I know it. Lord, I know you didn't say that the weapon wouldn't be formed against my baby, but you did promise me that the weapon wouldn't kill her. Right there in your book of Isaiah, fifty-four, seventeen, you said it, Lord. You said it wouldn't prosper! Please give me strength to see this thing through."

Then Esther wept. Her pleas flowed from her heavy heart. Each time her tears landed on the tweed carpet beneath her, they formed tiny reflective puddles, then seeped into the carpet's grain.

"Save her, Lord. Save my baby. Please wake us all up from this terrible nightmare," she whispered directly into God's ear.

That night Esther praised God some more. She thanked him some more for her blessings, and she asked forgiveness for the moments when her faith dipped below the plumb line and for all the times she plotted Ambro's demise. Afterward, she lay there on the floor and cried some more, until her waterlogged eyelids remained closed in a soothing slumber steeped with prayer. An hour or so flew by before she awoke, topped off her final prayer requests, and pulled her weighty body up off the floor, only to collapse into bed for some real deep sleep.

Esther was alone in the house that night because James was working the three-to-eleven shift at Providence Hospital. When Esther fell asleep, she dreamt that it was Sunday morning and she was sitting in church. She wore her favorite purple hat with the wide brim, her purple nightgown, and her multicolored bathrobe, with its lavender terry cloth belt tied tightly under her big bosoms. She wore her matching terry cloth slippers too, because even in a dream, girlfriend had to look good. When awake, she'd always laughed and said that God wanted her to look good.

In her dream, it was raining in the church's sanctuary, and there was some kind of big commotion going on in front of the pulpit. She tried to get up off her pew and move closer to see what was happening, but she couldn't. Her body felt clumpy, and she was sheepish. Wads of sand granules threatened to leak out of her pores if she moved. She didn't want to get up and run the risk of totally disintegrating. That was when two angels with widespread wings swooped inside the church through the opened top half of a stained glass window. They flew in on an angle right over her head and then glided right down in front, toward the commotion. The gust of wind they produced perfumed the church with the smell of lilacs. Esther said that the strong gust of wind almost knocked her hat clear off her head.

The angels calmed the crowd, looked over at Esther, and smiled. Then they seemed to take something away with them as they flew upward and back through the rainbow rays of the stained glass window. Just beyond the window's frame, the angels turned to powder and blended into the light blue sky. Shimmering white doves appeared and followed close behind. Esther had struggled to see what the angels were carrying away, but she had to duck when they flew back over her head again, as she didn't want to lose her hat. When she looked over at the crowd, the worshippers were now kneeling and quietly praying at the altar. The raindrops slowed to a drizzle.

Buzzzzz! The dream vanished with the sudden screech of her alarm clock. Esther's body felt like someone huge had wrapped their arms around her. Her drowsy mind was shrouded in both confusion and relief all at the same time as she slowly realized she'd been dreaming. Her soul felt light, though. She looked over to find James sleeping soundly in his blue-and-white pin-striped pajamas, and she was surprised to see him there. Esther hadn't heard him come in the house, let alone get into bed, which was her habit without fail. Her heart pounded away, but it felt good, somewhat tingly. The sensation was satisfying. Sweat beads dotted her forehead.

James, who had his heavy arm fastened tightly around her waist, started nudging her to shut off the alarm. She wanted to shake him and tell him about the dream, but she couldn't talk yet. Her subconscious was still downloading information. So, with her open palm, she reached over, smacked the little black button on top of the alarm clock, and struggled to free herself from James's grip. She shoved her body out of bed with the goal of heading down the hallway to the bathroom. It was Sunday morning, time to get ready for church.

At the instant her reflection filled the bathroom mirror, her mind fully processed the dream. She strongly believed in the phenomenon of prophecy and was certain that God often communicated with her in her dreams. Just what were those angels carrying? she pondered, while replaying the image in her mind, trying to unravel the mystery. Suddenly, she clutched her cheeks with both hands. Her eyes filled with alarm. In a desperate, loud whisper, Esther shouted out, "*Jubi!*"

Chapter Thirteen

Life and Eternal Life

The Sunday before Esther's dream . . .

"Girrrl, what in the heck's got into you? I thought you was gonna kick me out the bed," Ambro said to Jubi in a playful tone. The afternoon sun rays beamed in through the dirty bay window of his one-room flat. He chuckled and struggled to hold on to the crusty floral sheets that entangled them both. He also had a hold on Jubi's waist with his heavy arm. She struggled to break free from his naked grip by mustering up her silent disgust. Finally, she unraveled herself from the sheets and rolled off the tattered mattress that lay on the dusty hardwood floor. She headed for the bathroom. Everything in Ambro's flat was dingy, beaten up, and worn. Its decor included dirty beige walls, ripe sixties-style furniture, a tattered mattress, and a rusty, singing radiator that clanged rather than give out any heat in the winter. The couch had a heavily stained lima bean-green plaid slipcover on it, left behind by the previous dwellers. Even under the influence of hallucinogenics, Jubi thought the idea of sitting on it was nauseating. Because the renters in the house had become so scummy, the owner had instituted weekly rates. Ambro was always in arrears.

The owner of the house, Mr. Hirsh, also owned the old Stardust Inn down on the corner of Fulton and

Pennsylvania Avenues. The Stardust used to be a big, fancy white-folks-only place in the 1950s. By the time the 1960s rolled around, Mr. Hirsh had grown a nice little side business, renting the rooms in his house to impromptu star-crossed lovers for the night or by the hour. But by the time types like Ambro were the typical clientele, the Stardust was a run-down eyesore for entrepreneurial wannabe pimps, and the big fairy-tale plantation-style abode . . . well, it wasn't even near what it used to be.

While Jubi was in the bathroom, Ambro was still in a chuckling mood. So he unraveled himself from his dingy sheets and propped himself up into a sitting position. He grabbed his T-shirt, resting on a mound of funky, wrinkled clothes growing on the floor beside him, and slid it on. Sitting on the mattress's edge, he folded his body into a crouching position, with his legs spread apart, so his nudeness from the waist down could be clearly ascertained.

Ambro purposely sat that way because he thought it was funny or sexy or something. He grabbed his crushed, almost empty pack of cigarettes, pounded one out, and crunched it between his lips. He set it aflame with a matchstick; he then blew out the match and haphazardly discarded on the hardwood floor. The floor bore many scars. Slowly, he drew one long puff of smoke deep into his lungs. The sensation of heat was so satisfying, he tilted his head back and creased his eyes shut in a puffer's display of lust. For a moment, he forgot he was waiting to show his *lust* to Jubi when she came out of the bathroom.

When Jubi reappeared, clad in her bloomers and bra, her stride was cut short by Ambro's glaring welcome. There he was, sitting and puffing on his Kools, with his top half shrouded in a wrinkled T-shirt and swirled cigarette smoke, and his bottom half laid bare. His penis dangled proudly off the side of the mattress. Dust bunnies danced around the eye of the tiger as it bobbed up and down in response to his hearty laugh.

Jubi stood there. It was lucky for her that no flies buzzed nearby, because her bottom jaw had swung open and hung in the open air. She was stunned by his Kodak moment. When she could move, she rolled her eyes and her neck. She was in the middle of sucking her teeth at him when a little voice of reason, the one that popped into her head from time to time, whispered in her head again. It said, *Girrrl, what are you doing here?*

Ambro and Jubi spent the coming week as usual, getting drunk, smoking weed, and lacing it with a little heroin. All the get high was courtesy of some dude Ambro knew who wanted to get next to Jubi. Ambro used Jubi as currency. She settled accounts too, but it made her vomit. Well, sometimes Jubi got high just to be getting high. In the beginning, she did it to be with Ambro. Then she did it because it was fun. When all the fun got sucked out of it, she did it to fight off despair.

Lately, fleeting thoughts of reason had been racing through her mind more and more, even when she was high. Strange voices confirmed sorry negatives and asked annoying questions, like: *Is this what you want to do with your life? What are you doing here? You're too young to be in this fix. If he jabs his finger up his nose or rearranges his testicles one more time, I'm gonna scream! If he tries to stick his yellow-caked tongue down my throat one more time, I'll puke on it.* Then the little voices would fly away, and she'd think, *I've really messed up. There ain't no fixing this now. Not my parents, not even God could ever reverse all of this. I might as well forget it.*

It happened during those moments when Jubi would lay prostrate on the floor, next to the mattress. She wanted to pray. She tried to pray, but she couldn't. In fact, she would feel stupid for even trying. How could she have the gall to speak to God, especially in her shape? She started yearning for her mother in secret. But anger still consumed her. *Heck, there ain't no God. 'Cause if there was, He wouldn't have let all this crap happen to me. Mama and Daddy are stupid, suckin' up to that preacher, giving them all their time and money instead of me—their own flesh and blood. They're old and stupid. They don't know nothin' about nothin'. Not nothin' I'm going through, anyway.*

She'd sink even deeper in the gutter. Ambro, and whoever else, could do whatever they wanted to her when she was in that state. To survive, she only had to exist in total darkness and get high.

After Ambro had finished with her, Jubi lay next to him, watching him sleep it off. His slumber kept him busy. He swiped drool off the corner of his gaping mouth one minute and swatted invisible flies the next. Throughout, he engaged in some kind of unintelligible conversation. His wild gestures occasionally rearranged the lint balls in his dried-up Jheri curl, which looked more like a sad Afro, now matted into a nappy pyramid. His entire nocturnal dance made it look like he was dreaming about being caught in a spider's web. And really, Ambro was caught in a web. He just didn't know it.

Jubi's voices of sanity crept in once more. This time they were short and sweet. They shouted, *Get the heck out!* Or they might have said, *Get out of hell.* Either way, she got the point. For the rest of that night, Jubi lay there, paralyzed, while her mind flirted with unfinished routes of freedom. She couldn't think clearly, but she had finally begun to plot her escape. Across town, while her mother lay prostrate on the floor, praying and dreaming of angels and doves, Jubi fell asleep with a silent, needy cry.

Then it was Sunday morning. A strong sun returned to shine through the bay window of Ambro's cold-water flat. Its rays filtered through Ambro's makeshift curtain, a faded cream-colored twin sheet that he had so stylishly nailed to the window's wooden frame. Jubi's eyes popped open on their own accord, and to her surprise, her brain brimmed with good thoughts, instead of bad ones. She wanted to go to church.

Such strange notions had come to her before, but she had always managed to talk herself out of them before they could penetrate the ozone of her reality. This day, however, she wasn't having any of that. She didn't exactly know why she wasn't having it, but she wasn't.

Now, her usual train of thought went like this: *You got the nerve to walk up in a church after all the stuff you did last night? All those people know you. They're gonna see you and shake their heads. You ain't got no business around no church folk. Shoot, them people are all hypocrites, anyway. They ain't got no business judgin' you. If I were you, I wouldn't give 'em the chance. Chile, them folks don't wanna see you! And what about your mama and daddy . . . ? Are you not remembering y'all's last fight? What they said to you? Chile, they really don't wanna see you! If you walk into that church, you're gonna embarrass them. And it's just like you to be so selfish. Girrrl, you ain't thinking clear! All you need is a cigarette, a beer, and to get your funky butt back in the bed. It's too early for all this mess!*

Jubi could've thought of all that stuff—she had before—but this morning she just wasn't having it. It was about 7:00 A.M., and Ambro was still in his funky coma. As usual, he would be that way until about two o'clock that afternoon. That was when he'd stretch, scratch his testicles, expel gas, and roll off the mattress, looking for a cigarette, a reefer roach from the night before. Then he'd look for her.

Everything Jubi did, she felt, was an abomination before God. She knew better, but she was powerless to stop doing any of it. She certainly wasn't worthy of walking into the church and being around all those *good* kids, those perfect kids she'd grown up with, who had stayed in school, who had stayed in church, who had stayed on the right track. *I turned my life into trash, and they didn't. I bet not even God can help me change things now. How in the world can He undo all that's been done?* she wondered, but she kept it moving.

She dragged her nude, contaminated body off the mattress, headed for the bathroom, and did the best she could to clean herself up. Carefully, she inspected the two puffy eyes staring back at her from the bathroom mirror. Her eyes had dark circles around them like the dog on *The Little Rascals*. She rubbed them hard, trying to erase reality away. Her hair looked like a brown, matted imitation fur collar. Her honey-brown skin wasn't creamy or supple; it was crackly, dry, and ashy. But she was hell-bent on doing whatever she could do to pull herself together. This morning all systems were go. Jubi's determination seemed fueled by an unknown source. She felt little nudges in the small of her back. She felt protected, too, like if she fell backward, something would catch her. Not even Ambro could foil this plan.

***

As usual, Forest Unity Memorial Church was packed to the gills. If you didn't get there by 10:45 A.M., you needed to plan on standing for the 11:00 o'clock service. Esther was always early enough to pick her seat: fourth-row pew, right side of the church, at the end closest to the center aisle. That way she could look back, with ease, to see who entered the sanctuary. It was her prayer that one day she'd look back and see her Jubi walking in. James, he sat up front, taking his place on the deacons' row.

Ten minutes into the service, the choir had fired up the congregation with its second refrain of "I Need Thee Every Hour." The Holy Spirit was in the house, and Esther, as usual, was getting her praise on. With her eyes shut, her head tilted slightly back and upward, her body swayed from side to side. She extended her right hand upward to swirl gentle currents of air around her softly spoken "Hallelujahs." She was in another world when she praised God, and that world was perfect. Esther's weary mind floated on a cloud. It was praise and worship time.

The organ wove a tapestry of traditional hymns. Operatic voices harmonized with soulful baritones, sopranos, and the rest. They sounded like angels were in the air. Esther lost awareness of everyone around her. Then, suddenly, right at the peak of her praise, her right ear perked up at the sound of something even sweeter. "Excuse me. Excuse me, please. . . . Thank you." It was a soft, polite voice. Esther homed in on its familiarity and felt a wisp of the movement that it caused. Afraid of disappointment, she hesitantly looked to her right. Esther couldn't believe her eyes. Jubi was pressing her way, sliding into Esther's full view.

Esther was sure she wouldn't see or hear from Jubi for months, maybe, after the fight they had had. But just like the first time Esther held her baby in her arms, all the prior pain evaporated. Esther's body flushed warm, as if she had slowly dipped herself into a warm, soapy bubble bath. Esther's heart felt lighter, and it fluttered with thankfulness. Jubi gave her mother a trembling smile. Tears rolled down Esther's cheeks. She held out her arms to receive her newborn babe once more. Jubi folded into her mother's softness. With delight, she breathed in her mother's lilac scent. She was the perfect fit under Esther's wide-brimmed purple hat.

From the pulpit, the pastor, Reverend Charles A. Wicker, Jr., a tall, thick chestnut man with a charismatic persona, had taken notice of what was going on. He let out a loud "Hallelujah," which ignited the praise of the entire church, because everyone else was watching too.

Not a word was spoken between mother and child—none was needed. James, who had been standing during the praise and worship, was filled with emotion and fell back down into his seat. He wiped tears of joy from his eyes using one of the cotton handkerchiefs that Esther always kept snow white and perfectly creased for him.

The service progressed, and Jubi fell into the worship mode like she had never missed a Sunday, let alone three years' worth of Sundays. All the while, she absorbed the smiles, pats, and hugs that came her way. She was astonished. Instead of feeling like an outcast, she felt like a star. When she started singing and clapping along with the congregation, Esther's heart swelled with happiness. Her baby's voice and her baby's memory of God's hymns had remained intact. The devil had thrown them in the fire, yet they were neither singed nor contaminated with smoke.

Soon, it was time for Reverend Wicker to preach. And preach he did. The "Amens" and "Glory hallelujahs" resonated on every beam of the church's cathedral ceiling. Oddly enough, the sermon was on the prodigal son. "Open your Bibles and turn to the Gospel of Luke, chapter fifteen," he said amid the sound of fluttering pages. Making the connection to Jubi coming home, the parishioners clapped their hands like clashing cymbals throughout the sanctuary. In praise and thanksgiving, folks sprang up and down from their pews, as if they were on pogo sticks. Esther's tears were a continuous flow.

The sermon tingled underneath Jubi's skin and caused her to breathe fresh air again. She felt like she had been shut up in a dark tomb all this time, and Reverend Wicker's words seemed to roll away the stone sealing the tomb. After a while, she couldn't hear anything but his voice, not the clapping around her, not the "Amen" shouts, not even her mother's spirit-filled "Hallelujah" praises. All she heard was the story of the prodigal son coming home.

Once again, Jubi felt a push in the small of her back, followed by a warm, soothing sensation. Then she felt a stronger shove, but when she turned to look behind her, it didn't seem likely that anyone close by had nudged her. Jubi had been holding on to her mother's hand throughout most of the service, but another nudge caused her to pull her hand loose. Esther took notice and moved to comfort her daughter by caressing her. Slowly, Jubi began to rise to her feet. She didn't want to stand up; she *had* to stand up. Jubi couldn't control what was happening. Esther was puzzled but kept silent. In fact, she couldn't speak, and Jubi wasn't saying anything, either. She just stood there with a look of need on her face. Then, gently, Jubi pushed past her mother's lap and headed for the center aisle. With her arms stretched out and tears tumbling down her face, Jubi made her way down front to the pastor. Everyone who witnessed Jubi's out-of-order behavior froze in whatever position the Holy Spirit caught them, perplexed, and their eyes fixed on the scene. After all, this wasn't the time when the preacher called people to the altar to accept Jesus as their Lord and Savior. Pastor hadn't beckoned forward those who wanted to join the church. He had made no signal to anyone to come down front. In fact, he was still in the heat of his sermon, and the prodigal son hadn't quite made it home yet.

Reverend Wicker's face was flushed and covered with tiny pimples of sweat. They were lodged in the deep character creases of his forehead. During the heated sermon, Reverend Wicker glided his huge, tall frame down from the pulpit like a graceful butterfly. Then he sprinted back and forth across the front of the church, emphasizing each of his sermonic points with a firm finger propelled in the air. The reverend was at the far right end of the altar when he spotted Jubi coming down front. He stopped mid-sentence and rushed to the center stage to meet her. He stretched out his arms to receive her.

"Come on, baby. You come on, Jubi. Come on home to Jesus," Reverend Wicker shouted, wearing a compassionate look. The congregation roared with excitement, but Jubi really couldn't hear it.

"Please, pray for me," Jubi struggled to shout, but her voice trembled as she cried. "Please pray for me. Help me! Help me!" Jubi repeated. Her pace slowed as she supported herself in her journey by leaning on each pew, one in front of the other. She was nearly overcome with emotion.

Reverend Wicker's feet stayed firmly planted in place, for he believed that she needed to make it to him and to the altar on her own. He fought the urge to go get her. Instead, he kept his arms locked in position, stretched out, patiently waiting for the special delivery of Jubi's body and soul. Reverend Wicker sent her a little strength by projecting his thick baritone voice her way. It rumbled like thunder in a fierce storm. "Come on, Jubi, you can make it!" Then he shouted to the folks in the congregation, "Get up! Get Up!"

Jubi finally reached him and floated into his arms like a falling feather. She didn't weigh much more than one hundred pounds.

"Get up and help me pray this child back to Jesus!" the reverend shouted, placing his right hand on her forehead, cradling her upper body in the nook of his left arm like she was a rag doll. The deaconesses rushed to Jubi's feet with a huge white linen cloth to cover her legs for modesty.

The deacons quickly surrounded the two of them, and a crowd of church folk formed around them all. James, who had stayed back, gathering his own strength, parted the sea of worshippers to get to his baby girl. Both James and Reverend Wicker held Jubi in their arms, almost off her feet. More members of the congregation came running to the front, shouting godly praises and clapping. There was not a dry eye in the sanctuary. The prayer wall of parishioners formed a swaying cluster around Reverend Wicker, James, Jubi, the deaconesses, and the deacons.

Esther, however, stood frozen in place in her pew. She suddenly realized her dream was unfolding. She

looked up to notice a cone of soft light streaming downward from the center stained glass window. It shined
a spotlight on the clustered congregation below. The
dust particles that danced in the light looked like powder crystals. "My dream," she shouted, then threw her
head back and her hands up in the air to God. One of
the seasoned deaconesses ran over to her and started
fanning her with a church fan, but Esther was clearly
unaware of her presence.

The organist, respectful, softly played "I Need Thee
Every Hour." Members of the choir, the few still left in
the choir loft, gently chimed in with the lyrics on cue.
The cone of light looked like a sparkling, colorful wa-
terslide. It streamed in, the colors of a rainbow.

Jubi's entire trip to church that day had been a spiritual tug-of-war. Something had no doubt pushed her to
the church, but she had also felt the pull of a negative
force trying to keep her away. And she was more familiar with the negative force, because that was the force
that usually won. Even in the center of this God-fearing
human prayer wall, with hands clamped all about her
torso, she could still feel the tug of evil. She couldn't believe how even at that moment, she harbored thoughts
that didn't belong in her head. But they made the
rounds in her brain, anyhow, like painted horses on
a moving carousel. She pondered how maybe she was
a lost soul who would stay lost, and as soon as all that
praying stopped, her dreadful life would resume. She
thought about Ambro waking up and finding her gone,
and the beating she'd take because of it. Then her need
for some get high surged, and her body was filled with
tiny electric shocks.

The intense praying created a concerted hum, vi-
brating her human shell. It sounded like the hum of an
electric mixer, and it formed a fortress of safety around

her body, but the pangs of needing Ambro and needing to get high still managed to prick her flesh. Here Jubi was in God's house, and yet the devil still had a stranglehold on her. It let her know that this was a knock-down, drag-out fight with the devil himself. He had already captured her soul, her dignity, her dreams; now he wanted what was left. He wanted to suck the breath right out of her lungs.

Something pricked her side again, and the cries of a weak kitten jetted out of her mouth. "God, help me. Help me!" By this time, she was no longer supporting her own body. A sheet of tears hampered her eyesight. She couldn't feel her head or her legs, only the blood pumping throughout. Her heart didn't hurt anymore, like it had when she walked into the church an hour ago. And Jubi couldn't imagine a sensation more soothing than the sound of her daddy's voice, softly chanting in her ear, "I love you, baby. God loves you, Jubi. Come on home, Jubi. Come on home. We love you. We'll never stop loving you."

Esther, still paralyzed in her pew, continued to pray from where she stood. She continued to keep her eyes on the light that intensified over the nucleus of the crowd. Suddenly realizing that it had come to take her baby away, she frantically thought to herself, *Oh my God. Is this what I prayed for?*

Ever since Esther had had Jubi, she had acknowledged the fact that Jubi was a temporary gift from her God, a life that she would love and nourish and give back to Him. But she had thought that *giving back* meant transforming Jubi into a disciple for Jesus, a spokeswoman, a minister of music, perhaps—not death. Was her Jubi on this earth only for a short season, most of it spent in turmoil? Selfish streams of guilt horrified her as memories of how young Victoria had left this world so unexpectedly frightened her. Were there similarities between Victoria and Jubi about to unfold, she feared? Then she remembered the fact that her dream turned out to be the premonition of Victoria's earthly departure. Was Jubi's earthly life meant to end even before it had really got started?

And as terrible as all that seemed, there was even more at stake. Could Esther, as Jubi's mother, just stand back passively—the way she had just lain there on her back and let that Ella woman snatch Emmett's seed from her body? Decades earlier she had failed to stand up to her mother. Back then she didn't even know what she was supposed to believe in—the stand she was supposed to take. Now, faced with this, was she supposed to stand back and watch her baby leave this earth? *Is that why I can't move?* Esther thought. This was a faith test like no other. *This is too much,* she argued with God. It didn't even hold a candle to the faith test Esther had faced while waiting for God to bring her baby back to her.

I can do something about this. Esther scrambled for answers in her mind. *If I could just run down there and grab my baby. I can stop this. I can save her.* But the more she wanted to run, the more she couldn't move. Interfering was against God's will. She felt like her body was ripping into equal halves, letting her innards spill out and dissolve into grains of sand. Valuable time was getting away. *Lord, I ain't no Abraham,* she argued. *I can't sacrifice my only child. I can't. Don't ask me to. Please, don't ask me.* It was going to take every ounce of faith she could muster to get through this. Could she do it? Could she let Jubi go like that?

"Oh my God! My Lord and Savior, how can I just say, 'Let thy will be done,' when I know you've come to take my baby? How?" Esther said aloud. She begged for strength; tears plummeted down her aged olive face. The deaconess, puzzled by what she heard, fanned harder.

Jubi held on to Reverend Wicker's robe as if her life depended on it, because it did, which made him turn up the intensity. She could feel the rapid pounding of his heart. Anointed by his own tears, Reverend Wicker shouted, "In the name of the Father, the Son, the Holy Spirit, Lord, redeem this child for your wonderful service. Save her to do your will—here on earth—if that be your will in heaven." The veins in his temples plumped up thicker as he shouted, even louder, more deliberately, "In the Name of all that's holy, Lord, God, the Christ, spare her life! Use her."

With his words piercing the air about him, a rush of electric energy surged through Jubi's body. The impact elicited from her a fierce scream. Reverend Wicker's right hand was now lifted upward into the cone of light. Someone would comment later that it was as if he was waiting for God himself to reach down and take hold. Reverend Wicker's open right hand was extended to the Lord's as gradually his left arm, which cradled Jubi's back, loosened its grip. Slowly, he began to collapse against the tightly knitted prayer wall. The shifting weight caused Jubi to open and wipe her eyes. She looked up into Reverend Wicker's face just in time to see his eyelids close shut. He was looking into her face as they closed. Everything happened in slow motion.

Jubi screamed out once more. "Somebody help me! Help me," she shouted as the two of them descended to the plush red carpet beneath them.

One of the deacons shouted into the crowd, "Somebody, call an ambulance! Reverend Wicker's not breathing."

Deacon Thomas, who was one of the doctors at the same hospital where James and Esther worked, penetrated the prayer wall and knelt by the pastor's side. Reverend Wicker's head was now resting in Jubi's lap, and she gently cradled it, wiping off his beaded sweat with her hand. She was crying and was confused about this strange turn of events. Without haste, Deacon Thomas methodically loosened the reverend's collar and unzipped his robe. He placed two fingers on the side of the reverend's neck, feeling for a pulse. Meanwhile, the praying never ceased around them. Approaching sirens blared from the street just as Deacon Thomas was forced to conclude that there was no pulse.

The deacon's eyes welled up as he gently laid the pastor's forearm across his chest. He looked up at the other deacons and slowly shook his head no. Then he glanced over at Jubi with the same despairing look on his face. Jubi's eyes bulged with fright and disbelief. She fainted. The Reverend Charles A. Wicker, Jr., pastor of Forest Unity Memorial Church of Baltimore, had gone home to be with the Lord. As word of his passing traveled throughout the cluster of parishioners at the front of the church and then to those still standing in the pews, wails of disbelief filled the air. The paramedics rushed in and took over the scene.

Some several hours later, Jubi came to in a hospital bed, with her mother and father by her side. Jubi spent the next three weeks detoxing in Providence Hospital's special detox unit, aptly called Cloud Nine. When she was discharged, James and Esther took their baby girl home.

"I am the vine, and you are the branches. If you stay joined to me, and I stay joined to you, then you will produce lots of fruit." Esther recited this Bible verse for the first time at Reverend Wicker's home-going service. She read it at the request of Beola. For as far as the reverend's widow was concerned, it was one soul in exchange for another. The grieving congregation was in agreement as well. The work and the calling of one very seasoned, dedicated shepherd was done on this earth. And his last assignment from the Lord was to solidify the calling of another, just beginning. It would be the testimony that poured from the lips of genera-tions to come.

The second time Esther read that scripture aloud was during Jubi's car ride home from the hospital. James was driving, taking it in too. The words, and the promise, brought smiles and silent confirmation to all three. Esther then flipped her Bible's pages to another verse and read, "Faith without works is dead." And so Jubi's ministry would begin.

Chapter Fourteen

Testimony on the Vine

Los Angeles, 2031 . . .

"Well . . . Joy . . . baby girl, now you've got the whole story," Julie said, "and all the sordid details." She shook her head and laughed. Julie took a big relaxing breath and a well-earned stretch, as the two of them, Julie and her baby girl, Joy, rested on the snow-colored Victorian couch that dressed up their elegant suite at the Beverly Wilshire in Beverly Hills.

"Yeah . . . honestly . . . whew!" Joy said. "You know, Mama, I imagined a lot of things whenever I read Grandma Jubi's testimony, but I never imagined anything close to that." Joy snuggled up close to her mother, like she did when she was a toddler.

"Well, honey, like your great-grandmother Esther used to say, 'Faith without works is dead!' And your grandmama struggled hard to reclaim her faith and build her legacy." Mother and daughter reveled in the intimacy of reliving their family's roots.

"Ever since her first album," Julie said, "your Grandma Jubi has insisted on her life's testimony appearing on the inside jacket of every project she's ever produced—the CDs, the books, you name it. She promised herself a long time ago that the world would know how God saved her life using prayer and that Reverend Wicker. You know, that man was only in his fifties when he died on that Sunday?"

"He was?" Joy said. At sixteen years old, she hadn't quite decided if fifty was too young to die or not. But, then again, Grandma Jubi was fifty-eight years old. Grandpa Will was pushing sixty, and the two of them didn't show any signs of being old or kicking the bucket, Joy felt. She had watched them keep a hectic touring schedule of singing and preaching around the country and abroad. Grandpa Will was a fantastic minister and a musician.

Joy loved the part of the story about how her grandparents actually grew up together, being a part of Forest Unity Memorial Church. She tried to picture just what they must have looked like as children and then as teens, her grandpa Will, young and energetic, playing the drums for the choir, and her grandmother wowing the congregation with her singing. That must have been cool, Joy thought. And she wondered what their wedding must have been like with that handsome preacher marrying them in front of a huge crowd cheering them on. Well, that was how her grandmother often described it. The vestibule was lined with church portraits of all the pastors who had served the church. They hung proudly. That Reverend Harris was quite a looker, she thought. And of all the preachers, the folklore surrounding his tenure was the juiciest. Someone had said that he might have even gone to jail at some point. But all that was neither here nor there on this special day.

"And you know what your Grandma Jubi always says, girl?" Julie said, looking straight into her daughter's ginger-brown eyes.

"Yeah, Ma," Joy said in an annoyed tone, because she knew what was coming next. "She says that if you got a calling on your life, you'd better stay close to the vine and get to it. So God can bless you."

"Okay then. And what else does your Grandma Jubi say?" Julie had decided to quiz her daughter some more.

Joy's eyeballs slightly rolled up in her head, because in her estimation this longtime ritual had been played out. She recited her answer in a monotone voice. "She says that since God had a calling on her life, we all have callings on our lives—since we live because God let her live."

"And what else?" Julie prodded further. She tickled her daughter's ribs while she said it.

Joy erupted in giggles. She playfully shielded her side and strained to get the answer out. "So we better not mess it up?"

"*Ding, ding, ding* . . . You win the prize!" her mother shouted in a whisper. They both laughed and hugged.

"Seriously, though," Joy asked her mother, "but what about our . . . well, these spiritual callings? How do you know what it is? What am I called to do?"

"Baby, a calling is a desire that won't let you go. If you feel a passion to do something, and it's positive and godly, then there's your calling. Just keep searching for your gifts, child. You'll find them."

Joy pondered that, and Julie gave her daughter a bear hug.

Time interrupted the moment. "Okay now," Julie said in a rushed tone after accidentally glancing at her watch. "It's time for you to get ready. You know we don't want to be late and miss your grandma's big moment. A Grammy Lifetime Achievement Award ain't no joke."

Not pleased by the interruption, but understanding, Joy whined in a sarcastic tone, "Okay, Ma. No, we don't want to miss that." "Hey," Joy added quickly to save herself from her mother's wrath. "Did you look at my dress? I think it needs ironing. And when you gonna wake up Daddy?"

By this time Julie was in the suite's main bedroom, and she hollered, "I'll wake him now, while you're in the shower. And I'll check out your dress too in a minute. And when you do get dressed, go down the hall and check on your grandparents, see how they're getting along."

"Okay," Joy replied, knowing her mother would say that.

"We all need to be in the lobby by six-thirty sharp," Julie yelled.

"Okay, Ma," Joy lobbed back, slightly irritated.

The magic of their time together had worn off. Now her mother was getting on her nerves. No doubt about it.

A short time later Joy emerged from the other bedroom, dressed up. Her olive skin looked sensuous adorned in lilac. She was scurrying through the main room of the suite when she picked up on its silence. She spied the couch and knelt down in front of it. She was being careful not to crease her beautiful dress by fanning it out beyond her toes.

"Lord, I know that prayer works. I know that you've blessed us. I know that you proved it by saving my grandma and letting all of us be born. But could I pray for one more blessing? I would like to ask you to give one more Grammy for Grandma's latest CD, *Jubilee's Gems from the Father*. I know you know about it, since all the songs came from you. So maybe you'll want to reward her again tonight." She thought for two seconds. "Now, if you decide to give it to somebody else," Joy sighed, "who maybe hasn't had a chance yet, well,

I'll be disappointed, but I won't be mad. I'll love you, anyway. Amen."

"Joyyy." Julie's muffled yell came from behind the double French doors of the bedroom. "You dressed yet?"

"Yeah!"

"Go check on Grandma and Grandpa, like I told you. The limo is almost here."

"I'm goin', Mama. Goin'."

Joy bounded to her feet and did a kind of Skip to My Lou to the front door, enjoying the bounce of her dress. When she opened it, delight dropped her bottom jaw.

Surprising her was a lovely vision of purple chiffon, lace, and silk, garnished with a rich ginger-hued smile that matched her mother's. "Grandma Jubi! You're ready already!" Joy said, grinning.

"Yeah, I'm ready." Jubi laughed, turning on a dime, heading for the elevator. When she reached out to push the elevator's button, her left wrist glistened with a gold bracelet. It was encrusted with glistening sapphires. The bracelet was a family heirloom. Family folklore had it stamped with slavery blood. For the awards ceremony, the bracelet lent the perfect pop to her outfit. It matched Jubi's rainbow-tinted shoes and shawl.

"You look beautiful, Grandma Jubi," Joy said, giddy and mesmerized in the moment.

"Yeah, that's right." Jubi chuckled. She Madonna vogued to accent the point. Joy might not have known the exact reference, but the move was comical, so she laughed. "And you do too, baby girl," Jubi said. She added, "Now, come here." And she pulled her granddaughter into her outstretched arms for a loving squeeze. The elevator chimed its arrival. Its doors opened to welcome them in. The chime caused Jubi to switch gears. Quickly, she called out, while holding the doors open, "You'd better c'mon!"

Grandpa Will was in tow, midway to the elevator, boasting a huge, easy smile. He was suited down in a perfect French-cut tux and proudly swagging in a sleek pair of wingtip shoes. Definitely the Hershey-chocolate complement to Jubi's seasoned beauty, Will Promise was tall, distinguished, and handsome. He smiled and threw a playful wink at his granddaughter. Playfully cosigning his wife, he said, "Okay, we'd better all rev up our engines naw." He was talking to Joy's parents, who were bringing up the rear. The elevator chime caused them to break into a half sprint. Everyone was tickled by the sight.

"Yeah, that's right," Jubi joked. "You better not make this diva late!"

About the Author

Yvonne J. Medley is a features writer and photographer, and is currently concentrating on the sequel to her debut novel, *God in Wingtip Shoes* (April 2012, Urban Books/Kensington), her upcoming collection of novellas and novel-lattes, *Two Old White Ladies in Africa: And Other Life Journeys,* and her screenplay, titled *Journey to Nowhere.* She has worked on staff at the *Washington Times* and has freelanced for several national and local publications, such as the *Washington Post, People* Magazine, *Gospel Today Magazine,* and *A Time to Love Magazine.* Medley garnered recognition for controversial pieces on racism and the church, and the psychology of sexually abusive clergy. Her work has been cited in online encyclopedias and reference links, and there have been several news stories printed about Medley as an author.

Medley travels the country, interviewing and writing about intriguing personalities, as well as *everyday* heroes, proving that everyone has a riveting and beneficial story to tell. One only needs to make a quality effort to unearth it.

About The Author

She conducts her Life Journeys Writing Workshops, designed to empower and encourage incarcerated men and women, as well as youth, adults, and fellow writers within the general population. Some of these workshops have been supported by the Maryland Humanities Council's One Maryland: One Book program. Medley is the founder of the Life Journeys Writers Club, serving writers in Southern Maryland and beyond. She also teaches ESL (English as a Second Language) and ABE (Adult Basic Education) to adult learners. Medley is a volunteer for Point of Change Jail & Street Ministry, Inc., dedicated to uplifting and impacting the lives of incarcerated men and women, their families, and providing aftercare support and life skills training.

Medley conducted Life Journeys Writing Workshops for the Maryland Writers' Association's Twenty-Second Annual Writers' Conference; the State of Maryland's Big Read, featuring Ray Bradbury's science fiction masterpiece *Fahrenheit 451* (sponsored by the National Endowment for the Arts); and the Reginald F. Lewis Museum of Maryland African American History & Culture; as well as for various educational programs and churches.

Medley's other offerings include *God in Wingtip Shoes*, a novel; *The Prison Plumb Line*, a novella; and her novel-lattes, titled *The Number Hole* and *The Counselors*. Medley is a wife and a mother of four, and lives in Southern Maryland.

To contact her, visit www.yvonnejmedley.com

Suggested Discussion Questions

1. Why didn't Jubi tell anyone about the date rape?

2. When she discussed with Jubi the facts of life, should Esther have done anything differently?

3. Did Esther suffer from denial? If so, why?

4. Was the Stones' church family a good support system for the family, or was it fearful of the family's trauma?

5. Do you feel that Esther forgave Mama Adele? Why or why not?

6. What's the purpose of Forest Unity's FISHH Ministry?

7. What is the significance of the passing of life and death at the altar?

8. What, if anything, should happen to Ambro?

9. Who or what killed Victoria?

10. Does God give everyone a calling?

11. What's your life's calling, your passion?

Reader's Group Guide Questions

12. Will Promise waited for Jubi. Is that realistic?

13. Regarding Victoria, what are the pros and cons of your children having an outside adult confidant?

14. How did Julie and Joy benefit from Jubi Stone's life experience? Who was/is the vine?

UC His Glory Book Club

www.uchisglorybookclub.com

UC His Glory Book Club is the spirit-inspired brain-child of Joylynn Jossel, author and acquisitions editor of Urban Christian, and Kendra Norman-Bellamy, author for Urban Christian. This is an online book club that hosts authors of Urban Christian. We welcome as members all men and women who have a passion for reading Christian-based fiction.

UC His Glory Book Club pledges our commitment to provide support, positive feedback, encouragement, and a forum whereby members can openly discuss and review the literary works of Urban Christian authors.

There is no membership fee associated with UC His Glory Book Club; however, we do ask that you support the authors through purchasing their works, encouraging them, providing book reviews, and of course, offering your prayers.

We also ask that you respect our beliefs and follow the guidelines of the book club. We hope to receive your valuable input, opinions, and reviews that build up, rather than tear down, our authors.

What We Believe:

—We believe that Jesus is the Christ, Son of the Living God.

—We believe the Bible is the true, living Word of God.

—We believe all Urban Christian authors should use their God-given writing abilities to honor God and share the message of the written word God has given to each of them uniquely.

—We believe in supporting Urban Christian authors in their literary endeavors by reading, purchasing, and sharing their titles with our online community.

—We believe that everything we do in our literary arena should be done in a manner that will lead to God being glorified and honored.

We look forward to the online fellowship with you. Please visit us often at *www.uchisglorybookclub.net*.

Many Blessings to You!
Shelia E. Lipsey,
President, UC His Glory Book Club

Notes

Notes

ORDER FORM
URBAN BOOKS, LLC
78 E. Industry Ct
Deer Park, NY 11729

Name: (please print):_____

Address: _____

City/State: _____

Zip: _____

QTY	TITLES	PRICE

Shipping and handling-add $3.50 for 1st book, then $1.75 for each additional book.
Please send a check payable to:
Urban Books, LLC
Please allow 4-6 weeks for delivery

ORDER FORM
URBAN BOOKS, LLC
78 E. Industry Ct
Deer Park, NY 11729

Name:(please print):_____

Address: _____

City/State: _____

Zip: _____

QTY	TITLES	PRICE
	3:57 A.M Timing Is Everything	$14.95
	A Man's Worth	$14.95
	A Woman's Worth	$14.95
	Abundant Rain	$14.95
	After The Feeling	$14.95
	Amaryllis	$14.95
	An Inconvenient Friend	$14.95
	Battle of Jericho	$14.95
	Be Careful What You Pray For	$14.95
	Beautiful Ugly	$14.95
	Been There Prayed That:	$14.95
	Before Redemption	$14.95

Shipping and handling-add $3.50 for 1st book, then $1.75 for each additional book.
Please send a check payable to:
Urban Books, LLC
Please allow 4-6 weeks for delivery

ORDER FORM
URBAN BOOKS, LLC
78 E. Industry Ct
Deer Park, NY 11729

Name: (please print): _____

Address: _____

City/State: _____

Zip: _____

QTY	TITLES	PRICE
	By the Grace of God	$14.95
	Confessions Of A Preachers Wife	$14.95
	Dance Into Destiny	$14.95
	Deliver Me From My Enemies	$14.95
	Desperate Decisions	$14.95
	Divorcing the Devil	$14.95
	Faith	$14.95
	First Comes Love	$14.95
	Flaws and All	$14.95
	Forgiven	$14.95
	Former Rain	$14.95
	Forsaken	$14.95

Shipping and handling-add $3.50 for 1st book, then $1.75 for each additional book.
Please send a check payable to:
Urban Books, LLC
Please allow 4-6 weeks for delivery

ORDER FORM
URBAN BOOKS, LLC
78 E. Industry Ct
Deer Park, NY 11729

Name: (please print):_____

Address: _____

City/State: _____

Zip: _____

QTY	TITLES	PRICE
	From Sinner To Saint	$14.95
	From The Extreme	$14.95
	God Is In Love With You	$14.95
	God Speaks To Me	$14.95
	Grace And Mercy	$14.95
	Guilty Of Love	$14.95
	Happily Ever Now	$14.95
	Heaven Bound	$14.95
	His Grace His Mercy	$14.95
	His Woman His Wife His Widow	$14.95
	Illusions	$14.95
	In Green Pastures	$14.95

Shipping and handling-add $3.50 for 1st book, then $1.75 for each additional book.

Please send a check payable to:

Urban Books, LLC

Please allow 4-6 weeks for delivery